HER ROGUE ALPHA

PAIGE TYLER

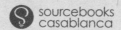
sourcebooks
casablanca

Published by Sourcebooks Casablanca, an imprint of Sourcebooks, Inc.
P.O. Box 4410, Naperville, Illinois 60567-4410
(630) 961-3900
Fax: (630) 961-2168
www.sourcebooks.com

Printed and bound in Canada.
MBP 10 9 8 7 6 5 4 3 2 1

With special thanks to my extremely patient and understanding husband. Without your help and support, I couldn't have pursued my dream job of becoming a writer. You're my sounding board, my idea man, my writing partner, my critique partner, and the absolute best research assistant any girl could ask for.

Love you!

Prologue

Kabul, Afghanistan

"SPREAD OUT A LITTLE, GUYS." LIEUTENANT JAYSON Harmon cursed as he led his four Special Forces teammates toward the downtrodden goat farm on the outskirts of Kabul, Afghanistan. "I know you like each other, but jeez, one frigging grenade will get you all."

The guys—Derek Mickens, Kyle Griffen, Kellen Tredeau, and Connor Marks—grinned but followed his orders. The four enlisted Special Forces operators had logged more time sitting on toilets than he had running missions. They knew what the hell they were doing, but he appreciated them humoring him anyway.

It wasn't much of a mission. They were going out with some of the local Afghan National Police to gather up a cache of illegal weapons, but he was just thrilled Captain Donovan had finally allowed him to run an operation on his own. Jayson knew his commander and best friend was just watching out for the FNG—effing new guy—but it was time to stop coddling him. He'd completed the same Special Forces training as everyone else on the team. This was his third deployment, and it was time to let him do his job.

The captain grudgingly agreed with him, mostly because this was such a low-risk operation. But, hey, it was a mission, and Jayson would take it where he could get it.

The three ANP officers ahead of them quickened their pace through a series of low corrals and paddocks, pushing aside a random goat as they headed toward the main barn structure that supposedly held the collection of automatic weapons they were there to recover. The local police chief had described the area as more of an equipment dump than a weapons cache, and said he didn't expect anyone to be guarding it and doubted they'd have to worry about booby traps. It was a nice piece of intel, but Jayson wouldn't believe those details until he confirmed them for himself.

He was about to yell at the Afghans to slow down a little when a horribly familiar whooshing sound jerked his attention to the left.

"RPG!" Mickens shouted.

Jayson had about half a second to throw himself forward as the rocket-propelled grenade raced straight at him and slammed into a thin wooden fence behind them. The rocket warhead exploded, the blast wave picking him up and throwing him through the air like he was a toy.

He didn't feel the searing pain in his back until he slammed into a wooden water trough and finally hit the ground; then, the agony did its very best to make up for lost time, ripping through him like a thousand red-hot knives. His vision wavered like someone was dragging a heavy black curtain across him right there in the goat-crap-filled corral. He fought the darkness trying to drag him under. Gunfire echoed in his ears, making him nearly deaf. He could barely hear his men swearing up a storm around him. He couldn't pass out, not yet. He'd led his guys—his friends—into an ambush, and now he had to get them out.

He reached behind him, trying to figure out how badly he'd been hurt, praying his tactical vest and equipment pouches had limited the damage, but froze when his hand encountered something warm, torn-up, and numb where the base of his spine had been.

Shit.

He shook off those thoughts. It didn't matter how bad it was. He just had to last long enough to make sure his guys made it out of this alive.

Jayson lifted his head out of the muck in the corral, shocked at how hard even that simple movement was. It was like his upper body weighed a ton. It didn't help that his damn legs wouldn't do a thing he told them to do. That was when he realized he was fucked up beyond all repair.

He gritted his teeth and shoved with his arms until he raised his head enough to see what the hell was happening. The scene that met his eyes almost made him want to say the hell with it.

A constant stream of bullets was tearing up the ground around them. Two of the Afghan police lay dead fifteen feet ahead of him. The third guy was nowhere to be seen. He'd either escaped or been blown to pieces. Being on the national police force in this country didn't earn these guys any love.

Jayson twisted his head to the left just in time to see another RPG slam into the ground and explode right where Connor had been taking cover behind a low stone wall. He went flying backward, his face and upper body peppered with the frag from the grenade. But like the tough-ass soldier he was, he was back on his feet in a flash and popping off shots at the roof of the barn where the attack was coming from.

But Connor's angle was all wrong. His rounds merely hit the edge of the mud wall along the roof, not doing much more than making a mess. He was never going to get a clear shot on the insurgent and his RPG launcher from down here, not with his M4.

"Connor, stop shooting!" Jayson shouted over the sounds of battle. "Take Kyle and work yourself around to the right. The 40mm grenade launcher is the only thing we have that can take out that asshole on the roof."

Every one of his guys turned and looked at him in shock, though he wasn't sure whether it was because he'd shouted so loud or because they'd thought he was dead.

Derek—the team's medic—immediately headed in his direction, but Jayson clumsily waved him off. "Cover Kyle and Connor. If they don't get that guy on the roof, we're all dead."

Derek hesitated, clearly torn between his medic responsibilities and the orders he'd just been given. But ultimately he did what he had to do and turned back to start laying down suppressive fire on the roofline.

Kellen was on the squad radio, probably giving a situation report to Landon. Oh shit, the captain was gonna be so pissed at him. The first time Jayson had a chance to prove himself capable of leading the team and instead he'd walked them right into a damn ambush. Landon was never gonna let him run a mission again in his life.

He pushed that self-pitying crap aside. Nobody cared right then how he'd gotten them in this mess; they just expected him to get everyone out.

Just then he heard the familiar hollow thump of the grenade launcher going off. A few seconds later, he saw the explosion on the flat roof of the barn. Three more high-explosive grenades quickly followed, each landing squarely on top of the building.

No more shooting came from the roof, but that didn't mean they were out of the woods yet. There were still at least ten insurgents running around the goat farm peppering them with automatic weapon fire from their AKs. Jayson ordered Connor and Kyle back into a better defensive position, then started directing their fire on one specific target after another. He pulled his Beretta 9mm and started shooting at the nearest insurgents as the rest of the team did the same. Even though every one of his guys was bleeding from multiple wounds by then, they did some serious damage.

It was as he was trying to reload his pistol—a damn near impossible task with his screwed-up back—that Jayson realized something was wrong with his eyes. His vision was starting to go dark around the edges, like he was staring down a long, pitch-black tunnel. He blinked his eyes trying to fix the problem, but it only got worse.

He looked down to get a fresh clip out of one of the pouches on his tactical vest and saw that he was lying in a pool of his own blood.

"Oh, fuck."

That was all he could manage as his pistol slipped out of his nerveless fingers and thumped to the ground. A few seconds later, he fell to the dirt next to his weapon.

Darkness was closing in. He was about done for. It wouldn't be long now.

Then he felt hands on his body.

"Hold on, Jayson!" Landon shouted. "Just hold on!"

Jayson was vaguely aware of someone doing something to his back. That would probably be Derek. SF medics were pretty frigging amazing, but they weren't magicians. Jayson tried to tell him there wasn't anything he could do, but he couldn't make his mouth work.

"I'm here now, and you're not going anywhere. Do you hear me?" Landon said. "Don't give up on me, Jayson. That's a fucking order!"

Jayson tried to fight his way back to his friend, to say good-bye if nothing else. Even though he could see Landon's face just above him and feel his friend holding his hand as if he were trying to pull him out of the darkness, it didn't help. The tunnel was so long, and he was so tired.

He felt his hand slip out of Landon's, and then the darkness swallowed him.

Chapter 1

Fifteen Months Later

JAYSON HARMON HATED POWELL AND MOORE. THEY were two of the most irritating field agents in the Department of Covert Operations, and whenever they came to the shooting range where he worked, he couldn't help daydreaming about both of them suffering from an accidental weapon discharge at the same time—preferably through really important and sensitive parts of their anatomies. It was a horrible thing for a weapons officer who ran the DCO's ranges to think, but the two men were such frigging asshats.

The DCO provided an unlimited supply of ammo for their field agents to maintain their weapon proficiency, and most of them took advantage of this generous job perk. Then there were Brian Powell and Aaron Moore. Both were average height and dark-haired with perpetual I-couldn't-give-a-flying-fuck expressions on their faces, and these two were the reason the DCO also had a minimum monthly ammunition consumption requirement. Asshat One and Asshat Two barely fired that minimum. It showed, too. They were the worst shooters he'd seen in the DCO by a mile. Jayson couldn't help but wonder how the hell they had even survived in the field as long as they had.

He'd tried to give them a few pointers the last time

they'd come to the range, but they hadn't been interested. Fine with him. He couldn't care less about the fact
that neither of them could shoot their way out of a wet
paper bag. But the way they loved making nasty cracks
about every shifter and hybrid in the organization was
something he had a hard time overlooking.

"Can you believe that hot chick Kendra let herself get
knocked up by a freak like MacBride?" Powell cracked
before blazing a few rounds downrange and missing his
target by nearly three feet.

Moore snorted. "As big as she's getting, I wouldn't
be surprised if a full-grown bear cub claws its way out
of her."

Jayson ground his jaw. It took everything in him not
to pull his sidearm as they continued insulting training
officer Kendra MacBride and her bear shifter husband,
Declan. As the weapons officer, Jayson had to be on the
shooting line whenever the range was active. If not, he
would have walked off a long time ago. Even though
he suspected these two assholes were only saying this
crap to get a rise out of him because his girlfriend, Layla
Halliwell, was a feline shifter, it still pissed him off.

He took a deep breath and tried to rein in his temper.
To be fair, it wasn't every day you learned some people
were born with animal DNA that allowed them to sprout
claws and fangs, see in the dark, run faster than a horse,
survive a fall off a three-story building, or any of the
other amazing things he'd seen shifters do since he'd
started working here. But just because shifters and their
man-made counterparts called hybrids could do all these
things, it didn't make them freaks. And it sure as hell
didn't give people like Powell and Moore the right to

call them names. It was like they were good enough to go into battle with but not good enough to treat with any kind of respect once you got back home.

"I bet those shifter bitches are absolute animals in bed," Powell said as he reloaded a magazine. "Can you imagine what that Ivy Halliwell chick would be like? It'd almost be worth sleeping with a freak like her to get some of that."

At the mention of Layla's older sister, Jayson smothered a curse and pushed away from the wall he'd been leaning against, ignoring the way the sudden movement jarred his injured back. He didn't care if he got his ass fired. There was no way in hell he was going stand around and put up with any more of this shit.

"Unload and clear your weapons, then get the fuck off my range," he ordered.

The two assholes were still laughing as they turned to look at him. Did they think he was joking?

Jayson pulled his Berretta 9mm from its holster and held it down at his side. He wasn't pointing it at them yet, but the message was abundantly clear.

Powell and Moore stopped laughing but didn't move. Instead, they both stared at him like they thought he was crazy.

"You can't throw us off the range," Powell finally said. "We haven't finished our qualification requirements yet."

Man, he'd like nothing better than to wipe that sneer off Powell's face. The guy had supposedly been in the military, but Jayson had no idea what kind of work he'd done. All he knew was that the army had kicked the asshole out for some reason. No shock there.

"I can do anything I want on this range. I run it," Jayson said.

Moore glared at him. "What the hell is your problem? Just because you're sleeping with one of those freaks doesn't mean we can't talk about them in front of you."

Jayson balled his free hand into a fist, more frustrated than ever that his shrapnel-shredded back kept him from walking over and punching both of the stupid fucks in their big mouths.

"Damn right it does. You come out here talking crap about people you don't know anything about," he ground out. "If I ever hear either of you making a crack like that again, it's going to be the last thing you ever say."

Jayson prayed they *would* say something. He had a bucketload of hostility and anger inside him that had been building for well over a year now, and he was just itching to empty it all over these two idiots. But after a few more moments of silence, Powell and Moore unloaded their weapons and walked away, muttering under their breaths.

Jayson kept his Beretta out until both men had disappeared down the gravel road that led to the main part of the DCO complex. He knew he'd just made enemies of the two men, who wouldn't hesitate to sucker punch him—or worse—when he wasn't looking, but so be it. Feeling the anger that was now so much a part of his life engulf him, he turned and put all fifteen rounds in his weapon through the center of the twenty-five-meter target. When that burst of violence wasn't enough to calm him, he dropped the empty clip, smoothly yanked another from the pouch at his side, and reloaded, then blazed through another fifteen rounds.

That seemed to do the trick. At least he wasn't seeing red anymore. He reached down to pick up the empty 9mm clip and jerked nearly rigid in his boots as a lightning bolt of pain raced down his spine to the twisted nerves that currently called his lower back home.

"Shit," he muttered.

Gritting his teeth, he slowly straightened up and breathed through the pain. When it had receded to a dull throb, he holstered his Beretta. Picking up Powell's and Moore's guns and unused ammo, he forced his tingling legs to respond to orders and slowly walked back to the building where the weapons were kept. The discomfort was yet another reminder of the fact that no matter how hard he worked on his physical therapy or how many muscle relaxants and pain pills he took, he was always going to have a screwed-up back.

Dwelling on it wasn't going to do anything but put him in a bad mood again, so when he got inside, he instead focused on the tasks he needed to do, like cleaning his Beretta and the weapons Powell and Moore had been firing, as well as a few others that had been used earlier that day in a training exercise.

Ignoring the stool, Jayson stood beside the table instead and broke down the 9mm by habit. Maintenance was usually the part most people hated about target shooting, but he didn't mind. It was cathartic in a way. And outside of pricks like Powell and Moore, he got to spend a good deal of his time working with field agents who actually cared about being able to shoot straight and hit what they were aiming at. It was damn tough training people to go out on missions when he'd never get a chance to go himself, but it was better than not being involved in anything important at all.

At least that's what he kept telling himself.

The continuous throbbing in Jayson's back as he stood at the worktable cleaning the Beretta reminded him that he'd pushed himself too hard today—again. The little railroad spike of pain when he'd bent over before was just the frosting on the cake. He was going to pay for all of it tonight. Usually, if the muscles in his back tightened up this much by noon, it almost guaranteed they'd be spasming uncontrollably by the time he went to bed that night. He wouldn't be sleeping much, that was for sure. No matter what he did, he was in some kind of pain. It was like a shadow that followed him wherever he went.

Fucking great.

He had no one to blame but himself. Even though he was walking better now, his doctors warned him to use his cane as much as possible, but he hated leaning on the damn thing when anyone was around. He didn't want to look weak in front of people, especially assholes like Powell and Moore. Of course, he rarely used his cane at home either, at least not when Layla was there. Of all the people he hated looking broken in front of, she topped the list. Unfortunately, when he pushed himself too hard, he ended up limping a lot, which made him look weak anyway.

Jayson set down the slide he'd just cleaned and ran his hand through his short, dark-blond hair with a sigh. He still did all the physical therapy as well as the breathing and visualization techniques he'd learned, but those things didn't mix well with a full-time job. Truthfully, it was getting harder and harder to find the motivation to keep doing them anyway. On good days, he wondered if he was going to be living with the pain for the rest of his life. On bad days, he wondered if what he had could even be called a life—and why he even bothered getting out of bed.

It was during those dark times that he was glad the doctors had pulled him off the heavy-duty narcotics. He didn't want to think about where his head would be if he had access to bottles of the mind-numbing crap he'd been living on before he'd met Layla. Right now, he was making do with over-the-counter painkillers and prescription muscle relaxants.

And Layla's constant support.

He wasn't sure how much longer that was going to last since he seemed to be blowing the only chance he had with her. When she walked out of his life… Well, something told him he wasn't going to last too long.

Jayson swallowed hard and picked up the barrel of the Beretta, practically attacking it with the cleaning cloth. He could see himself pushing her away even while he was shouting at himself to stop messing up the only good thing he had going in his life. Yet he couldn't seem to stop.

He didn't understand what the hell was wrong with him. He was in love with Layla, had been since the moment they'd met. He loved every inch of her, from her feline grace and beauty to her quiet strength and patience. But every time he opened his mouth to tell her that, the dumbest shit possible came rolling out. And when he wasn't saying something provoking and hurtful, he was ignoring her.

A few months ago, when Layla had first confessed she was a shifter and worked for a secret organization called the DCO, they'd been on the verge of sleeping together. These days they barely talked, much less touched. He hadn't kissed her like a man was supposed to kiss his girlfriend in weeks.

He knew she was just about at the end of her rope with him. He was surprised she'd put up with his childish crap this long. On good days, he was an angry, broken man without much of a future. On bad days, he was barely tolerable, even to himself. Why the hell a woman like Layla hung around with him in the first place was a mystery to him. Sooner or later, she was going to wise up and figure out he was a lost cause, then leave his ass.

The mere thought of the one bright spot in his life not being there was depressing as shit. Having Landon and John Loughlin, the director of the DCO, help him land this gig had given some purpose to his life lately, but there were days having a job involving open access to loaded weapons didn't seem like the best thing for a guy like him. All he had to do was pick one up and put it to his head…

He determinedly pushed those thoughts aside, refusing to let his mind even go down that path. He knew from experience—in his first few months after coming back from Afghanistan—that depression was a self-fulfilling prophesy. The more you thought about how shitty things were, the bleaker things looked.

He finished cleaning the Beretta and moved on to the other weapons that had been used this morning. He kept everything carefully segregated as he pulled off the slides and took out the various parts, checking each piece for damage and unusual wear marks as he did so. He was so lost in the rhythm of it that he didn't even realize someone had come into the building until he heard the sound of footsteps on rough concrete. He looked up and saw Dick Coleman, the DCO's deputy director, standing there.

"Thought I'd find you here." Dick smiled, nodding at the disassembled weapons on the table. "You want some help with these?"

He didn't wait for an answer. Instead, he took off his suit jacket and draped it over the back of a nearby stool, then rolled up his sleeves and began cleaning one of the Colts. Jayson wasn't surprised. While Dick might be the second most powerful man in the organization, he was easy to talk to and always willing to lend a hand as well as an ear. The guy was a good thirty years older than Jayson and had the gray in his hair to prove it, but they never had a problem finding something to talk about.

Dick held one of the .45 barrels up to the light to inspect the chamber area, his gray eyes narrowing as he checked it for wear. "I didn't notice you in the cafeteria for lunch, so I thought I'd come down and see how you're doing."

"I wanted to get these cleaned up first," Jayson said. "I was planning to go up later to get something."

One look at Dick's expression told Jayson his boss knew he was full of crap, but the older man didn't call him on it.

"You spend too much time down here by yourself," Dick said. "I appreciate all the work you do for us, but no one expects you to work your fingers to the bone, you know."

How could he tell his boss that he didn't like going to the cafeteria during the normal rush because he hated the idea of everyone watching him slowly shamble across the room with his tray?

Dick picked up another barrel and ran a bore brush through it. "I see the lessons you're giving Layla on that SIG Sauer she's partial to are really paying off. She looks great on the training exercises."

Jayson grimaced. Layla's training was a love/hate issue for him. He wanted her to succeed, but it also reminded him that she was moving toward a life he could never be part of. Knowing she was doing things he used to be able to do and couldn't do now was hard as hell. He knew it was shallow and petty, but knowing that didn't change the way he felt.

Jayson hadn't been the one who'd taught Layla to shoot though. As much as it hurt to think about anyone other than him teaching her anything, at the end of the day, he was proud of her and everything she'd accomplished. He wouldn't dream of trying to take credit for it.

"Nah," he said. "She's doing that all on her own."

"If you say so." On the other side of the table, Dick didn't look convinced. "You know, when John told me that Layla was going to train to be a field agent, I thought it was a mistake. Even if she is a shifter, she's still a psychologist, one with nothing in her background to even suggest she'd have the skills to be an operative. But I was wrong. She's learning faster than almost anyone I've ever seen. In fact, I heard John mention she'll be going on a mission soon."

Jayson almost dropped the lower frame piece he was

working on. Of all the things Dick could have said, that was the one thing Jayson least wanted to hear.

"That's good," he mumbled.

While he was thrilled for her, he couldn't stop the nagging voice in the back of his head that kept reminding him that once Layla proved herself ready for full-time fieldwork, she'd be one step closer to the very worst part of this whole deal—getting a partner.

No matter how proud of her he was, he was never going to be happy about her going into the field with someone other than him. It would almost certainly be a man because all the female shifters were paired up with guys who were ex-military or ex–law enforcement. Jayson tried not to be jealous and failed miserably—mostly because he knew how close DCO agents had to get to do their jobs. That's how his former A-team commander-turned-DCO-agent Landon Donovan and his partner Ivy had ended up married, even though no one in the DCO "officially" knew it. Wolf shifter Clayne Buchanan and his fiancée Danica Beckett had gotten together as a result of some mission to hunt down a serial killer in California, while Declan and Kendra MacBride had fallen in love while on the run from crazed hybrids in the rainforest of Costa Rica. Heck, even Angelo Rios, another former Special Forces guy, and his quiet hybrid partner, Minka Pajari, had gotten seriously close during their first mission in Tajikistan.

The thought that Layla would be out there spending a bunch of time with another man—laughing, bonding, and probably realizing she was wasting her life with him—just about tore out his guts.

On the flip side, Jayson also worried that Layla would

end up with an asshole partner who wouldn't watch her back—like Powell or Moore. If she was paired with one of those idiots, he'd never be able to sleep again.

"What kind of person do you think Layla would match up well with?" Dick asked, as if reading his thoughts. "As a partner in the field, I mean."

Jayson's grip tightened on the slide as he tried to breathe through a pain in his chest that hurt more than any back spasm ever could. Asking him which man he thought would be a good partner for Layla was a question he couldn't—wouldn't—answer.

If Dick noticed his reaction, he didn't mention it. "Personally, I think the two of you would make a great team."

Another spike of pain stabbed him. He swallowed hard. "Yeah, well I don't think that's ever going to happen."

Dick glanced up from the spring he was meticulously cleaning. "But what if it could?"

Jayson frowned. "What do you mean by that? You know how screwed up my back is."

Dick shrugged and went back to cleaning. "Some of our doctors have been working on a serum that might be able to repair the damage."

Jayson froze. His heart began thumping harder even as he told himself to be wary. "You mean a hybrid serum?"

"Basically, yes. But it's nothing like the stuff that was used on Tanner and Minka," he added quickly. "While the basis for this new drug is the hybrid serum we've been studying, our doctors have refined it. They've eliminated the negative side effects, like the rage, and have optimized the serum so that the person who takes it gets the strength, speed, and healing abilities of a shifter without any of the more extreme physical attributes, such as claws and fangs."

Jayson stared at him, afraid to believe what he was hearing. If what Dick said was true, a serum like that could heal his injuries. "And this stuff is safe?"

Dick nodded. "Absolutely. It's already gone through a thorough review and animal testing. Now that we're ready for human trials, I immediately thought of you."

Jayson didn't say anything. Was Dick telling him this because he thought a veteran with a screwed-up back would be a good candidate or because he thought he was desperate enough to agree to take an experimental drug?

Jayson's first instinct was to say hell no. He didn't like being the crippled guy everyone stared at when he walked down the street, but he wasn't crazy enough to voluntarily take a drug that might kill him. He'd heard what the hybrid serum had done to Tanner Howland and Minka Pajari. Besides having to fight the animal inside them for control every day, they were also subject to violent rages. He didn't want any part of a drug like that. But as Dick went on to explain how thoroughly the new serum had been tested and how it wouldn't merely heal the damage that fucking RPG had done to his back, but also help him get back to the man he'd been before—maybe a little better—Jayson found himself considering it.

"At least think about it," Dick suggested when Jayson didn't say anything. "I won't lie and say there aren't any risks involved here. But you're a soldier and you understand that sometimes you have to take some of those risks. Look me in the eye and tell me that the possibility of you walking without pain stabbing you in the back every time you take a step or covering Layla's ass in a firefight on a mission—hell, maybe even picking her up and carrying her across the threshold someday—isn't worth a little risk?"

Jayson couldn't tell him that. Because when Dick put it that way, of course the risk was worth it. But there was also the minor fact that something could go wrong when he took the drug. Then there wouldn't be any issues with back pain or covering Layla's ass in a firefight or carrying her across a threshold either. Because he'd be dead.

—∿∿—

Layla carefully wiped the dust off the large picture frame sitting on the top shelf of the bookcase in Jayson's living room. The photo of the tall, handsome soldier dressed in military camouflage with gleaming stars on his collar and the smiling, beautiful woman at his side was one of the few keepsakes Jayson still had of his parents. He treated it like the most precious thing in the world, so she did too.

Jayson had told her about his parents a little while after they'd first met, back when he'd still been at Walter Reed Army Medical Center. They'd died in a house fire several years earlier while he'd been finishing up his senior year at West Point. He'd barely had the chance to process what had happened, bury his parents, and come to grips with the fact that the only family he'd ever had was gone before he had to ship out for Special Forces training less than a week later. He never talked about it, but Layla got the feeling that not having the time to grieve properly had been the hardest part of the whole thing for Jayson.

After she finished dusting, Layla looked around,

checking to make sure she hadn't missed anything. That was unlikely considering she'd been cleaning for the last three hours. Luckily, she'd finished training with Ivy and Landon around noon, so she'd been able to come over and clean up before Jayson got home. Even though he knew she was just trying to help him out, he still got touchy about her cleaning his apartment, like he thought her doing it meant he was less of a man. Trying to make a relationship work with Jayson was harder than she'd ever imaged it would be. She'd been in love with him practically from the moment they'd met, but to say he was pushing her away as hard as he could was an understatement. She knew it was all wrapped up in a complicated knot thanks to his injuries, his lack of self-worth, and, at some level, a fear of losing her. Sometimes she expected him to come home, find her there, and tell her to get out and not come back. There were times when it was that bad. The thought of him breaking up with her brought tears to her eyes.

Cursing under her breath, Layla tossed the disposable dust cloth in the trash can in the kitchen, then washed her hands. She was just checking the lasagna she'd put in the oven earlier when she heard Jayson's heavy footsteps on the stairs in the hallway. He sounded like he was limping more than usual. Damn, she hated that he'd gotten an apartment in a place without an elevator, but he was so stubborn. Then again, that was part of why she loved him so much. He never let anything stop him from doing what he wanted.

She was still thinking about all the different reasons she loved such an adorable, frustrating guy as keys jangled in the lock and Jayson opened the door. That's when she remembered why he'd caught her eye the first time she'd seen him, at Ivy and Landon's wedding. He was absolutely gorgeous. Tall, with broad shoulders and well-muscled arms, he had dark-blond hair, piercing blue eyes, and a square jaw covered with just the perfect amount of stubble. Then there was his mouth… There were books written about lips that kissable.

Layla didn't have to fake the smile that tugged up the corners of her lips. No matter how crazy things were between them on any given day, seeing Jayson always made her happy. She hurried across the room and wrapped her arms around him in a welcoming hug. That's when she was reminded of the second thing that had attracted her to him at her sister's wedding—his scent.

Shifters had a tremendous advantage over the rest of the world when it came to their senses. Since the day she'd gone through her change when she was seventeen, Layla had been able to see, hear, and smell things that the rest of humanity never even noticed. And when it came to Jayson's scent that was a pity because he smelled better than anyone else in the world.

As she hugged him, Layla surreptitiously buried her face in the crook of his neck and inhaled deeply. *Mmm*, he smelled so good. It would be tough to describe his scent to anyone else, even another shifter or hybrid. None of the workplace smells could ever cover his natural, yummy aroma, not even the metallic odor of the guns he handled or the sharp smells of smokeless powder and cleaning solvents. When she was this close to him, all she could smell was his personal musk. It was so perfect that sometimes it was hard not licking him.

Layla hadn't been able to do something that intimate in a long time—not since she started field training and Jayson had started working at the gun range. Hugs like this were all they managed these days. Though she had to admit, a good hug could go a long way for her.

"You worked late." She reluctantly pulled away from him, not wanting to push her luck. "Somebody having problems getting through their qualification course?"

Jayson looked around the living room of his small apartment, and she tensed, knowing he could tell she'd been cleaning. She braced herself, waiting for him to get upset. But it didn't happen. Instead, he smiled and shook his head.

"Nah. Just had a lot of weapons to clean. Then a shipment of 40mm grenades came in and I had to get them inventoried and locked away in one of the ammo bunkers before closing up for the day. They aren't something I like to leave sitting out on my desk like a box of doughnuts."

She couldn't help but laugh, both at what he'd said and in relief that he didn't seem upset at her for cleaning his place. "I don't know, 40mm grenades might be less dangerous than doughnuts—at least as far as my hips are concerned."

Jayson chuckled as he followed his nose to the kitchen. Opening the oven a crack, he took a sniff.

"Mmm, smells good." He turned to give her a big smile. "Is that homemade lasagna? Special occasion or something?"

Layla had seen the hesitation in his stride when he'd walked over to the oven. Which meant he'd either pushed himself too hard at work today or moved the wrong way and made his back flare up again. Either way, he was in pain. That made his obvious good mood all the more surprising.

She followed him into the kitchen. "No special occasion. Do I need to have a reason to do something nice for you?"

Jayson floored her yet again by wrapping his arms around her and pulling her close. "No, you don't need to have a reason. I'm just glad you're willing to put up with me, considering that I can be such a jackass sometimes."

Layla opened her mouth to tell him he was never a jackass, but before she could say anything, Jayson dipped his head and kissed her. Not a little peck on the lips either, but a real, honest-to-goodness kiss. It took her a second to get over the shock, and when she did, she melted against him. It had been so long since he'd kissed her like that, and while she had missed his touch, she hadn't realized how much until that moment.

He slid one hand into her long hair, tugging that little bit like she loved as his tongue tangled with hers and made her moan. Heat pooled between her thighs. God, it had been so long.

She reached down to massage his hard-on through his cargo pants when he suddenly pulled his mouth away from hers. The kiss ended so abruptly that she almost fell over. She caught herself just in time and looked up at him in confusion.

Jayson didn't seem to notice. Or if he did, he didn't let on. "Need some help getting the rest of the dinner made?"

She'd rather he turn off the oven and take her to

the bedroom so they could get to work on dessert, but she didn't say that. Jayson hadn't been romantic with her in weeks, and she was never sure if it was because he wasn't attracted to her anymore or because he felt he wasn't physically up to the task. The one thing she did know was that the fastest way to upset him was to push too hard.

So as difficult as it was, she put her arousal on hold and nodded. "Yeah, that'd be great. Can you make the salad while I fix the garlic bread?"

He flashed her a grin. "Babe, I live to make salad."

She couldn't help laughing at the silly words.

Within minutes of working side by side in the small kitchen they were laughing and joking like they used to do before their relationship had fallen off the rails for reasons Layla didn't really understand. She couldn't even remember the last time she'd heard Jayson laugh. Months at least. It wasn't until now that Layla realized she had missed that as much as she'd missed his touch.

Not that there wasn't some touching too. As he stood beside her cutting tomatoes for the salad, their arms and hips would occasionally come into contact, and she could feel the spark that was always there between them. It reminded her of why she fought so hard to stay with him and how good it could be—when it was good.

Layla was spreading garlic butter on the bread when Jayson leaned over and kissed her neck, then slowly ran his warm mouth up to her ear, making her shiver all over even as he whispered softly to be careful with the knife. She put down the knife and turned her head to capture his mouth in a quick kiss.

He returned the kiss with a laugh. "We're going to burn dinner if we're not careful."

She couldn't care less about the dinner. Man cannot live on lasagna alone, and a woman definitely needed a few good kisses every now and then, she thought as she gazed up into Jayson's twinkling, blue eyes. This was the guy she had fallen in love with. A part of her wondered why he couldn't be like this all the time and why he was like this right now.

She resolutely pushed those thoughts aside. Right now, Jayson was laughing and joking and happy. When he was like that, she couldn't help but be happy too. It was on the tip of her tongue to tell him how she felt about him, but the same thing that always held her back stopped her this time too. She was afraid he didn't feel the same. The thought of him rejecting her love hurt so much it made her heart ache.

So, instead, she gave him another kiss, then busied herself by taking the lasagna over to the table. As they ate, Jayson told her about his day, including his run-in with Powell and Moore.

Layla gaped. "You pulled your weapon on them?"

She hadn't had much in the way of interactions with the two men, but she knew there was a good chance Powell and Moore were working directly for the people on the Committee who were in charge of the DCO as well as behind the hybrid research facilities. She had no doubt that Jayson had been justified in pulling his weapon on them, but she wasn't sure they were the kind of people you wanted as enemies.

Jayson must have picked up on her concern because the smile disappeared from his face. "I know I should have found a better way to deal with the situation." He pushed a big piece of pasta onto his fork with a chunk of bread. "But it's not in me to stand around and let someone say that kind of crap about my friends."

She smiled. "I know, and I appreciate that you were sticking up for Ivy and me and the rest of the shifters. Just watch yourself around those two, okay? I wouldn't put it past them to try and get back at you somehow."

She expected Jayson to disagree and say she was worrying for no reason, but he surprised her by nodding as he helped himself to more lasagna. "Yeah. I think I'll be watching my six for a while when it comes to Powell and Moore."

Layla relaxed. Was it too much to hope Jayson's good mood was permanent? She was itching to ask him what had happened today, but she was so happy they were having such a good time that she didn't want to jinx it.

"Dick mentioned that you're doing well in your training," Jayson said as he set his knife and fork on his empty plate. "He said you'd probably be heading out on your first mission soon."

Suddenly, the lasagna didn't taste nearly as good as it had just a few seconds earlier, and she pushed it aside. Of all the subjects Jayson could have brought up, this was the absolute worst.

Layla hadn't been looking forward to telling Jayson about the mission because she knew he probably wouldn't handle it well. It was something they were going to have to talk about soon, considering she was on standby to leave at any moment, but a part of her had been hoping she might put off telling him until tomorrow morning—preferably while they were lying naked in his bed.

"Do you know where you'll be going?" Jayson asked softly. "Or who you'll be going with?"

She took a deep breath and let it out slowly. She'd stopped talking to Jayson about her training because he always got so depressed after their conversations. In some ways, he was like the sick kid stuck at home while all his friends got to go out and have fun. Layla didn't think of what she was doing as having fun, but as a former Special Forces soldier, Jayson almost certainly did.

She would have dropped out of the training if she could have, anything to take at least this one burden off Jayson's shoulders. But she'd made a deal with the DCO director more than two months ago to become a field agent if he would hire Jayson and give him a job at the DCO. John Loughlin had done his part, so she would do hers. Even if things hadn't gone the way she'd expected.

None of that mattered now. What was done was done. And whatever she said now would almost certainly ruin this night beyond repair.

"I'm going with Clayne and Danica," she told him. "They've been chasing an arms dealer for weeks. I'm supposed to provide backup when they finally catch up to him, but I don't know exactly where that will be or when."

She held her breath, waiting for Jayson to flip out because she hadn't told him about any of this before now, but to her surprise, he didn't say a word. He simply sat there, nodding his head and gazing off into space like he was thinking over what she'd just said.

"I know you can't give me any details, but this guy you're going after, is he dangerous?" Jayson finally asked.

Layla mentally cringed, not sure how she should

answer his question. Of course the guy was dangerous. The DCO wouldn't be going after him if he wasn't. The guy had a reputation as a stone-cold killer and a businessman who would sell weapons to whomever could pay him the most.

But if she told Jayson that, he'd lose his mind for sure. On the other hand, she hated lying to him. Besides, she was a terrible liar. Jayson would see right through her.

"He's a scary guy," she admitted. "He specializes in selling chemical weapons technology and is responsible for the sudden increase in that kind of stuff showing up in places like Syria, Northern Iraq, and the Sudan. The worst part is that no one is even sure exactly what this guy looks like. Based on the name he goes by, the analysts assume he's from a Slavic nation, maybe Yugoslavia before it broke up, or Poland. All they can say for sure is that he's very good at knowing when he's being tracked and that it rarely ends well for the people who go after him."

Jayson's eyes widened in alarm. Crap, she probably should have left out that last part.

"Fortunately, I'm just there to help run the operation from a remote command post," she added quickly.

Jayson slowly let out a breath, the panicked look disappearing from his eyes. "So you won't be directly involved in apprehending the guy, right?"

She shook her head. "Nope. I'm only going to keep an eye on everything with cameras to make sure this guy doesn't turn the tables on Clayne and Danica."

While she wasn't exactly thrilled at the idea of going up against someone as dangerous as the arms dealer her first time in the field, it didn't make a lot of sense to send her halfway around the world just so she could sit at a computer and watch other operatives do their job. She didn't say that to Jayson, though.

Across from her, Jayson was staring off into space again, lost in thought.

"You okay?" she asked.

He jerked, snapping his head up to look at her. "Yeah. Why?"

"Because you look like you're a million miles away," she said. "I know you don't like the idea of me being a DCO agent, but…"

"It's not that," he said. "I mean, I'm still not thrilled about you going into the field, but I'm dealing with it. I was actually thinking of a conversation I had with Dick today."

Layla's stomach clenched. Jayson's relationship with the DCO's deputy director had made her uneasy from the first time she'd seen them together. Even though she, Ivy, Landon, and every one of their other friends had told him that Dick Coleman was dangerous, Jayson seemed to consider the man a friend.

"What did you talk about?" she asked.

Jayson shrugged, picking up his glass and taking a long drink of iced tea. "He was telling me about a new drug he thought might be able to heal my back."

Layla's heart started beating faster. There was only one "miracle" drug that could ever heal a shrapnel-shredded body. "A new drug? As in a hybrid serum?"

Jayson met her gaze, his blue eyes steady. "Not exactly."

"What does that mean? Either it is or it isn't."

Jayson sighed. "Okay, the drug *is* based on a hybrid

serum, but Dick assured me it's nothing like the stuff that was used on Tanner and Minka."

"Dick assured you?" Layla shouted, finding herself on her feet and having no clue how she got there. "And you believe him? That serum kills people. Or drives them insane. You know what Tanner and Minka went through, and they were the lucky ones! You can't seriously be considering letting him put that stuff into you."

Jayson stood, wincing as he straightened up too quickly. But he paid no attention to it. "Yeah, actually, I am. His scientists have worked out all the bugs, and they don't expect any negative side effects. I won't even get fangs and claws. Dick would never let me take this drug if he didn't think it was safe."

Layla suddenly couldn't breathe. This was what Dick had been planning all along. The deputy director had befriended Jayson because he knew a disabled soldier would willingly take an experimental drug for a shot at being whole and healthy again. He'd been planning to use Jayson as a test subject for the next generation of hybrid serum from the day they'd met.

Anger like she'd never felt consumed her, and she felt little stabs of pain on the tips of her fingers as her claws extended too fast. Dick was flat-out using Jayson's insecurities about his injuries to manipulate the hell out of him, and if the deputy had been there right then, she would have ripped off his lying face.

"Don't you see he's using you?"

Jayson flushed beneath his tan, and Layla immediately regretted her choice of words. She'd made it sound like she thought he was the kind of guy who could be used in the first place—a victim. It was the worst, most hurtful thing she could have said.

"I'm sorry," she said. "I didn't mean—"

"Yes, you did," he shot back. "Dick isn't using me. On the contrary, he's doing everything he can to help me. He's not looking at me with pity. He's not reminding me to use my cane. And he's sure as hell not telling me to stop fighting and get used to being a cripple."

"Don't call yourself that!" she snapped.

"Why not? It's what I am!" He muttered a curse and ran his hand through his hair, making it stick up every which way. "Look, I might barely be able to walk some days, but I'm not blind. I know how much you and everyone else hate Dick, and maybe you have your reasons. But knowing what it's like having people prejudge and dismiss me two seconds after seeing my limp, I'm willing to give him the benefit of the doubt. Regardless of what you think, he's not using me. He's giving me a chance to flip the script and get my fucking life back."

Layla knew it would be better to let it go for now and try to talk to Jayson when he'd cooled off. He had to believe Dick was being honest and that this drug could fix him. Because if he didn't, he'd be admitting he was never going to get any better than he was right now. But how could she let it go? How could she let the man she was in love with take a drug that might turn him into something she didn't even recognize—or worse?

"Get your life back, huh?" she asked. "By taking a drug that could end it?"

When he didn't answer, Layla stepped closer and took his hand. She wanted him to know that she was there and wasn't going anywhere.

"I know how hard your injuries have been on you, but are you so desperate to get back what you had that you're willing to risk your life without even thinking about us?"

"I am thinking about us," he said softly. "What kind of life do you think we're going to have if I can barely walk?"

"Our life will be just fine." She squeezed his hand. "I don't care about your physical limitations as long as we're together."

He yanked his hand out of her grasp with a snort. "That's easy for a person to say when they can jump out a two-story window and land on their feet. It's even easier for a person who's likely to be somewhere on the other side of the world in the next few days, chasing arms dealers and saving the world. But it's not nearly as easy for the person left behind." He shook his head, the pain in his eyes breaking her heart. "Layla, I can't even pick you up and carry you to my bed."

Tears stung her eyes and she blinked them back. "Then we'll walk there together."

"There are some days I'm not even sure I can manage that." He shook his head, his blue eyes as sad as she'd ever seen them. "You don't get it. You never will."

He picked up their plates and slowly walked across the kitchen to put them in the sink.

She followed. "Jayson—"

"Maybe you should go," he said in a voice so low she barely heard it even with her keen shifter hearing.

Layla froze. Her heart felt like someone had ripped it out and stepped on it. The pain was so intense, she had to grab the edge of the table for support. Thirty minutes ago, she thought things were back to the way they used to be. Now, it looked like this might be the end for them.

She turned to leave, tears blurring her vision. She hoped Jayson would stop her before she reached the door, but he didn't. She paused, her hand on the knob, then turned to look at him. He was still standing at the sink, his back to her.

"I know I don't have any right to ask this, but could you at least wait until I get back from wherever it is I'm going on this mission until you do anything?" she asked. "Please."

Jayson didn't answer.

Stifling a sob, she whirled around and jerked open the door. His soft voice stopped her.

"I'll try, but I can't make any promises. This is a decision I have to make on my own."

The words were like a knife in her already trampled heart. "Then the decision should be a lot easier for you to make without me around to complicate things."

Layla bolted out the door and ran down the hall. She didn't even make it to the stairs before regret overwhelmed her. *Why the hell had she said that?*

She was about to turn around and go back, but before she could, her phone rang. She dug in her purse to glance at the screen and cursed when she saw the number for the DCO operations center. *Crap.*

"Halliwell."

"Agent Halliwell, this is control," the man on the other end said. "Your mission is a go."

Great.

She sighed. "When and where do I report?"

"Your flight is already waiting for you at the

Andrews MIL-AIR terminal. You need to be there in an hour."

She wasn't sure how the hell she was going to make it all the way to Andrews AFB at this time of night. Just getting through the gate could take fifteen minutes sometimes.

"Where am I going?" she asked.

"That information will all be provided when you get to Andrews."

Layla looked back at Jayson's door as she hung up. She wished she didn't have to leave things like this, but she didn't have a choice. She just prayed Jayson wouldn't do anything stupid before she got back.

Chapter 2

"WE WON'T LET HIM DO ANYTHING STUPID," IVY PROMISED her sister. "Now stop worrying about Jayson and focus on your mission, okay?"

Ivy could barely hear her sister over the roar of the C-5's engines in the background as Layla promised she'd be careful. Sighing, Ivy put her phone away. She still hated the idea of her sister being a field agent, but she understood why Layla was doing it. And if Layla had to go out on her first mission with anyone other than her and Landon, Ivy was glad it was Clayne and Danica. She just wished her sister wasn't preoccupied with Jayson.

"What was that about?" Landon asked from the driver's seat of the DCO-issued sedan they were using for tonight's op, his night vision binoculars glued to the huge house they were surveilling.

She and Landon had been sitting outside the home of Thomas Thorn, former senator and current member of the DCO Committee, as well as owner-slash-CEO of Chadwick-Thorn, for the past two hours. Well, *home* was a poor choice of words. Manse, mansion, estate, small zip code—all those terms were more accurate. The immense Mediterranean-style house occupied a coveted chunk of Washington, DC, property positioned near Embassy Row and the Naval Observatory.

"Layla's on her way to meet Clayne and Danica for

her mission. She's worried about Jayson because Dick is trying to convince him to take a drug made from the latest hybrid serum, claiming it can heal his back."

Landon lowered his binoculars to give her a shocked look, his dark eyes wide. "Are you frigging kidding me? Please tell me Jayson isn't seriously considering doing it."

Ivy shrugged. "It sounds like he might be. When Layla tried to talk him out of it, Jayson got so upset, he practically tossed her out."

Landon cursed, digging in his pocket for his cell phone.

"What are you doing?" she asked.

"I'm going to call Jayson and tell him to stop being a dumbass."

Ivy reached out and caught his arm. "Don't do that."

"Why the hell not?" Landon demanded. "Someone needs to tell him that he's going to kill himself with that damn serum."

Ivy glanced at Thorn's place, checking to make sure nobody was moving around outside. She and Landon were there to get an idea of how many security people Thorn employed, how often they walked the grounds, and if there were any obvious weak spots in the estate's security before they came back to break in. It would end up being a wasted trip if they missed something because they were arguing about how to deal with Jayson.

"You can't call Jayson because it won't do any good," she said. "You're not his A-team commander anymore—you're his friend. You can't order him around. Besides, you know Jayson well enough to realize you can't keep him from doing something he wants to do—especially once he's gotten it into his head to do it. If you call him and tell him he's being stupid, you're going to push him into making the worst possible decision even faster than he normally would."

Landon's jaw tightened. "Well, I have to do something. I can't just stand by while Dick pumps that crap into Jayson's body."

Ivy slid her hand up to his heavily muscled shoulder and squeezed. "We are going to do something. We're going to call John and let him know what's happening. He'll tell Zarina and she'll figure out a way to stop this."

Landon looked doubtful as he shoved his phone back in his pocket. Ivy didn't blame him. While the Russian doctor Zarina Sokolov had single-handedly done more to stop the DCO's secret hybrid research than anyone, this was a tall task to ask.

"She might be able to stop it for now," Landon agreed. "But like you just said, it's hard to keep Jayson from doing something he really wants to do. If we stop him this time, what's to keep him from going back to Dick next time, or the one after that? How do we protect him from himself?"

Even though Jayson's injury wasn't Landon's fault, he blamed himself anyway. He'd sent his friend on the mission that had ended with Jayson getting blown up and ultimately chaptered out of the army. But while Landon wanted to help his friend so badly it hurt, it seemed that every time he tried, it usually resulted in Jayson getting pissed off.

"We can't," she said softly. "The only person who has any chance of doing that is Layla."

"If he'll even listen to her," Landon muttered. "It doesn't sound like things are going too well between them right now."

"No, it doesn't." Ivy's heart went out to Layla. Her sister had fallen really hard for Jayson. She didn't even want to think how badly Layla would be crushed if the two of them broke up. "We just have to hope they can make it work, for both their sakes."

Landon picked up his binoculars and went back to watching Thorn's place. She and Landon had been immersed in the former senator's world ever since getting back from Tajikistan two months ago, looking for evidence that would tie him to all the illegal crap that had been going down at the DCO for years, especially with the hybrid program. Unfortunately, they hadn't found anything in his offices or the dozens of research facilities they'd slipped into over the past few weeks.

The only other place left for them to check was Thorn's home. Normally, breaking into a private residence wouldn't be a big deal for her and Landon. B and E was their area of expertise. Unfortunately, getting info on the layout of Thorn's place had turned out to be harder than they'd thought. They didn't want to walk in there and set off an alarm on a security system they didn't even know was there.

"I guess John was right about Thorn's new hybrid serum being further along than we'd guessed," Landon said, not taking his eyes off the house.

Ivy frowned as she scanned the roofline. The tile-and-slate roof was seriously steep, and she wasn't crazy about the idea of traversing it. Hopefully they'd be able to find a better way in.

"Did you really doubt it?" she asked. "If that mysterious shifter Adam told John that Thorn and his new collection of mad scientists got their hands on samples from those hybrids we went up against in Tajikistan, I'm sure they did. That would have given them a big head start."

A muscle in Landon's jaw flexed. If he were a shifter, he probably would have growled. They'd been so sure that all the research from Tajikistan—with the exception of the intel they'd collected for John and the one nearly feral female hybrid they'd brought back and put into Zarina's care—was gone. Powell and Moore must have managed to get Thorn blood samples from those totally badass hybrids over there without anyone knowing it.

"Yeah, well, I get the feeling John knows a lot more than he's telling us," Landon muttered.

Ivy didn't disagree. John had been working closely with Adam and his crew of hidden shifters to find hard evidence on Thorn. Even with Adam around to watch out for John, Ivy wasn't comfortable with the idea of the director of the DCO putting himself at risk. Thorn wasn't the kind of man you wanted to mess with.

Movement out of the corner of her eye suddenly caught her attention. She snapped her head around just in time to see someone moving quickly across the rooftop. The person was too lithe and graceful to be anything other than a woman.

"Someone's on the roof," she said. "Just to the left of the big chimney."

Landon turned his binoculars in that direction, immediately locking on the woman as she ran straight up the steep roof without disturbing a tile, then scurried along the top ridge. In less than ten seconds, she'd made it all the way across the mansion and was sliding down the slate toward one of the third-floor windows, through which she promptly disappeared.

"I'll be damned," Landon whispered. "I think Thorn is about to get robbed by a shifter."

Ivy didn't argue about the shifter part. Even from a distance, the woman's grace and confidence made it obvious. Ivy wasn't sure she was a criminal though. "Do you think Adam sent her?"

Landon didn't take his gaze off the house. "Maybe, but wouldn't he have told John? Think we should move in for a closer look?"

"No. Let's watch and see what happens. If she's one of Adam's shifters, we'll get a report on what she finds. If she's really a thief trying to rob Thorn, we'll get a chance to see how good his security actually is."

Ivy only hoped they didn't shoot first and ask questions later.

───

Dreya Clark couldn't believe how easy it had been to get into the Thorn mansion. After sneaking past perimeter security, cameras, motion and thermal sensors, and the occasional guard, breaking into the house itself had been a joke. Then again, people usually didn't bother with security alarms anywhere but the first floor. Not that she was complaining. She liked when rich people made it easy for her to steal things. It made taking them that much sweeter, like she was only doing what these rich snobs were begging her to do.

She slipped through the third-floor window and landed lightly on the dark hardwood floor, then stood there, checking the place out with her nose. She immediately pinpointed the location of Thorn and three security guards. They were all on the first floor. Good. Even though that rich bastard had an office downstairs, she was more interested in the private study up here.

She ran down the hallway in that direction, her soft-soled shoes soundless on the floor. Letting herself into the room, she quietly closed the door behind her. As she caught sight of historic Georgetown and the White House just beyond through the big picture window, she had to admit that the view was spectacular.

The room was dark, but her freaky eyes let her see as clearly as if the lights were on. Dreya would have loved to pull an old book off the shelf that covered one wall and curl up in one of the comfy-looking chairs, but she wasn't there for that. She was there to steal something. Even so, she couldn't help running her gloved fingers along each book as she made her way past the bookcase. Man, it would have been nice to swipe some of them. Unfortunately, none of her regular fences worked with rare books.

She moved over to check out Thorn's desk but didn't find anything interesting, unless you counted a little black book full of names, addresses, usernames, and passwords.

"Mr. Thorn, you silly man. Didn't anyone ever tell you that you're not supposed to write down your passwords?" she said softly. "It's very bad for security."

Even though she didn't give a crap about credit card pins and bank account numbers, she flipped through the book anyway. She broke into places to steal stuff for the fun of it, not to transfer money to a Cayman bank account. She stopped when she came to numbers related

to access doors and security systems. Those she memorized. Sometimes it was nice being a freak, like now,
when she could store dozens of different numbers in her
head like a computer.

In the very back of the book was a long alphanumeric
code. There was nothing to indicate what it was for, but
it looked interesting, so she memorized that one too.
Then she put everything back exactly the way it had
been and turned her attention to the real reason she was
there—the diamond.

Dreya surveyed the room, taking in the hardwood
floors, marble accents, and old paintings mounted
everywhere. She sniffed the air, letting her nose lead her
to the painting on the far wall—a large, fancy portrait
of George Washington sitting on a horse. She leaned
closer and inhaled deeply. The scent lingering on one
side of the frame told her that Thorn handled the picture
too frequently for it to be anything other than a cover
for a safe.

She swung the painting aside and studied the exposed
safe behind it with a smile. People like Thorn didn't buy
cheap crap, that was for sure. But this same model had
been in the last two houses she'd hit, so she knew it
well. She shrugged off her small backpack, keeping an
ear open for movement from downstairs as she took out
her tools.

The safe had an electronic keypad designed to lock
out anyone who punched in the wrong combination of
numbers three times in a row. Luckily, she had equipment that allowed her to bypass the entire keypad
interface and communicate directly with the computer
chip that controlled the locking mechanism. Thank God

Thorn wasn't the old-fashioned type who liked those twirling combination dials. Those things could be a real bitch to deal with.

Pulling the electronic safe cracker out of her bag, she attached it to the side of the safe and flipped it on, then let it do its thing. If Rory Keefe—her best friend, mentor, and fence—was right, she'd open the door to find the biggest honking diamond she'd ever seen. That was saying something, since she'd stolen a lot of big diamonds in her time.

After the lights on the box turned green, she double-checked to make sure all the alarms were deactivated, then yanked open the safe.

Inside, there were two black boxes. One was a standard velvet jewelry case. The other was made of plastic. Knowing the diamond had to be in the jewelry box, she took it out and opened it. She almost gasped at the sight of the enormous, pear-cut diamond pendant set in gold. The stone was flawless and had to be close to forty-five carats. Dreya couldn't imagine what it was worth or how the hell a man like Thorn had gotten his hands on it. Diamonds this size always carried a story with them. She wondered what one this rock had.

Telling herself there'd be plenty of time to look up the stone's pedigree while she was figuring out how much to sell it for, she closed the jewel case with a snap and dropped it in her backpack. She swung her gaze back to the safe, tilting her head a little as she considered the other box inside. Curiosity getting the better of her, she took it out and opened it. Or tried to, anyway. Frowning, she held it up, inspecting it more closely, and realized it wasn't a box at all. It was a solid, rectangular piece of metal with a pencil-sized hole in one end and a small, narrow slot that looked suspiciously like a computer connection of some kind on the other.

She chewed on her lip, weighing the piece of metal in her hand and wondering if she should take it. If it weren't valuable, it wouldn't have been in Thorn's safe. And while it wasn't something she'd probably ever be able to sell, the reality was, she liked taking valuable crap from rich people.

Shrugging, she tossed the funny box in her backpack along with everything else. Then she slipped her arms through the straps, gave the place a once-over, and headed for the door. She could have closed and locked the safe, then put the painting back into place. But why do that? It was no fun stealing stuff if the person you took it from didn't know it.

Dreya poked her head out the door to make sure the coast was clear, then darted down the hallway to the window. Hopping onto the roof, she climbed up the thin wire she'd left dangling from the eaves, then scampered back across the way she'd come. She was walking down the side of the road toward her motorcycle when she got a strange tingling along the back of her neck. She stopped and spun around but didn't see anyone along the dark street. But her instincts—and her nose—told her someone was back there somewhere staring at her. And the scent they were putting off was the freakiest thing she'd ever smelled before.

Pulse suddenly pounding, she hurried to her bike and climbed on, then pulled her helmet over her long, blond braid and hauled ass. She glanced over her shoulder as she zipped down Embassy Row but still didn't see anyone. She always took the license plate off her bike before a job, so no one would be able to track her. Besides, it was too dark for anyone to get a good look at her face anyway.

She slowed down after a few miles. She needed to chill out. Now that she was on her bike, there was no way anyone could catch her—if there had even been someone back there in the first place. It had probably just been her freaky side getting nervous.

But if that were the case, why was her freaky side telling her that something bad was coming her way?

Layla sat beside Danica in the operations truck, staring at the multiple monitors set up along one wall and trying to keep her eyes open. She'd traveled through the night, getting to Glasgow, Scotland, early that morning and immediately meeting up with the rest of her team. They'd set up surveillance on the warehouse where their mysterious arms dealer, Kojot, was supposed to meet a group of people who wanted to buy some really nasty weapons for reasons that probably wouldn't make sense to anyone but them. It was nearly lunch and so far, no luck.

Two of the monitors showed the interior of the warehouse, which was fairly dim, even at this time of the day. Two others gave a view of the main streets leading away from the building. The last monitor showed nothing but a blank brick wall at the moment, since the feed on that one was coming from the remote controlled drone currently sitting idle on a nearby rooftop waiting for the coordinates from Layla.

"So, what's going on with you and Jayson?" Danica

asked, sipping her coffee. "I hardly ever see you two together around the training complex anymore."

Layla stifled a groan. She didn't really feel like discussing her screwed-up relationship with anybody right now, even if Jayson and that damn hybrid serum had been the only thing on her mind since leaving DC. But if there was one person in the world she could talk to about this—outside of Ivy, of course—it was Danica. At least they were alone. If Clayne or the other two agents on the mission, Foley or Hightower, were in the van, there was no way in hell she'd talk about her relationship troubles. All three men were out checking to see if the DCO had any new intel on why the meeting hadn't gone down yet though. At least, that's what Layla hoped they were doing. Considering how poorly Clayne and Foley got along, it was also possible they'd gotten in a fight with each other in the middle of the street and were all in a Scottish jail somewhere with Hightower standing between the two men, trying to keep them from killing each other.

"If you don't want to talk about it, it's okay," Danica added when she didn't say anything.

Layla shook her head. "I don't mind talking about it. In fact, getting some of this stuff off my mind would probably help. Sometimes it all seems so complicated that I'm not even sure where to begin."

"Let's start with something simple then. Are you in love with him?"

"Yes," Layla answered without hesitation.

Danica glanced at her. "Is he in love with you?"

"I don't know." She swallowed hard. "I know he cares about me, and I used to think that was enough.

But as hard as everything has been lately, I don't know if it is anymore."

Danica let out a sigh. "He's pushing you away, isn't he?"

Layla blinked. "How did you know?"

"Because I've seen it before." Danica snorted. "Hell, I've done it before." At Layla's confused look, she continued. "When I fell in love with Clayne—I got put into an impossible situation where I thought that being with him was going to hurt him. He wasn't going to let me go on his own, so I pushed him away. And when he refused to let go, I pushed even harder. I ended up saying some things that hurt him terribly to get him to let me walk away."

Layla frowned. "But if you loved him, how could you do something like that?"

"It was because I loved him that I could do it," Danica said. "I was wrong for him at the time and didn't want him getting hurt because of me. I don't know Jayson very well, and while your situation isn't anything like ours, I'm guessing he has similar reasons for pushing you away."

Even though Layla didn't want to admit it, on some level, she knew Danica was right. "He feels like he's not worthy of me because he's disabled. I mean, I hadn't even met him until after he was injured. I told him that's crap and that I don't care about it, but nothing I say gets through to him."

It didn't help that she was a shifter. It was hard enough for people who weren't physically challenged to accept someone who could do the things she could. In Jayson's eyes, she must seem superhuman. She'd always embraced her inner animal and dreamed of sharing that part of herself with someone who would love her in spite of it. She'd been so sure Jayson was that person. But instead, her shifter half was coming between them. Not because it disgusted him or freaked him out, but because it made him feel like he wasn't good enough for her. For the first time ever, she wished she were simply a regular person.

Danica went back to watching the monitors. "He's a man. For most of his life, his whole world was wrapped up in what he could do physically. In his eyes, that's all gone now. If you want him to get his head right, you're going to have to help him get to a place where he can stand on his own two feet again."

"I've been trying to get him back on his feet for months, but it's not working." She growled in frustration. "I helped him get his own place, so he'd see that he could still be self-sufficient. Then I helped him get a job at the DCO so he could still use his tactical skills. Heck, I even tried to get him a service dog to take care of, thinking that would help him, but Jayson refused to even go look at the cute little fur ball, saying he could barely take care of himself much less a pet. Nothing I do seems to help, and he's drifting further away every day."

Danica offered her a small smile. "I wish I could give you some magical piece of advice, but I can't. It's going to take more than getting him a dog—or a job. You need to give him a purpose, a reason to keep going and get out of bed every day."

"How the hell do I do that?" Layla demanded, especially when Dick was waiting in the wings with a syringe full of drugs that promised a shortcut back to everything Jayson used to be.

"You're going to have to prove to him that he's still the same man he used to be, injured or not."

That was easier said than done.

Layla was still pondering that impossible task when the radio on top of the monitors crackled to life and Clayne's rough voice filled the back of the ops van. "Everybody get ready. Our buyers are three minutes out and our target is probably in the area already. Layla, fire up the drone camera and find him."

Danica swiveled her chair around. "That's my cue. See you later."

As Danica hopped out of the van to meet up with Clayne, Layla grabbed the controls for the drone. She guided it off the roof, letting it hover above the building, so she could see the streets below. A few minutes later, two dark blue SUVs pulled into the warehouse. A little while after that, a van came down the street.

"There's a white van coming toward the warehouse from the East End side," she said softly into the radio as the vehicle moved slowly through the alley and entered the building. "The van doesn't have windows on the side or in back, so I can't see what's inside, but it's low on its shocks so they're carrying something heavy, whatever it is."

"Can you see the driver or tell how many other people are in the vehicle with him?" Danica asked.

Danica and the rest of the team were hidden in the warehouse, ready to make their move as soon as they verified this really was a weapons deal. Clayne and Danica would focus on the man they hoped was Kojot, while Foley and Hightower apprehended the locals who were there to buy the weapons. Foley and Hightower

had gotten the short end of the stick in Layla's opinion.
There were six buyers, all of them armed.

"Negative," she said. "All of the front windows
are tinted."

"Understood," Clayne replied in a low, gruff
voice that always made it sound like he was pissed at
something—which he usually was. "Let us know the
second you confirm we're dealing with weapons here
and not some drug deal or a truck full of stolen computers. If that's the case, we abort without response. It
might be Kojot setting a trap to see if we're on his trail.
We don't break cover unless we're sure it's him."

Layla followed the van on the monitors as it moved
into the warehouse, then pulled up next to the two SUVs
and stopped. The buyers looked nervous as heck as they
moved to form a semicircle around the front of the van.
She supposed she couldn't blame them. If the intel on
Kojot was right, he was one hell of a scary dude.

A minute later, the driver's side door opened and a
man in jeans and a T-shirt stepped out. He wasn't a big
guy, but he was in good shape and definitely moved
like a person who wasn't concerned with all the armed
men standing around him. He didn't necessarily look
like a cold-blooded killer, but Layla supposed he could
be Kojot. It would have been much easier if she'd had
audio as well as cameras.

One of the buyers moved over to the back door of the
closest SUV and took out an iPad. He moved his fingers
over the screen for a moment, then held it up so Kojot
could see. Kojot must have liked what he saw because
he nodded and tossed the keys for the van to one of the
other buyers. The buyer and one of his buddies headed

for the back of the van while their friends continued to keep a tense eye on the arms dealer.

"The deal is going down," she reported over the radio.

"What's in the van?" Clayne growled.

Layla glanced at the other monitor showing the inside of the warehouse. Crap, it wasn't positioned right. When the doors of the van swung open, she couldn't see inside.

"I don't know," she said. "The camera is at the wrong angle."

"We need to know what's in that van before we blow our cover," Clayne said tersely. "Figure out a way to ID what's in there."

Layla wanted to ask him how the hell she was going to do that since he was the one who'd been so adamant about her staying in the operations truck, but pointing out the obvious would probably only piss him off. She was half a second from jumping out and hauling ass for the warehouse when she remembered the camera drone.

"I'm moving the drone in for a look," she said, grabbing the controller.

The image on the monitor feeding from the drone immediately jumped all over the place as she put it in motion. Clearly it didn't like the idea of diving near ground level to look through windows like a Peeping Tom.

"Hurry up before they close the doors and leave," Danica urged.

Layla darted a glance over at the stationary camera monitor. Kojot was tapping something into the iPad, no doubt transferring funds to some account that even the DCO would have a hard time tracking. Another few minutes and they'd be out of there.

The hell with it. Turning back to the controls for the

drone, she sent it diving down into the alley behind the warehouse at insane speed. A split second later, she was rewarded with a long-distance view into the back of the van through one of the warehouse windows. The dark green boxes were definitely military and the stickers on them had universal symbols for *Danger*, *Caution*, and *Explosive*.

"They're weapons," she announced. "The boxes are about the right size for shoulder-fired, surface-to-air missiles."

She had no idea what a group of people in Glasgow wanted with surface-to-air missiles, but it wasn't something she liked to think about.

Clayne immediately gave the order to move. A moment later, he, Danica, Foley, and Hightower dropped to the first floor of the warehouse from their hiding places upstairs and ordered everyone to freeze. No one obeyed that order, least of all Kojot. The arms dealer took off in the opposite direction. Clayne and Danica followed, the wolf shifter quickly gaining on the bad guy.

Layla went back and forth from one monitor to the next, looking for Kojot, and caught a flash of movement at the south end of the warehouse as he ran down a flight of stairs. How the hell had he gotten all the way across the warehouse in just a few seconds?

"Kojot is heading down the stairwell on the south side of the warehouse," she called over the radio.

On the monitor, Danica immediately turned and ran in that direction. Clayne, on the other hand, was standing in the middle of the warehouse, his head tilted to the side and a pissed-off expression on his face. Then he tore across the room, growling so loud that Layla could hear him without the benefit of the radio.

"He's a fucking shifter!" Clayne shouted as he raced down the stairs ahead of Danica. "Kojot knew we were here all along and still had the balls the go through with the deal. He's probably been onto us for months."

Layla's eyes widened. No wonder they hadn't been able to catch the mysterious arms dealer. It was hard to sneak up on a person when he could smell you coming. She couldn't believe the DCO never even had a hint he was a shifter. Just how good was this guy?

In the warehouse, an engine roared to life. She looked over at the monitor just in time to see the white van spinning up dirt and debris as it raced for the exit on the west side. Foley and Hightower were trapped behind one of the SUVs, locked in a shoot-out with the buyers who'd stayed behind. As the van sped away, Foley switched targets, shooting at the escaping vehicle and trying to hit the tires.

"Foley, stop!" she shouted. "That van is full of weapons. You hit something sensitive and you're going to turn the neighborhood into a combat zone."

"I know that!" Foley ground out. "But we're pinned down and those weapons are getting away. If we can't stop them, you're going to have to do it."

Layla expected Clayne to countermand the order as lead agent on the mission, but he didn't say anything. Maybe he hadn't heard Foley.

"Clayne, did you copy that?" she called. "Foley and Hightower are pinned down and want me to go after the van full of weapons. Do you copy?"

"Layla, you gotta go now!" Hightower shouted. "We're okay here. You can't let those weapons get away."

She was up and out of the operations truck before Hightower even finished. Clayne would probably make sure she never went on another mission as long as she lived, but if this was the only one she ever got on, she was going to do it right.

She thanked God that whoever was driving the van had decided to escape out the west side of the building. If he'd gone the other way, she would have had to run all the way around the building. She would never have caught up to them, shifter or not. As it was, the white van was already out of the alley and pulling onto Ingram Street. Fortunately, the van couldn't accelerate very quickly with all those weapons in the back.

Layla ignored the people on the street staring at her and ran faster. It wasn't until then that she realized she didn't have a plan for what she was going to do when she caught up to them. Stopping a moving van while on foot hadn't been part of her field training.

She had her 9mm SIG Sauer, but she'd just berated Foley for shooting at a vehicle full of weapons. Besides, she wasn't sure she could aim very straight while running flat-out like she was.

Heart pounding, she sprinted around to the driver's side door. As she gripped the handle and wrenched it open, she realized her claws were out. Crap, she hadn't even felt them extend.

It was hard to keep pace with the van, but she managed it as she grabbed the surprised driver by the scruff of the neck and yanked hard, tossing him out of his seat and onto the road.

The van immediately swerved into oncoming traffic. Layla quickly hopped in and got control of the wheel just as the guy in the passenger seat finally figured out what the hell was going on. She stomped on the brakes as he pulled his gun, making him fly forward. His head bounced off the windshield, then he slammed back into the seat, leaving him unconscious.

Pulse racing, Layla pulled the van over to the side of the road. Okay, that had been way more intense than any training scenario.

She was just climbing out as the sound of sirens reached her ears. She glanced at the guy in the passenger seat to make sure he wasn't going anywhere for a while, then looked around for the one she'd tossed out. From the way several people two blocks down Ingram Street were looking underneath a pricey-looking four-door BMW, she guessed that guy wasn't going anywhere either.

Layla bit her lip, not sure what to do. The sirens were getting closer. Did she stay at the scene or not? Unfortunately, this situation hadn't exactly come up in her training, and they sure as heck hadn't talked about it during the mission briefing Clayne had conducted.

The pounding of running footsteps interrupted her musings, and she spun around to find Danica coming her way. Relief coursed through her. She'd never been so happy to see anyone in her life.

"I know I was supposed to stay in the truck, but they were getting away with the missiles," Layla said quickly.

Danica waved her off as she caught her breath. "Don't worry about it. The situation changed and you did the right thing. Outstanding job catching these guys."

Layla smiled, relieved. "Thanks."

She was about to ask Danica if she and Clayne had

apprehended the arms dealer, but right then, three police cars weaved their way through the crush of vehicles crowding the street and stopped in front of them.

Crap.

"What do we do?" Layla asked.

Danica reached into her pocket and pulled out her Department of Homeland Security badge. "Follow my lead. And try to lie as convincingly as you can."

Chapter 3

"YOU CAN'T JUST GO BARGING IN THERE. I NEED TO announce you!"

Jayson ignored Dick's secretary, walking past her and pushing open the deputy director's big oak door. He hated to blow her off like that, but he wasn't feeling very polite right now.

"Were you serious about what you said?" he demanded as he came to a stop in front of Dick's desk.

The deputy director looked up from whatever he was writing on the notepad in front of him as if just realizing Jayson was there. *Right*. Like he hadn't heard the fuss his secretary had made.

"I'm sorry, Mr. Coleman. He just blazed right past me." The plump, blond woman gave him a disdainful glare. "I tried to stop him, but he wouldn't listen."

"That's okay, Phyllis." Dick gave her a nod. "I'll take it from here. Close the door as you leave, please."

Phyllis gave Jayson another scathing look, then turned and walked out, closing the door behind her.

"Was I serious about what?" Dick asked, a trace of irritation in his voice.

"Were you serious when you said that if I take your new drug, and it works, you'll pair me up with Layla?"

Dick sat back in his chair, his expression changing to something between curious and appraising. "Once we're able to verify the drug has worked—in some kind of field test—then yes, I'd be open to pairing you and Layla up as a team."

"Then I want to take the drug," Jayson said. "Now."

He expected Dick to ask why the sudden rush, but the deputy only regarded him thoughtfully. "Are you sure, Jayson? This isn't exactly a situation you can back out of once you've started."

Jayson nodded. "I'm sure."

Dick considered that for a moment, then nodded. "Let's go, then."

Getting up from his chair, the deputy director headed for the door. Jayson took a deep breath and followed. He had to move a little faster than he liked to keep up with Dick, which made his back twinge and tighten up, but the deputy director didn't seem to notice, and Jayson refused to show any weakness.

As they left the operations building and walked down the sidewalk to the facility where the DCO conducted their shifter and hybrid research, Jayson's heart beat faster. He knew this was rash, stupid, and probably insane, but after everything that had happened last night, he didn't have a choice. No matter what, something had to change. And taking Dick's hybrid serum would definitely change things, one way or the other.

Last night had been a complete and total disaster. Not only had he been a grade A asshole, but he was also pretty sure he might have destroyed whatever was left of his relationship with Layla.

He should never have brought up Dick and that damn hybrid serum. He'd known Layla wouldn't be thrilled with him taking a drug that hadn't been tested on humans, but when she immediately assumed that Dick was *manipulating* him into taking it, something inside him had snapped.

He'd wanted to tell her that he was frightened too, but for different reasons. He was more scared of being a cripple for the rest of his life than he was of Dick's hybrid serum. He was terrified of her going after dangerous international arms dealers without him and scared of her spending more time with another man—even if it was her DCO partner—than she did with him. Most of all, he was afraid of sitting in a chair, watching his life—and the woman he loved—drift away from him.

But he hadn't said any of that. Instead, only anger and frustration had come out of his mouth, and before he knew it, Layla was gone, slamming the door on him and their relationship. He'd immediately gone after her, but by the time he'd gotten to the door, her phone had rung. He couldn't hear everything she said, but he'd heard enough to know her mission was a go.

He'd spent the whole night sitting in his living room berating the hell out of himself and waiting for the phone to ring. It hadn't.

It wasn't until the sun peeked through the windows that morning that everything became crystal clear to him. One miserable night was all it took to illuminate very clearly that he was never going to be the kind of man who could sit at home and wait patiently for his significant other to come back safely. One night of not knowing and he was ready to explode.

Now he finally realized why none of the relationships he'd tried to have while he was in Special Forces had survived a single deployment. Some people simply couldn't deal with the stress of knowing the person they cared about was in danger on the other side of the world. Last night, he'd figured out he was one of those people. If Layla was going to be out there, he had to find a way to be with her. If that meant taking Dick's serum, then so be it. Because living like this wasn't even an option.

He was so lost in thought that he didn't realize they'd reached the lab until the familiar medicinal stench smacked him back into awareness. That's when he saw the DCO's resident hybrid expert, Dr. Zarina Sokolov, standing there with a guarded expression on her face.

"Is there something I can help you with?" Zarina asked Dick in a Russian accent that could be icy cold when she wanted—like now.

Dick didn't seem to notice that the temperature in the room had dropped a few degrees. "I need you to get Jayson ready for the hybrid serum protocol."

Zarina lifted a brow. "I wasn't aware the DCO's hybrid serum protocol was ready yet."

Dick smiled. "I guess no one told you, then. There have been a few breakthroughs in the past couple weeks. I'd appreciate it if you got Jayson ready. I'd like to start as soon as the doctors arrive with the serum."

Zarina's blue eyes darted to Jayson, then back to Dick. "And the serum is safe?"

"I'd never let any of our people take a drug that wasn't completely safe," Dick said. "Now, if that's all, I need to make a phone call."

Dick gave Jayson a nod, then walked out of the lab, leaving him alone with the Russian doctor.

"Jayson, this is insane. You shouldn't be agreeing to this. You've seen what this serum can do to people." she said.

Jayson had to admit, he was a little concerned that the one person who probably knew more about hybrids than anyone in the world wasn't involved in the development of this latest serum—concerned, but not enough to make him reconsider his decision.

"I know what the risks are," he said. "I'm willing to accept them."

She regarded him thoughtfully for a moment, then gestured to one of the examination tables. "Let's get you ready then. I'll need you to take off your shirt and climb up there."

He hesitated, not liking the idea of Zarina—or anyone—seeing his scars. "I thought I was just going to get an injection?"

"You will be getting an injection, probably more than one. I need your shirt off so I can attach the EKG and use the defibrillator on you if your heart stops beating. It will also make it easier to get adrenaline or epinephrine into you quickly if necessary."

None of that sounded very good, but then again, neither did living his life as a cripple. So he pushed those thoughts out of his head and shrugged out of his shirt as Zarina walked over to the built-in cabinets along the wall. He tossed the garment on the back of a nearby chair and climbed onto the exam table, flinching as his injured muscles quivered in complaint when he lay back on the cold paper.

Zarina closed the drawer she'd been rustling around in, then turned toward him, a big syringe in one hand and a vial in the other. Without a word, she shoved the needle in the top of the bottle and pulled out the plunger, filling the syringe with the thick, yellowish liquid. When she was done, she set down the empty vial, then picked up a gauze pad from the counter and walked over to him.

"What is that?" he asked.

She swabbed his left bicep with the alcohol wipe. "Gamma globulin. It's to boost your immune system and help your body handle the stress of taking the serum."

She shoved the needle in his arm and pushed in the plunger. He inhaled sharply. Damn, it felt like she was injecting him with a Jell-O shot made out of battery acid.

"That kind of burns, Doc," he said with a laugh.

Zarina pinned him with a look as she pulled out the needle and massaged the area with her fingers. "The hybrid serum will be much worse."

She walked back over to the counter without waiting for a reply. Jayson snorted. She must have been absent from medical school the day they taught bedside manner.

It turned out that Zarina had a better bedside manner than Jayson had given her credit for, at least compared to the two doctors who came in with Dick thirty minutes later. They ignored Jayson as if he weren't there, instead asking Zarina a few medical questions that he really didn't understand before finally nodding at Dick.

"Are you ready?" Dick asked.

Was that excitement in Dick's voice? Jayson had to admit, right then, there was a part of him that wondered if Layla was right about the deputy director using him. But as Dick leaned over the table, his gray eyes full of concern, it was hard not thinking the man genuinely cared about him.

"I'm ready," Jayson told him.

Standing behind Dick, Zarina looked uneasy.

Knowing she was worried only made Jayson worry too, so instead he focused his gaze on the high ceiling. The two doctors approached the table, one on either side. A moment later, he felt each of them shove a needle deep into the muscles of his biceps.

At first, he didn't feel anything besides the pain that came with getting stuck by syringes. Maybe Zarina had been messing with him about the serum being worse than the yellow goo she'd pumped into him.

That's when the burning started—first in his arms, then all over. Within seconds, the fire spread through his entire body. He gripped the edges of the table. *Shit.* Maybe this was going to kill him.

He closed his eyes and forced himself to take slow, deep breaths. That helped for a little while. At least until the muscle spasms started. The pain was excruciating then. But it was nothing compared to how much it hurt thinking he might not ever see Layla again or have the chance to be her partner—they would have been awesome together.

He felt someone grab his left hand and squeeze tightly. He opened his eyes to see Zarina standing beside the exam table, concern on her face. On his right, Dick grabbed his other hand.

Jayson wasn't sure how long the pain lasted, but at some point, it began to recede—slowly at first, then faster as the minutes—or was it hours?—ticked by.

Through the fog surrounding him, he heard the doctors talking to each other about the readings displayed on the various pieces of medical equipment hooked up to him and comparing notes about his reaction to the serum.

As the pain finally disappeared completely, he looked over to see Zarina still holding his hand. Dick was on the far side of the room, a cell phone up to his ear. Jayson heard him saying something about the first phase of the test being very successful.

Jayson was so focused on what Dick was saying that he didn't realize Zarina had released his hand until one of the doctors who'd administered the serum came up and began poking and prodding him like he was a piece of pizza dough.

"It's been two hours and the results seem nominal so far," the man said to Dick as the deputy director hung up the phone. "We need to move on to phase two and get him into a field environment as soon as possible. It's the only way we'll know for sure whether the serum worked."

The doctor didn't even look at Jayson as he spoke. Why should he? To them, he was just a two-legged lab rat. A rat they anxiously wanted to get into the field in order to evaluate the success of their experiment. Normally, that kind of dismissive, condescending bullshit would have pissed Jayson off. But right then, he'd have liked nothing better than to go into the field. And he knew exactly where he should go—to meet up with Layla.

"I never thought we'd get in here so easily," Ivy whispered to Landon as a member of Thomas Thorn's security staff led them up the marble stairs to the third floor of the former senator's home.

"No kidding," Landon muttered. "Though I have to

admit, coming in through the front door almost seems like cheating."

On the way up the steps, she and Landon passed several plain clothes detectives, two uniformed police officers, and three crime scene techs. None of them looked happy to be there. From what John said when he'd called, Thomas Thorn was royally pissed that someone had waltzed into his heavily secured home while he'd been there and made off with a family heirloom.

When they reached the third floor, the guard led them to a room at the end of the hallway. Thorn and his head of security, Douglas Frasier, were over by the far wall near a big picture frame that had been swung back on a hinge to reveal an open safe. A tall, dark-haired man in jeans and a leather jacket who exuded pure cop stood near the big window, and from the way he was clenching his jaw, he was obviously angry about something. He wasn't the only one. Ivy could practically hear Thorn's teeth grind together as he took in the empty safe. As for his paid muscle, Frasier looked like he was waiting for a live chicken to walk by so he could bite off its head.

The detective frowned when he saw her and Landon. "This is a crime scene. I'm going to need you to step outside."

"That's not necessary, Detective. I asked them to join us," Thorn said. "These are Agents Donovan and Halliwell from the Department of Homeland Security. They're here to help with the investigation."

Detective Hayes looked like someone had just handed him a lemon to suck. "DHS is working home break-ins these days?"

"This is Detective Braden Hayes," Thorn said,

interrupting before either she or Landon could respond. Probably a good thing, since Landon would have almost certainly said something snarky in response to the sarcastic tone in the detective's voice. "He handles major robbery for the Washington Metropolitan Police Department. You three will be working together."

Hayes's eyes narrowed. "Burglary is a police matter. DHS has no jurisdiction here. Unless you're trying to tell me that this case has terrorism implications that I don't see."

"This isn't an issue of jurisdiction or terrorism," Thorn snapped. "This is about someone breaking into my home and stealing something that's extremely valuable to me. You *will* work together, you *will* find the thief who took my property, and you *will* get back what they took. If you can't do that, Detective, I can call the MPD brass and have someone else assigned to this case. Is that clear?"

The detective's jaw tightened, but he didn't say anything. Obviously, he was smart enough to realize this wasn't a battle he could win. Even for a former senator, Thorn possessed a tremendous amount of influence in the DC area. Add that to the power that came with his position as CEO of Chadwick-Thorn and his place on the DCO Committee, and Thorn could easily make life a living hell for the detective if he wanted to. The only problem was, Braden Hayes seemed like the kind of man who loved tilting at windmills, even if the windmill always won.

She'd better step in and say something before the two men decided to drop their pants and compare dick size. "What do we know about the thief so far?"

Hayes and Thorn continued their staring contest for another long moment before the detective finally turned his gaze on her. "Unfortunately, we don't know much of anything about the thief at this point. We can't even say for sure how many of them there were."

"No evidence left behind, I'm guessing?" Landon asked.

Hayes shook his head. "Nothing. No fingerprints, hair, fiber, or trace materials. No footprints anywhere on the grounds, no obvious signs of forced entry, and not a single mark on the safe. No one would even know it had been tampered with if it weren't for the fact that it was left hanging open."

"How did the thief get in?" Ivy asked as she wandered around the study.

"We're still looking for his entry point into the home, but right now it's looking like he came in through a third-floor window in the hallway, by way of the roof. I was up there earlier with some of the security staff. You'd have to be a psycho to walk around on that tile, but that seems to make the most sense. I'm thinking the thief lowered himself down from the edge of the roof somehow and came in through a window, but how he did it is beyond me."

Ivy's estimation of the detective went up a few notches, not just because he'd actually figured out how the shifter had gotten into the home, but also because he'd been committed enough to clamber around on the roof and confirm his suspicions.

"About all I can say for sure is that the thief is good," Hayes added. "Based on the time line established by the security people working last night, the thief couldn't have been on the property for more than fifteen minutes."

"What did he take?" Landon asked.

"This," Frasier said, handing Landon a photograph

of what looked like a flawless diamond. "It was last appraised for twenty-five million and is worth considerably more than that now."

Ivy blinked. While she couldn't tell the exact size of the diamond from the picture, it looked huge.

Landon handed the photo back to Frasier. "Was anything else taken?"

"No," Thorn said quickly—too quickly. "Just the diamond."

Ivy's kitty alarm immediately went off. Thorn was lying, she was sure of it. And something told her that the former senator was more interested in getting that other item back than he was the diamond.

Detective Hayes hung around a few more minutes before announcing he was going to start checking the usual fences to see if they'd heard of anyone looking to sell a diamond.

He handed Landon his card, then gave both of them a nod. "If you'd like to compare notes, give me a call."

The moment Hayes left the room, Thorn looked at Ivy expectantly. "Was the thief a shifter?"

"Could be," she said. "Especially if Hayes is right about how the person got into the house."

"Could be?" Thorn frowned. "I thought shifters could identify other shifters purely by scent?"

Ivy gave him a bland smile. "My sense of smell isn't that good. I have feline DNA, not bloodhound. If it was a shifter, they weren't here long enough to leave much of a scent trail behind. Not that it would have mattered. With all the cops and crime scene techs running around here, whatever traces left behind have been obliterated by now."

Thorn swore. "I want you two to stick close to Hayes. I get the feeling he already has a few ideas about who this thief might be. If so, figure out who he is before Hayes can pick him up."

Landon exchanged looks with her. "What do you want us to do when we identify him?"

"Get the information to Frasier." Thorn's mouth twisted into an evil smile. "He'll take care of it from there."

A chill ran down Ivy's spine. Whatever the female shifter had taken, it was obviously something the former senator was willing to kill to get back.

Hayes was waiting for her and Landon outside.

"I thought you were going to talk to some fences," Landon said drily.

"I'd appreciate both of you staying out of the way on this case, regardless of what Mr. Thorn said," Hayes said, then added, "I'll give you as much credit as you want, as long as you don't interfere in my investigation."

Hayes didn't wait for an answer, but simply walked over to his silver Dodge Charger and got in without a backward glance. Landon chuckled as Hayes drove off. "I think I like this cop. He reminds me of Clayne— without the claws and fangs."

Ivy silently agreed. "Unfortunately, I get the feeling that Hayes is as stubborn and relentless as Clayne too. If there's someone out there who could catch a shifter cat burglar, it would be this guy. Normally, I'd be all for that, but in this case, it's going to get the shifter killed, and probably Hayes too."

"Then I guess we're going to have to ignore his request and interfere in his investigation," Landon said.

Chapter 4

"I DON'T UNDERSTAND," JAYSON SAID AS HE PULLED ON his shirt. "If you need me in the field so urgently, why not just let me go meet up with Layla? I could hook up with her and get the adrenaline rush or whatever the hell you said I need to activate the serum."

Dick gave him a placating smile. "The doctors and I already explained it to you. We need to put you in a very specific field environment, one in which you're going to be exposed to the proper amount of stress to make your adrenaline, norepinephrine, and cortisol hormones spike, not to mention all those other hormones and neurotransmitters the doctors mentioned. The situation in Glasgow is already resolved, so it wouldn't do any good to send you there."

"So send me on another mission with Layla," Jayson insisted.

Dick sighed. "Jayson, think this through. We don't have time to screw around waiting for the right situation to develop somewhere in the world. Moreover, the doctors have a very legitimate concern that being around Layla your first time in the field might actually delay the process. She's too much of a calming influence on you, and your body wouldn't react to the stress the way we need it to in order for this to work."

Jayson almost growled in frustration. After all the crap he'd gone through, he really didn't feel like waiting any longer.

"Look," Dick said softly, pulling him off to the side and out of hearing range of the two old doctors who were still eyeing him like a lab rat. "I promise we're going to get you into the field with Layla as soon as we can. Until then, you need to work with me on this other mission so we can see if this serum really worked."

Jayson understood what Dick was saying, even if he thought the man was completely wrong. Sure, there was still some pain in his lower back, but he was able to move around better than he had in a long time. He could even bend over and touch his toes. He felt some pain, no doubt about it, but to be able to do something like that was frigging amazing.

The doctors said that was only the first step in a very long process though. The new hybrid serum had been designed to make small, incremental changes to his body because it would be less stressful on him and less likely to lead to a violent rejection scenario. They'd told him that if the drug worked the way it was supposed to, he could expect even more healing in his back, followed by the emergence of shifter skills. It would take time— and the right application of stress-related hormones.

Jayson knew he was indebted to Dick—the man may have given him the greatest gift he could have ever asked for. If that was the case, why did he suddenly feel so wary?

Dick put a hand on his shoulder much the same way Jayson's late father used to do. "Jayson?"

He nodded. "Let's do this."

"That's what I like to hear." Dick smiled and squeezed his shoulder. "Come on. Everything's set up in the main conference room."

As they left the lab a few hours later and walked over to the operations building, Jayson thought about Layla. Even though Dick hadn't given him details, it sounded like the mission in Glasgow had gone well. That meant she was probably already on her way back. If he were lucky, she'd get there before he left. Hopefully by the time she returned, he'd have figured out how he was going to explain to her what he'd done and why. While he was thrilled with how everything had turned out, he realized now that his decision to take the drug had been reckless. Layla was still going to be furious with him, but maybe this time he'd be able to get her to understand why he'd taken such a huge risk.

When they got to the operations building, Dick led him into the conference room. One of the big screens on the wall at the front displayed a map of Russia and Ukraine while the other four displayed photos of various people. A pocket-protector type was at the table manning the computer and leafing through folders.

Jayson sat down just as Powell walked in. The hairs on the back of his neck stood on end as Powell took the seat across from him. It didn't take a genius to figure out why the asshat was here. Powell was going to be his partner on this mission.

You have to be fucking kidding me.

From where he stood at the head of the table, Dick directed a laser pointer at the screen with a photo of a smiling kid who looked about seventeen. The picture looked like it had come from a high school yearbook.

"This is Dylan Palmer," Dick said. "He's the son of Norman Palmer, the counselor of political affairs at the U.S. Embassy in Kiev, Ukraine. Four days ago, Dylan didn't come home. Given what's currently going on over there, the embassy immediately sent someone to look for him, thinking he might have been kidnapped. They quickly realized they had a much bigger problem on their hands."

Dick nodded at the guy manning the computers and a blog came up on another screen. Jayson quickly scanned it. There were posts about Russian aggression, autonomous regions, cease-fires, and military atrocities.

"Dylan fancies himself an investigative journalist," Dick continued. "Apparently he'd heard rumors about all the bad stuff going on in the Russian-controlled territories around Donetsk and decided he needed to experience it firsthand. He loaded up his iPad and ran off to a frigging war zone to do a little snooping and write the next Pulitzer-worthy story. The best the embassy can tell, Dylan has been in Donetsk for at least two days."

Jayson winced. He watched a lot of news these days—the perk of not being able to sleep at night. The fighting in Ukraine had been headline material for weeks, and even though the media had grown bored with the subject and moved on to the next big thing, the fighting there was still going on.

Most of eastern Ukraine was populated with people of Russian ancestry who had ties to their native country. Western Ukraine, on the other hand, was predominantly populated by Ukrainians who had loyalties of a completely different nature and a tendency to look toward Western Europe for direction, as opposed to Mother Russia. The battles with pro-Russian forces against the separatist forces along the border of the two distinct parts of the country had been bloody and violent. If the kid had been looking for a place to find a gritty story, he'd definitely gone to the right area.

Dick pointed the laser at a photo of a dark-haired girl about the same age as Dylan. "Everything indicates that Dylan is with his Ukrainian girlfriend, Anya Zelenko, and possibly several of their friends, but nobody's saying much, and the embassy doesn't want to stir up anything because they fear the militias running the region will hear about it and start actively looking for him."

"Why hasn't the embassy sent some of their people in to go get the kid already?" Powell asked. "The CIA could be in and out of there in a couple hours."

"I'm sure they could," Dick agreed. "But unfortunately for Dylan, the U.S. is currently taking a hands-off approach to the whole region and has no desire to call attention to the fact that there's an American citizen, the son of a diplomat at that, running around what is essentially Russian-held territory. They're disavowing any and all knowledge or involvement in this situation."

"So Dylan is on his own?" Jayson asked.

"Except for us, yes."

"Donetsk is a pretty big city," Jayson pointed out. "Do we have anything as far as the kid's current location?"

"His father got a text from him about two days ago saying he was somewhere around the international airport near a small town called Oktyabrsky," Dick said.

The blog disappeared from the screen to be replaced by a map of the area.

Jayson narrowed his eyes, trying to remember why Oktyabrsky was important. Then it hit him. "I remember seeing that place in the news. Didn't both sides shell the hell out of that city?"

Dick nodded. "That particular area is still seeing a lot of violence and militia activity. The majority of the region's citizens are stuck in the middle, trying to keep their heads down and survive. There's no government control in the autonomous regions so militia groups are vying for control and whatever power they can get."

Militia groups. That was a nice way of saying they were a ragtag collection of current and former military who had the weapons and know-how to make sure they came out on top in a crappy situation.

"But none of that matters," Dick added. "This is a simple track, bag, and drag mission. There should be no reason to even come into contact with any of the militia groups, much less engage with them."

Jayson wasn't so sure about that. He'd learned from experience that it was rarely a good idea to assume you could avoid contact with any group in possession of a large amount of weapons.

"Besides, that punk kid is probably hiding in a basement somewhere, pissing his pants and scared to death," Powell snorted, his gray eyes hard. "All we need to do is find him and get him back to daddy. We should be in and out of there in a few hours."

Jayson wondered if he should suggest that Dick and Powell go together since they both seemed to think this mission would be such a breeze. He bit his tongue and instead asked how many different militia groups occupied the area, where they were headquartered, how large their territories were, who might be willing to help them, and most importantly, the best route to get the kid out of Donetsk once they had him.

Powell got bored about halfway through the

questions and got up to leave, telling Jayson he'd get their gear ready.

"For whenever you get tired of talking and decide to start doing," he added snidely.

That was when it really hit Jayson. He was going to a war-torn part of the world with that asshat to do a mission that wasn't exactly going to be a walk in the park.

"Are you sure sending me out on a mission like this is a good idea?" Jayson asked after the briefing was over. "We don't even know what I can do."

"If we don't send you now, we're never going to know what you can do," Dick said. "Like you said, this kid doesn't have anyone else to help him. He's a political liability. If we don't go over there, he's probably not going to make it."

That was what had Jayson worried. If the serum didn't work and he couldn't do the job, Dylan might not make it anyway.

"You know Powell and I don't exactly make the best teammates, right?" he asked. "I'm completely new at this—at least as far as DCO missions are concerned—and from my few run-ins with him, Powell doesn't seem much more experienced than I am. Shouldn't I be going out with someone who's been on these types of missions before, someone who can work with a shifter?"

"You have enough field experience for both of you," Dick said. "Powell is just there to back you up and let me know how you did."

Jayson nodded, but he was still concerned as hell.

Dick must have seen it on his face, because he frowned. "What's eating you all of a sudden? You were Special Forces. You're used to this kind of stuff. You don't worry about who you're going with or what the mission is going to be. You just go."

That had been true until that day in Afghanistan when they were lured into a trap and blown up. His head was spinning at a thousand miles an hour. He'd just admitted to himself a little while ago that taking the hybrid serum had been rash—and stupid. Was he making another rash, stupid decision by going out on this mission so soon after taking the drug, especially with Powell as a partner?

Dick sighed. "I need you to do this for me, and I need you to be a success. There are people on the Committee who didn't view you as a suitable candidate for the new serum. They thought you were too damaged. I put my neck out and said they were wrong. I told them that you aren't only a major asset to this organization, but that you're also a war hero who needs a new lease on life, not just a job. A hand up, not a handout. If you can't do this, the Committee is going to use that serum on people they think fit their mold. You're the prototype for the kind of person who should be getting this treatment. You need to do this, for both our sakes and for the sake of other amazing people out there just like you."

Jayson ground his jaw, hating what the situation was forcing him into. But Dick was right. He'd stuck his neck out for Jayson, and Jayson couldn't let him down—even if his gut was telling him he was making a huge-ass mistake.

Layla walked into the DCO operations building with her emotions in a tangled knot. She'd called Jayson last night to tell him she was on her way back from Glasgow, but he hadn't answered his cell or his home phone. She'd tried to tell herself not to worry, that Jayson had probably taken a stronger pain med and was just sleeping. She'd stopped by his apartment this morning before coming to the complex, hoping to catch him before he went to work, but he wasn't home. He wasn't in his office or on the shooting range either, and he still wasn't answering his phone. That's when her instincts screamed that something was terribly wrong.

As she hurried down the hall to Kendra's office, Layla's fear that Jayson had taken Dick up on his outrageous offer grew more intense. But if he'd taken the hybrid serum and something awful had happened, wouldn't Ivy have called her?

She quickened her step, practically running the rest of the way to Kendra's office. The DCO's resident jill-of-all-trades was sitting at her desk dialing the phone when she rushed in, but the minute she saw Layla, she stopped and dropped the receiver back in its cradle.

"I was just calling you," Kendra said. "It's Jayson."

Layla tensed, praying her instincts were wrong but knowing they weren't. "What about him?"

"Dick talked him into taking that damn hybrid serum," Kendra said. "I was out yesterday at my ob-gyn appointment and didn't even find out until this morning."

Layla's heart plummeted. *Oh God.* "Is he okay? Where is he?"

"I don't know if he's okay or not. Dick sent him straight out the door on a mission with Powell."

Of all the people Dick could have teamed Jayson up with, he had to pick that jackass. "What kind of mission?

Shouldn't they have waited to see if Jayson had a reaction before sending him into the field?"

"You'd think so, wouldn't you? I don't know what kind of mission it is or where they went, but I'm hoping Zarina can tell us something." Kendra put a hand on the arm of her chair and pushed herself to her feet. She might still be in her second trimester, but she looked like she could have given birth to the twins at any minute. "Want to come to the lab with me?"

That was a silly question. Of course Layla did. The moment they were outside, she had to force herself to keep pace with Kendra and not run ahead. She didn't want to waste even the slightest amount of time.

Zarina was typing something on her computer when they hurried into her office a few long minutes later.

"Is Jayson okay?" Layla asked without preamble.

"He seemed fine when he left," Zarina took off her reading glasses, then stood and came around the desk. "But that's probably thanks to the antidote I gave him right before Dick's doctors injected him with the serum."

Layla's eyes widened. "You made an antidote? I didn't think you even had a sample of the serum."

"I didn't," Zarina said. "I gave Jayson something I've been developing for Tanner in the hope that it will reverse some or all the hybrid changes. When I realized I'd never be able to talk Jayson out of taking the serum, I gave him the antidote hoping to counteract it."

Oh God. Zarina had essentially given Jayson one untested and dangerous drug in the hopes of counteracting another untested, dangerous drug.

"Did it work?" Layla asked.

"Well, he didn't die the minute the serum hit his

bloodstream, which is probably what would have happened if I hadn't given him the antidote." Zarina shook her head, her mouth tight. "Other than that, I don't know how successful my drug was. It might have completely halted the hybrid transformation or simply slowed it down."

Layla almost growled in frustration. Damn Dick Coleman. "But Jayson lived. That has to count for something, right? If he was fit enough to go on a mission, that has to mean he's going to be okay."

Zarina's smile was sad. "I wish I could tell you that was the case, but I can't. Without being able to study his blood and DNA, I have no way of knowing what the hybrid serum will do to him long-term, or how his body will handle the interaction of the serum and my antidote."

"Could this get any worse?" Layla moaned.

She'd meant the question to be rhetorical, but Zarina answered anyway. "Yes, it can. Jayson's body could violently reject either drug at any time. It might be the next time he falls asleep or the first time his body goes into fight-or-flight mode. The truth is, I don't know what's going to happen to him. I won't know until we get him back here and I can examine him. The sooner the better."

From Zarina's lips to God's ears, Layla thought. First, they had to find out where Jayson had gone. Unfortunately, the Russian doctor didn't know. And Dick, weasel that he was, happened to be out of the office for the next several days. His less-than-friendly secretary wasn't much help either, but luckily Kendra had a lot of friends in the intel division and tracked down the analyst who'd been in the conference room during the mission briefing.

Layla freaked when the guy told them that Jayson and Powell were on a completely unsupported rescue operation in pro-Russian parts of Ukraine. They hadn't even taken a satellite phone with them to call for backup if something went wrong. Was Dick trying to get them killed?

"I have to go over there and get him," Layla said as soon as she and Kendra were in the hallway.

"First, we have to talk to John and tell him what's going on." Kendra glanced at her. "Jayson's going to be okay."

Not if she didn't get him out of Ukraine and back here so Zarina could monitor him, Layla thought. But if anyone would know what to do in this situation, it was John. She only hoped he was in his office. She hadn't seen him around the complex in weeks.

Thankfully, he was. To say he was shocked when they told him about Jayson was an understatement.

"Shit," he muttered. "I knew Dick was working with Thorn, but I never guessed he'd do something this insane. He could have killed Jayson with that serum."

"He still might," Layla said. "Zarina has no idea how Jayson's body is going to react to the drugs pumping through his veins. He could go into shock, flip out in a hybrid rage, or worse."

"And if the drug doesn't get him, the mission might," Kendra added. "Ukraine is a powder keg just waiting to explode, and sending Jayson in with Powell is worse than sending him in alone. If Jayson doesn't develop any shifter abilities—and Zarina has no idea if he will—he could end up getting killed over there."

In addition to all that, Powell was a flipping asshole who hated shifters and hybrids alike. Layla couldn't imagine him putting all that hatred aside if Jayson got into trouble. Powell would take care of himself first, and if there was one person in the DCO who was a firm believer in the organization's stupid prime directive about never letting a shifter's identity be compromised, it was that jackass. The man would kill Jayson just because he could.

"Even though they have a good head start, I'm confident I can find them," Layla said.

Kendra was already nodding as she made notes on a pad she'd grabbed off John's desk.

"No," John said.

Her stomach dropped. "What?" she asked, sure she'd misheard him.

"I said no," John repeated. "I'm sure you did well over in Glasgow, but you were pulling support duty, not leading a mission."

"I took down two of the Scottish buyers without help from anyone on the team," she protested. "I can do this."

"You don't have the training or experience to handle a solo operation like this," John insisted. "Worse, you're too close to the situation. I can't have you going over there and making a mistake that gets you in trouble because you're worried about Jayson. You're not going."

Layla's control over her inner feline started to slip again. Before she realized it, the tips of her fangs had elongated and her claws came out. She didn't even try to hide them. She'd never been this scared, frustrated, or angry in her life. The man she loved was in danger, and John was sitting there telling her she couldn't go help him.

"Who are you going to send, then?" she demanded, biting back a growl.

"I'll get a message to Clayne and Danica. They're closer to Ukraine than any other team, so I'll tell them to divert and go to Donetsk."

Layla wanted to point out that it could take a while for Clayne and Danica to be able to divert from wherever they were to get to Ukraine. Who the heck knew where those two had gone in their search for Kojot after he had escaped? If the last mission had taught her anything, it was that the arms dealer was slippery—and that Clayne was obsessed with catching him. If Kojot had disappeared down a dark hole in the ground, it was likely that Clayne would go in after him, and Danica would follow.

But it would be useless to say any of that to John. He wasn't going to let her go, no matter what she said. So she waited for him to leave for the operations center so he could get a message to Clayne and Danica, then she turned to Kendra.

"If Declan were the one in danger, would you be okay waiting around for someone else to go over there and help him?" she asked.

Kendra regarded Layla in silence for a long moment, then sighed. "John's going to have my head for this. Go get ready. I'll have you booked on a flight to Ukraine by the time you get to the airport."

Chapter 5

"I COULD HAVE GOTTEN AS MUCH OUT OF THAT OLD MAN in three minutes as you did in thirty just by punching him in the gut," Powell grumbled as they walked down the rubble-filled street. "Another complete waste of time."

Jayson ignored the DCO agent as he scanned the occasional damaged and blown-up building looking for a particular Russian Orthodox Church with a broken bell. It was where Dylan Palmer was supposedly hiding. Or rather, where someone was hiding him, if the information they'd slowly been gathering since reaching the small town of Oktyabrsky was correct. Jayson hoped he could trust the info, because he sure as hell wasn't going to get any help from Powell when it came to finding the diplomat's kid.

They'd landed in Kiev late last night, then taken a series of trucks and cars to get to the Donetsk region. Sitting that much had seriously tightened up Jayson's back, but the pain was nowhere near as bad as it used to be. If the hybrid serum did nothing but give him some relief from the discomfort, he'd consider it a win.

Unfortunately, while getting into the region had been easy, finding Dylan had turned out to be a lot more difficult than Jayson had hoped. It hadn't taken him very long to figure out this mission wasn't going to be the quick track, bag, and drag Dick thought. First, Jayson didn't speak more than a few words of Russian, which made talking to people difficult. And while Powell spoke the language better, Jayson didn't exactly trust him when he translated. Second, the citizens living in this part of the country were scared to death of strangers. And third, Powell was a steaming pile of shit.

The other DCO agent's idea of a plan was walking up to nervous people in the middle of the street and flashing a photo of the kid in their faces. If the person acted like they hadn't seen the boy, Powell generally resorted to threats of violence to get them to talk. Shockingly, Powell couldn't understand why that didn't work.

Of course, if he opened his eyes and looked around, Powell might have figured out why locals were so hesitant to talk. If Dylan were looking for a dark, soul-sucking place to write about in his blog, he'd definitely found the right town. It was hard to find a single building that hadn't been damaged in the fighting, and many of them were completely destroyed. The worst part wasn't the physical damage though. It was the fear that filled the face of every man, woman, and child.

According to the people who had talked to them, this particular area of the Donetsk People's Republic—or DPR—was under the control of an independent militia group run by a former Russian army colonel named Zolnerov. Normally the way places like Donetsk governed themselves would be none of Jayson's business, but when he saw people like Zolnerov using the situation to become powerful, it pissed him off.

Jayson had seen this before in half a dozen different places. The scared and suspicious looks, the locked doors and windows, the vacant shops, the nearly empty streets—even at midday. People who once praised the militia were now terrified of them. But no one would stand up and call them out because they feared being labeled a sympathizer, a traitor, or a spy. Many people had already left the town, and more were leaving every day. At this rate, a city that had a population of nearly two million would be a ghost town in a few years.

"This is stupid," Powell groused as they moved through another dilapidated block of houses and into the next neighborhood. "We've been at this for hours and the sun is going down. Face it, there is no church with a broken bell. That old man sold you a load of crap just to get away from you. How about I pick out the next person we talk to and question them my way?"

Jayson ground his teeth. He could only imagine the kind of person Powell would want to question—young and female.

Sure enough, Powell was already heading toward a girl who couldn't have been more than sixteen years old, hurrying along the nearly deserted street, when a flash of gold in the distance caught Jayson's attention. He grabbed a handful of Powell's jacket, hauling him back.

"What the hell are you doing?" Powell demanded.

Jayson really didn't want to get into a fight out here on the streets, not with all the DPR militia troops congregating on every block, but decking Powell was hard to resist. He ignored the urge and pointed at the building down the street on the left.

"What?" Powell asked stubbornly.

"Fancy building. Golden dome on one side, blown-out bell tower on the other."

Powell still seemed to be clueless.

"Russian Orthodox Church with a broken bell," Jayson said.

Powell stared at the building like he was translating a foreign language, then grunted. "Maybe you're not so worthless after all."

The black-robed priest near the altar turned when they walked into the church. Unlike the people on the street, the bearded, gray-haired man didn't look frightened, but instead seemed resolute and defiant. Luckily, the priest spoke English, and when Jayson showed him Dylan's photo, he nodded and motioned for them to follow. Powell slipped his hand behind his back and rested it on his gun but nodded to Jayson.

The priest led them out of the church proper and across the hallway to a room. He knocked twice on the door, then opened it to reveal a small office. Dylan was sitting on a couch against one wall along with two other teenage boys. He looked exhausted and scared, but at the sight of them, he immediately jumped to his feet and snatched up a heavy candlestick from a nearby table.

"Who are you?" he demanded, moving to stand in front of the other teens.

"Relax, killer," Powell said while crossing the room to look out the window at a group of militia soldiers across the street. "We're here to take you back to daddy. Get your shit together. We're getting out of here."

Not exactly the smoothest way to announce the plan, but Jayson had to admit Powell's simplistic approach got to the point quickly. Unfortunately, Dylan didn't seem impressed with either the approach or the plan.

"I'm not going anywhere." He set down the candlestick, an expression of youthful defiance on his face.

Tall and lanky, with blond hair and brown eyes, Dylan looked ready to fight him and Powell with his bare hands. "Not without my friends—and not without Anya."

"We're not here for your friends," Powell said tersely. "And who the hell is Anya?"

"Anya is the Ukrainian girlfriend," Jayson reminded Powell. "Dick mentioned her during the briefing."

Powell looked at Jayson like he had no idea what the hell Jayson was taking about. Jayson shook his head. Why did he even bother?

"Where is she?" Jayson asked Dylan.

"She got captured by the militia last night," the curly-haired kid on Dylan's right answered in heavily accented English.

Powell's eyes narrowed suspiciously at the kid. "Who the hell are you?"

"Mikhail Ivanov." He jerked his thumb at the stocky, dark-haired kid next to him. "And this is Olek Rudnik. We're friends of Dylan's."

"Mikhail is a blogger I was in contact with back when Anya and I were in Russia." Dylan swallowed hard, close to tears. "All we wanted was to show the world what they were doing to the people over here, and now they're going to put her in prison for the rest of her life for supposed crimes against the new republic. If they don't execute her for being a Ukrainian spy. I can't leave until I get her back."

"We were trying to figure out how to break into the local militia headquarters when you two busted in here," Mikhail added.

The priest explained that one of the many problems with the plan was that Dylan and his friends weren't even sure Anya was actually being held there. But logic didn't seem to apply in this case. Anya was in trouble, and Dylan was young and in love. Jayson couldn't blame him. Hell, he'd have probably done the same thing.

"If my dad sent you, that must mean you're CIA," Dylan said. "Can you help us get her out?"

"This is bullshit," Powell muttered. "Your girlfriend is probably already dead, kid. And as for you two"—he pointed at Olek and Mikhail—"you'd better get yourselves some paddles because you're going to have to row your own canoe up the damn creek."

"Canoe?" Olek frowned, clearly confused by the metaphor. "What the hell are you talking about?"

"He means that they're not going to help us," Dylan muttered.

"We didn't say that—" Jayson began, but Powell cut him off.

"Damn right we did. Let's go, kid. We're taking you home."

Dylan lifted his chin, the rebellious look back in his dark eyes. "I'm not going anywhere with you, asshole."

Jayson swore. If he didn't know better, he'd think this was a fake scenario Dick and those old doctors had come up with to drive his blood pressure through the roof and bring on phase two of the hybrid process.

"You're coming with us if I have to knock you out and drag you home in a fucking sack, you silver-spoon brat," Powell said, advancing on Dylan.

Just like that, the argument went from heated to out of control. Olek started shouting in Ukrainian while Mikhail did the same in Russian even as Dylan and Powell threatened each other in English.

Shit.

Jayson stepped between Dylan and Powell, shoving them apart just as the priest hurried over from the door where he'd been standing. He said something urgently in Russian, making frantic gestures with his hands, but Jayson was too busy trying to keep Dylan and Powell separated to pay attention. Suddenly, the front doors of the church burst open and slammed against the stone wall. The sound reverberated through the whole building and Jayson froze along with everyone else.

What the hell?

Powell immediately started for the door of the office, but Jayson stopped him with a gesture. Motioning everyone to be quiet, he walked over to the office door and opened it a crack. His stomach clenched. Five men dressed in the modified Russian uniforms of the local independent DPR militia were making their way up the center aisle. Two of them were carrying Vityaz submachine guns while the other three had AK-74M automatics.

Shit.

Jayson quietly closed the door. He and Powell weren't equipped for this. All they had were small P-96 pistols with a few spare clips. They'd come in here for a simple rescue, not a firefight. But it looked like they were going to get into one whether they wanted to or not because those troops were coming their way fast and there was nothing to slow them down.

Jayson reached around behind him and slipped his 9mm out of the holster, then jacked the slide back and chambered a round. He gripped the doorknob and started to turn it when he felt a hand on his arm. He looked over his shoulder to see the priest standing there looking at him intently. The older man pointed at Jayson and the others, then at the row of windows behind them before gesturing at himself, then to the door that led to the main part of the church and the oncoming soldiers.

Jayson shook his head, knowing full well what the priest was suggesting. But the older man shouldered past him and pulled open the door before Jayson could stop him. Back straight, the priest strode boldly into the church, saying something in Russian as he advanced on the soldiers.

If there weren't three terrified teens depending on Jayson to get them out of there, he would have gone after the priest, all that firepower out there be damned. The old man was going to get himself killed. Refusing to waste his sacrifice, Jayson turned and quickly motioned them toward the window. With the exception of Powell, no one moved.

"Go!" he hissed.

Powell opened the window just as the chatter of automatic weapons firing filled the church, echoing off the walls. In the silence that followed, something heavy hit the floor. Dylan and his friends stared at Jayson in horror, panic leeching the color from their faces.

Knowing they only had seconds until the soldiers charged into the office, Jayson grabbed Dylan and forcibly shoved him out the window. At least the kid was smart enough to keep quiet when he hit the ground. Olek and Mikhail quickly followed him out. Being the ass he was, Powell made sure he went next, forcing Jayson to wait to escape. The door of the office opened just as he dived out the window. The stab of agony in his back as he hit the ground brought tears to his eyes and a curse to his lips, but he didn't have time to lie there and wait for the pain to subside. There was no way the soldiers could have missed seeing him.

Ignoring the numbness in his lower body, he scrambled to his feet and took off running. If he hadn't taken the hybrid serum, he'd have still been lying on the ground waiting to get shot. As it was, he barely made it to the corner of the church before bullets chewed up the ground around him. He swore and ran harder, getting to cover before he took a round through the spine.

Powell and the kids were fifteen feet ahead of him. Dylan and his friends slowed, waiting for him to catch up.

"Don't stop!" Jayson shouted.

He didn't have to look behind him to know that the militia soldiers were on their tail. There was no way he and Powell could shoot their way out of this situation, not with three kids in tow.

"Mikhail!" he shouted as he followed them across a dimly lit street. "If you know a place nearby where we can hide, now would be a good time to show us."

The Russian kid nodded and sprinted ahead, motioning with his hand for everyone to follow him.

Jayson hadn't done a lot of cardio since his injury, and it showed. His lungs and throat were on frigging fire as he raced to keep up with them. It didn't help that he had to slow down and pop off a few shots at the soldiers chasing them every so often. A few of the men went down, but reinforcements quickly took their place. Cursing, he emptied the remainder of his clip at them, then turned and sprinted after Powell and the kids.

Jayson started to wonder if Mikhail had a clue where the hell he was going when all four of them suddenly disappeared right in front of him. He dug into what reserves he had left—which wasn't much—almost falling on his butt as he careened down a concrete-lined aqueduct that ran between a grimy industrial complex on one side and a slow-moving river on the other. A few seconds later, he slid to a stop at the bottom. Powell and the kids were bent over, their hands on their knees, gasping for breath.

"We have to keep going," Jayson ground out. "They're right behind us."

Mikhail pointed at a metal grate in the wall a few feet away. "There's a series of tunnels down there. We can get to the other side of the river if we go that way."

Powell shook his head. "If we disappear, those soldiers are going to know we're in the tunnels. They'll have people waiting for us on the other side of the river before we can get there."

Jayson hated to admit it, but Powell was right. The tunnels were a good escape route, just not for all of them.

"You, Dylan, and Olek take the tunnels," he said to Mikhail. "We'll lead the soldiers away from here and meet up with you later."

Dylan looked like he didn't think much of the idea. Neither did Powell. Jayson didn't give either of them a chance to complain. He shoved Dylan toward the grate, then grabbed Powell by the sleeve and motioned him back toward the top of the aqueduct. The man took off without comment.

"There's an abandoned library on the other side of the river straight across from here," Mikhail called. "We'll wait in the basement until morning. If you don't come, we'll know you didn't make it."

Jayson nodded. He waited until the three teens opened the grate and disappeared into the dark tunnel below, then he ran over to where Powell was waiting. They both took off toward the dilapidated industrial area.

"You'd better be right about this," Powell said. "Because you just let the only reason we're here slip away. If that kid bites it, this is going on your record, not mine."

"By all means, let's worry about your damn record at a time like this. Your concern for the lives of those kids is touching," Jayson shot back as they headed for the ramshackle buildings on the other side of the aqueduct.

The place looked like it used to be a steel factory or an oil refinery, judging by the big metal pipes and conveyor chutes running between the buildings and toward the river. As the last rays of the sun slipped behind the dilapidated structures, the gathering gloom had Jayson thinking of a set you'd see in a Batman movie—all dark, gritty, and gothic.

Jayson and Powell moved slowly enough to make sure they didn't completely lose the soldiers behind them. Unfortunately, their plan worked a little too well. One second they were jogging toward the entrance of the nearest building and the next shots were coming at them out of the darkness. Bullets smacked into the building all around them, an occasional glowing-red tracer round lighting up the night as it zipped past. *Damn, there must be at least a dozen troops out there.*

Before long, he and Powell found themselves being herded in first one direction, then another. They tried to break out of the noose closing around them by taking out four of the shadowy figures chasing them, but that still left eight to deal with, and he and Powell were forced up the stairs to the roof of the factory building they were in. Jayson's back screamed from exertion as he jumped from roof to roof, but the hybrid serum must have been doing its job because he could deal with the pain.

Soon enough, they ran out of rooftops and ended up trapped behind a crumbling brick chimney that exploded into pieces as round after round slammed into it from the other side. *Fuck*. This was so not how he'd thought this mission would go. He'd wanted to get a simple op under his belt to prove himself, then he and Layla would get teamed up together. But it looked like that wasn't how this was going to work out.

He'd been so worried about Layla going on a mission, and now it looked like he was the one who was probably going to buy it on the job. There had to be some irony there, but he couldn't see it. He didn't even want to think how much his death would hurt Layla.

Jayson loaded his last clip and gave Powell a look in the gloom. "I saw a scene likes this in a movie called *Butch Cassidy and the Sundance Kid*. It didn't exactly end well for either one of them, and it probably won't for us either, but we're going have to shoot our way out of here anyway. Maybe in the dark we can get past them and find some stairs down to ground level again."

"Screw that noise," Powell said. "You need to do some of that shifter shit and get us the fuck out of here."

Jayson snorted. Guess Powell hadn't gotten the memo that claws and fangs weren't part of his particular package.

"Sorry, guy." He ducked his head as a round hit a little too close for comfort, making shards of stone fly off the chimney and pepper his face. "I might be a shifter, but not that kind."

Powell stared at him in shock for a moment, then his lip curled in a sneer. "Well, if you can't do anything to get us out of this, I guess it's my job to make sure these guys don't get their hands on you."

Jayson had half a second to figure out what the hell Powell was talking about before the asshole lifted his weapon and pointed it straight at him. Powell was going to kill him so the DCO wouldn't be compromised by having a hybrid taken alive.

Bullshit. The fucker wanted to kill him because he was a piece of crap who knew he'd never get a better chance than now to take him out.

Jayson lashed out with his foot, the heel of his boot slamming into the center of Powell's chest and sending him flying backward across the rooftop, where he fell on his ass right in the line of fire. Jayson would have loved to hang around and see if the bastard took one through the head, but he needed to take advantage of the distraction while he had it. Spinning around, he ran for the far edge of the roof, keeping the chimney stacks between him and the militia soldiers as much as he could.

He didn't have a plan for what he was going to do when he reached the edge. He just prayed he wasn't going to have to jump. The thought was painful enough. The reality was sure to be even worse.

Bullets zipped past him, striking the next building over, the one that was way too far away to reach from his position. That was when he spotted one of those big horizontal pipes he'd seen from the ground sticking out from the side of the building. As round as a big telephone pole and at least thirty feet above the ground, it was still a good ten feet from the edge of the roof where he was standing. The very thought that he could possibly jump so far and somehow land on such a small, round surface, and still maintain his balance was insane.

But he was going to do it anyway. It was either that or get shot full of holes. He jammed his pistol in its holster and launched himself off the roof and through the air before he had time to think about how incredibly impossible the jump was.

The leap sent a stab of pain up his spine, but he barely noticed as he focused every ounce of concentration on the pipe. He didn't even try to land feetfirst. That would have been ridiculous for anyone but a cat shifter like Layla. He might have hybrid serum running through his blood, but he didn't think it would improve his agility that much.

He slammed into the pipe chest first, wrapping his arms over it as the air exploded from his lungs. For a moment, he thought he was going to slide right off, but by some miracle, he held on. He would have shouted in triumph if he hadn't been worried about the soldiers hearing him. He'd disappeared from view for the moment, and if the shooting on the roof behind him was any indication, Powell was still occupying the soldiers. But they'd come looking for him soon enough, and he didn't want to be hanging here like a kitty in a motivational poster when they did.

Gritting his teeth, he kicked his legs and crabbed his

way up and onto the pipe. Balancing on the small metal tube wasn't much different from some of the elements on the confidence courses he used to run back at Fort Campbell—minus the three-story drop underneath him. And the people trying to kill him, of course.

Ignoring all of that, he took a deep breath and moved across the pipe in a half crouch as fast as he could. Thankfully, it was completely dark now, so he couldn't see the ground far beneath him. Unfortunately, he also had no idea where the pipe led. Did it go all the way to the river, or was it some kind of outlet into the aqueduct?

Shouting from the building behind Jayson along with the sudden end of the shooting suggested that Powell was done for—and that he would be too if he didn't get the hell out of there. He stopped trying to be careful and ran along the pipe instead. Bullets buzzed past him, making him duck.

Jayson tried to remember how far this building had been from the river. How far had he run? Was he over the aqueduct now or not even close?

He had to be almost there, right?

He was still wondering that when a bullet clipped him in the right thigh. The impact twisted his body, and he felt himself start to fall.

Oh shit.

Jayson was still praying he'd come down on something that wouldn't kill him and bracing for one hell of a hard landing at the same time when he plunged into the river. It might not be concrete, but water was still fucking hard when you hit it from three stories up. He had just enough time to suck in some air before the cold, dark water closed in over his head.

—◦◦◦—

"Why the hell did you tell me about the diamond if you didn't want me to steal it?"

Dreya's words came out as something close to a growl as she glared at Rory from across the small office in the back of the shop. She'd come into his jewelry store expecting him to tell her he'd find her a buyer for Thorn's diamond in no time and that she'd make a nice chunk of change in the process. Instead, he'd taken one look at the gem and told her she'd made a mistake by stealing it.

Rory didn't bat an eye at the strange sound she had made. He simply leaned back against the front of the big, ugly, antique desk that occupied way too much of his small office and regarded her thoughtfully. Then again, he'd known she was different for a long time.

"I tend to recall we talked about a lot of things that night." He chuckled. "Though it's hard to remember everything considering we'd put a good dent in that bottle of El Tesoro."

Maybe so, but she wasn't going to let him off the hook just because he didn't have a problem with her being a freak.

"Don't try and blame this on tequila," she snapped, remembering back to that night a couple weeks ago when they'd hung out at a trendy little bar in Foggy Bottom and talked shop. "You were stone-cold sober and had to know that if you mentioned some guy right here in DC had a diamond that big, I'd go after it."

Rory eyed the diamond nestled comfortably in the palm of her hand. "Actually, I didn't know that. Color me stupid for thinking someone as smart as you would have the sense not to steal something from a man as rich and powerful as Thomas Thorn. I didn't tell you that story so you'd go after him. I told you so you'd stay away."

Dreya frowned and dropped the big diamond in the center of his desk, practically knocking a dent in the dark mahogany wood. "So you're saying you can't fence this diamond for me?"

Rory shook his head of salt-and-pepper hair. "I didn't say I couldn't fence it for you. I'm saying that no one can fence it for you. No one is going to go near that gem with a ten-foot pole. It's unsellable even to a private collector. Everyone on the planet knows that diamond belongs to Thomas Thorn. You're not going to find anyone willing to cross him, no matter how valuable it is or how badly they might want it."

Dreya swore, not even caring if it came out as a full growl this time. "Can't you…I don't know…find somebody who could cut it down into smaller stones, so it wouldn't be recognizable?"

Rory looked at her like he thought she was insane. "Right. I just told you that no one would be dumb enough to even consider buying Thorn's diamond, and you think I'll be able to find someone willing to take a cutting tool to it? Not going to happen."

Dreya flopped down hard in the seat in front of the desk and sighed, waiting impatiently for the tingle in her gums to away. That was all she needed, a mouth full of razor-sharp teeth. That would make her day just about complete.

She supposed she couldn't blame Rory. It had only been a little over seventy-two hours since she'd broken into Thorn's place, and already the world she and Rory lived in was buzzing with the news that the former senator had brought in some heavy hitters to find the person who'd stolen his stuff. Rory had every right to be scared. He was one of the better-known fences along the northeast corridor. If someone was going to start hunting for a jewel thief, there was a good chance they'd start with him.

She leaned forward and picked up the diamond pendant by its chain, watching the lights in the office twinkle off the facets. "What the hell am I going to do with this thing, then? Should I just hold on to it for a while, until it cools off a bit?"

Rory pushed away from the desk, then walked around behind it and sat down in a monstrous chair that matched the desk perfectly. They both looked like they'd be more at home in an English manor than a custom design jewelry shop in DC.

He leaned back and met her gaze, his hazel eyes serious. "You could hold on to this thing for ten years and it would still be too hot to move. You want my honest opinion about what you should do with it?"

Even though they came from two completely different worlds and Rory was fifteen years older than she was, he'd been the only one she could talk to back when her whole life had turned upside down a decade ago. He'd been making some custom jewelry for her mother at the time, so she had come into the shop on a regular basis. He'd let her try on whatever jewelry she wanted and even listened to her when she offered suggestions on how some of his designs could be improved. Not only did he take her opinions seriously, but he also let her use his bench and tools, so she could try out some of her ideas with real metal and gemstones.

When she'd come in one day after the freaky stuff had started happening, exhausted and a complete wreck, he'd immediately picked up on it. The next thing Dreya knew, she was in this very office, crying her eyes out and telling him about all the crazy stuff that was going on with her. He'd never flipped out or called her mom and informed her that Dreya was in need of a few Xanax and serious therapy. Instead, he'd just listened as she told him what she was turning into. She'd even shown him her claws and fangs. From that day forward, he'd stayed calm enough for both of them and had helped her learn how to deal with these things. Without Rory, she probably would have fallen completely apart.

Of course, she probably would have ended up in prison as well. Because in addition to teaching her how to design and make jewelry, Rory had also taught her how to be a thief—an extremely good one.

There were people in their circle of business acquaintances who believed Rory had taken advantage of a teenage girl and manipulated her into stealing for him. That was crap. Rory was the older brother Dreya never had and her best friend. If there'd been anyone using someone, it was her.

In the beginning, Rory had only wanted to teach her about the legit side of the jewelry business. These days, she ran a very exclusive jewelry boutique over in Foggy Bottom catering to people who had more than enough money to pay for the pieces she designed. The work was creative and rewarding and fed a very critical part of her soul. The pay was nothing to complain about either.

But she'd realized a long time ago that she had another half, one that wasn't interested in making jewelry—or money. That part belonged to the beast inside her with the fangs and the claws. The thing that growled and seemed happiest when she was way up in the air, doing incredibly dangerous and foolhardy stuff. She'd talked Rory into teaching her how to be a thief to keep that part of herself content. The thrill of climbing high-rises, breaking into places, and stealing things gave a purpose to the animal inside her that used to scare her so much.

None of that would have been possible without Rory and all he'd taught her. She owed him everything. So if he had something he wanted to tell her, she'd listen. She might not necessarily take his advice, but she'd always listen to it.

That said, the serious look on his face made her a little nervous. Rory was rarely serious, even when things were at their worst.

"Dreya, if I were you, I'd take that thing down to the Potomac right now and chuck it in the river. Then I'd get out of town for a while. And when I came back, I'd never breathe a single word of this to anyone ever again."

Of all the things Dreya thought Rory might say, that hadn't been one of them. "You want me to throw a diamond worth millions in the river, then just walk away. You're kidding, right?"

Rory held her gaze.

She considered arguing with him but changed her mind. He was obviously really worried, which meant she probably should be too.

With a sigh, she flipped her long hair over her

shoulder and grabbed her backpack from the floor beside her chair. Reaching inside, she pulled out the weird black box she'd stolen from Thorn's safe and put it on the desk in front of Rory.

"If you won't fence the diamond, how about this?"

He picked up the rectangular object and studied it with interest. Then he frowned. "What the hell am I looking at?"

She shrugged. "I was hoping you could tell me. It was in the same safe as the diamond, so I figured it had to be valuable."

Rory handed it back to her. "I don't have a clue what it is, so I couldn't even hazard a guess as to what it might be worth. But if a man like Thorn had it locked up in his safe, it probably isn't something you want to mess around with. My previous advice still applies—toss it in the river with the diamond and walk away."

Dreya opened her mouth to tell him she'd think about it when the doorbell chimed, letting them know a customer had come into the shop.

"Duty calls," Rory said. "I'll be right back."

Dreya stared at the diamond and the funny-looking black box that might be worth even more—or could be a piece of junk. Should she take Rory's advice and toss them? She didn't care about the black box, but the diamond was too beautiful to throw away. Hell, she'd rather take it and put it back in Thorn's safe.

She was just wondering how long Rory was going to be when a familiar voice drifted her way from the front of the shop. Oh yeah, she recognized those deep, sexy tones all right. Detective Braden Hayes, Metro PD. Unfortunately, she'd heard it too many times, most of them in an interrogation room down at the police department.

Dreya had never been arrested for any of her crimes because she was too good to ever leave any evidence, but Hayes had brought her in for questioning several times. That cop somehow knew she was a thief. He just couldn't get anyone else to believe him. That didn't keep him from trying though.

She stood and walked out of the office, heading down the hall until she could peek into the front of the shop. Rory and Hayes were standing in the center of the room, talking like they were old friends. As the two men chatted about stolen diamonds, Dreya leaned her shoulder against the wall and pondered the general unfairness of the world. Hayes was a handsome guy, with an athletic build, eyes the color of her favorite espresso, a strong jaw, and hair that just made you want to run your fingers through it. Why did he have to be a cop, and one who worked robbery at that?

Then again, maybe she was only attracted to him because he represented something dangerous and thrilling. Something told her that her other half—the one that liked heights and growling—would love to play games with him. She ignored the purr her freaky side let out and dismissed that thought immediately, having no desire to see where it led.

Since it seemed like Hayes wasn't going to be leaving anytime soon, she decided to go. She definitely didn't want to be in Rory's office with Thorn's crap in the event the detective decided he wanted to see what was back there.

Hurrying into Rory's office, Dreya scribbled a quick

note, then slipped the diamond and the black box into her pack, grabbed her helmet, and headed for the back door. For now at least, she'd keep them. There was always the possibility that Rory would change his mind and help her find a place to unload the stuff. Maybe she just needed to give him a little time to think about it.

Chapter 6

THE BUTTERFLIES THAT HAD BEEN FLUTTERING IN LAYLA'S stomach since she'd left DC only got worse as she worked her way west across Ukraine in the back of the military vehicle that Kendra had arranged. By the time she reached the outskirts of Donetsk, they'd turned into angry birds.

She kept telling herself that Jayson was fine, that he wasn't going to have a bad reaction to the hybrid serum, and that his Special Forces training would keep him safe. But every time she thought she had her fears under control, she had visions of Jayson getting a delayed reaction to the hybrid serum and convulsing in pain, or his back giving out completely, or Powell abandoning him in the middle of a fight. They scared her so much, she found herself shaking in terror, her claws and fangs fully extended.

It hadn't helped when Kendra called on the satellite phone and told her that both the intelligence communities and the Internet were alive with the news that a good portion of the Donetsk militia forces had gone on high alert over an insurgent attack in the same area where Jayson and Powell had been heading. Kendra didn't know anything more than that, but she warned Layla to be careful. If the militias were looking for outsiders, it was going to make her task even harder. To make matters worse, Kendra hadn't heard from Clayne and

Danica yet, so she didn't know if they'd gotten the message to head to Donetsk.

Layla forced herself to take a deep breath. Kendra's news didn't mean Jayson was hurt—or worse. Since he and Powell had been there to rescue a diplomat's kid, it wasn't surprising that they'd probably gotten into it with the locals. If either of them had been captured or killed though, the chatter on the Internet would have included that.

Her plan to find Jayson went out the window the moment she hopped off the military vehicle and slipped across the border into the DPR region. The whole area was crawling with militia soldiers. Most of them were patrolling the streets, but some were going from house to house, knocking on doors. Layla's grasp of Russian wasn't great compared to a native speaker, but she'd learned enough during her training to get by. The soldiers were looking for someone. It wasn't hard to figure out whom.

As she moved through the nighttime streets, she could hear explosions in the distance followed by the distinct sound of artillery fire. She expected it to send the civilians around her running for cover, but no one paid any attention to it. With all the fighting in Ukraine lately, she supposed they were used to it.

She kept her head down and walked faster to catch up with the group of people ahead of her so she could ask if they knew whom the soldiers were looking for. They were already talking about it among themselves, and fifteen minutes later, she had not only learned what happened to put the militia on alert, but, more importantly, that it had also happened in a Russian Orthodox

Church down the street where a priest had been "harbor-ing spies." While no one said they were Americans, her kitty-cat instincts told her they had to be talking about the diplomat's kid.

Her instincts were right. Layla was so grateful she almost fell to her knees and gave thanks right on the spot when she picked up Jayson's scent outside the church. She followed his trail, picking up Powell's as well as three other people's along the way. Their combined scents led her on a roundabout path through the outskirts of the city and into an industrial section, then down to an aqueduct near a river. The scents got muddied a bit there because three of the people had ducked into a tunnel that led under the river while Jayson and Powell had gone back toward the warehouses.

Her stomach lurched as she followed the trail up to the roof of the building. She didn't even want to imag-ine how bad the situation must have been for Jayson to willingly head up there. Her dread only increased when she found all the spent cartridges scattered around the rooftop.

She balled her hands into fists, ignoring the claws digging into her palms as his scent led her to a shattered chimney in the center of the roof. Jayson and Powell must have tried to take cover behind it—and it must not have worked because she saw blood to one side of it. One sniff told her it was Powell's. The DCO agent was nowhere in sight though. There were scuff marks on the roof where it looked like someone had dragged him away.

She ignored them and focused on Jayson. His scent led away from the chimney, toward the side of the building closer to the river, but disappeared at the edge of the roof. She frowned and leaned over the edge. There was no way he could have jumped from all the way up here unless...

Suddenly, her nose picked up a trace of his scent coming from the roof of the other building. Her frown deepened. Jayson couldn't possibly have jumped to the far roof. It had to be at least thirty feet.

Then she saw the steel pipe sticking out from the building. That was where his scent was coming from. She gauged the distance to the pipe. While it wasn't quite thirty feet, it was still far. But Jayson had been trapped on the roof with people shooting at him and nowhere else to go—jumping had probably been the only option.

Layla threw a quick glance around, making sure no one had snuck up on her, then took a running jump and leaped over to the pipe, landing as quietly as she could. While she didn't have a problem traversing the slick pipe as she followed his trail, the fact that Jayson had been able to do it—under the stress of combat, no less— was impressive as hell.

She'd almost reached the end of it when she picked up the tangy scent of Jayson's blood. She stumbled, almost falling.

Oh God.

Fear gripped her. Jayson had been shot, and she had no way of knowing how badly he'd been hurt because his scent trail ended here. She stared down at the river. Had he jumped or fallen? Had he survived the impact with the water? Had he been able to swim all the way to shore? If so, where had he gone?

Spinning around, she raced back along the pipe until she came to support bars attaching it to the building, then climbed onto the roof and practically flew down the stairs to the first floor.

It took two hours to scour the shore closest to the warehouses, and she still came up empty. Then it took her another hour to backtrack through the city and find a way across the river. She'd been tempted to take the tunnel she'd seen earlier but decided against it. There was too much chance of soldiers guarding it.

When she got to the other side of the river, she discovered she was right about the militia standing guard at the tunnel. Careful to stay out of sight, she sniffed around. She quickly picked up the scent of the three people who'd been with Jayson when they left the church, then his scent a little while after that. Layla leaned against a tree for support, dizzy with relief. Jayson had made it across the river. That had to mean the gunshot wound wasn't too bad.

Pushing away from the tree, she tracked his scent to an abandoned building three blocks from the river. Even in the darkness, Layla could see that the building had been heavily damaged by the fighting in the area. Part of the roof had collapsed and one of the walls was completely caved in. She skirted the worst of the damage and followed Jayson's scent to a stairwell. It was stronger in there, but so was the smell of blood, and Layla had to force herself not to run down the debris-cluttered steps.

She was so focused on finding Jayson that she completely shut out everything else. Movement off to the right caught her attention as she reached the bottom of the stairs, and she only had a split second to see a curly-haired teenage boy rushing her in the darkness before he swung a piece of metal rebar at her head.

Instinct honed by hours of martial arts training with Ivy and Landon immediately took over, and she grabbed the bar, jerking it savagely away from her attacker and tossing it across the room. Then she kicked out, catching the kid in the stomach and sending him flying backward.

Another teen immediately stepped out from behind a bookcase, wielding more rebar. With a growl, Layla spun in a tight circle and put her heel into his chest, slamming him back into the shelf and sending the books on it crashing to the floor.

She was bracing herself in case either of them came at her again when a familiar scent filled the room, immediately followed by the glow of a flashlight.

"Layla?" Jayson's voice was full of disbelief. "What the hell are you doing here?"

All thoughts of the two teens she'd put on the floor disappearing, Layla ran across the room. A third teen stepped out from behind Jayson and tried to get in her way, but she shoved the tall, lanky blond aside so hard he fell; then she slammed into the man she loved so hard they both almost went down. She didn't think but simply wrapped her arms around him tightly and buried her face in the crook of his neck, breathing him in.

Her whole body shook—with relief, pleasure, satisfaction, need, and, yes, hunger—as she realized he was safe and that they were together. The sensations were nearly impossible to describe, but she knew she'd never felt anything better in her life.

Layla had realized she was in love with Jayson before tonight, but the emotions she'd experienced before were pale compared to what she was feeling now. She would have happily stayed like this for the rest of the night, but a noise behind her made her stiffen.

She lifted her head to look over her shoulder. The teen she'd kicked in the stomach earlier had climbed to his feet and was glaring at her.

"Who the hell are you, and how did you find us?" he demanded in heavily accented English.

She growled as he took a step toward her and Jayson. Not because she felt threatened by him, but because he was getting too close to Jayson.

The big teen stopped short, a shocked look on his face. "Um…okay, I'm going to stop right here. Who are you?"

"This is Layla. She's a friend," Jayson answered for her. "She works for the same people I do. She's here to help, Mikhail."

Mikhail eyed her suspiciously, then glanced at Jayson. "How did she find us?"

"She's good at tracking people," Jayson said simply. "Why don't you, Dylan, and Olek take a look around outside to make sure all that noise didn't attract attention?"

Dylan and Olek looked as leery as Mikhail, but after a few moments, all three teens headed for the stairs. When they'd disappeared from view, Jayson placed the big flashlight on top of the bookshelf, then turned toward her. Layla braced herself for his anger, but instead, he gently took her face in his big, warm hands and kissed her.

The move was so unexpected she didn't respond right away. Jayson must have thought she was rebuffing him because he started to pull away. She grabbed the front of his shirt, tugging him close and kissing him back, trying to tell him with her actions what she'd never been able to tell him with words.

Jayson's arms went around her, his tongue slipping into her mouth to seek out hers. She shivered as his taste filled her, burying her fingers in his hair and urging him on. Jayson let out a groan and slid a hand down to her jean-clad ass, squeezing her bottom and fitting her more tightly against him.

Layla growled in approval as she felt his hard-on press against her stomach. She was wondering just how far they might take things when she heard movement in the collapsed building above them.

She and Jayson broke apart, pulling their handguns. He moved over to cover the stairwell, while she kept her attention focused on the ceiling, her ears attuned to any further noise coming from upstairs. A moment later, she heard Mikhail ask Olek if he was okay, Olek muttered something about falling over a pile of rubble in the dark. She let out the breath she'd been holding and shoved her gun back in its holster.

"It's okay. Olek fell," she said softly to Jayson.

Her lips were still tingling from his kiss, and all she wanted was for him to walk back over to her and pick up where they'd left off, but he stayed where he was and slowly eased his pistol into the holster behind his back. His heart was beating hard though, and that—along with the scent of his arousal—told her he was still hungry for her.

Layla smiled, about to ask why he was standing all the way over there with a hard-on in his jeans, when another scent caught her attention—blood. Then she saw the big stain on the upper right side of his pants. Her heart seized in her chest.

She was across the room and on her knees in front of him so fast that he actually took a step back.

"Whoa," he laughed. "Not that I'm complaining or anything, but is now seriously the time for this?"

Layla rolled her eyes. *Men.* She gave him a look and pointed at the dark stain on his jeans. "You're bleeding."

"Oh."

Layla almost laughed at the blatant disappointment on his face. A rain check was definitely in order for this particular position as soon as they got back to DC.

"Yeah, I got shot. The wound isn't infected though," he added. "The hybrid serum must have taken care of that for me. It's not healing up like I heard it does for shifters, but it stopped bleeding almost right away. I think it'll be fine."

She bit her lip. How the hell could she just come out and say Zarina had given him a drug that had stopped most, if not all, of the hybrid changes he'd probably been expecting?

"Do you mind if I take a look anyway?" she asked.

"Go ahead."

She extended her claws and reached for his jeans, but he grabbed her hands.

"What are you doing?"

"I'm going to tear open your jeans so I can check the wound."

His mouth curved into a smile. "You don't have to rip them. It's not like I brought extra clothes with me, and I'm pretty sure I'd attract a lot of attention walking around flashing bare leg and a bloody bandage."

He had a point.

When she reached for his belt, she thought he might

stop her again and insist that he could do it. But he didn't complain as she undid the buckle, then the buttons on his jeans. While easing his pants down his hips was certainly fun, it would have been a lot more pleasurable if not for the present circumstances.

She only pushed them down to mid-thigh, just enough to bare the bandage-wrapped wound. He'd done a good job, which wasn't surprising since all Special Forces guys had combat medic skills, but blood still seeped through the material.

"Do you have any more cloth so I can put on a fresh bandage?" she asked as she untied the knot and slowly unwrapped it.

Motioning behind her with his head, he said, "Yeah, there's some in the back room. I was trying to catch a few hours of sleep when you ran in and scared the hell out of me."

She winced. "Sorry about that."

Layla swallowed hard as she unwrapped the last of the material to expose the ragged bullet wound in his upper thigh. She wasn't usually the squeamish type, but seeing Jayson's blood made her feel queasy. She could clearly see the entrance and exit wounds, and while the edges were red and angry, they didn't look infected. Jayson was right. Most of the bleeding had stopped, though she doubted it had anything to do with the hybrid serum. Most likely, the constriction of the capillaries due to swelling was responsible for that. She didn't point that out to him, though.

"I'll be right back," she said as she straightened up.

She went into the back room to get more material only to stop midstep when she saw the folded piece of carpet Jayson had been using as a bed. Sleeping on that would have been murder on her back. She couldn't imagine what it was doing to his.

Beside the carpet, there was a half-filled bottle of water, a stack of candy bars, and some torn strips of material from what looked like a T-shirt. She grabbed the water and material and walked back into the main room. Kneeling down in front of Jayson again, she gently began to clean the wounds. Looking at them still made her feel a little ill, and she forced herself to focus on something else. Like Jayson's legs. Even as crazy as the situation was, there was still something sexy about being so close to all that muscle. Other than when he wore shorts, she'd never really gotten a very good look at his legs. He had some seriously sexy thighs, wounded or not.

She did her best to keep her eyes averted from his underwear—and everything in there that seemed to be working hard to get out. Yet something else she hadn't seen much of lately. Oh, if this had been another place, another time.

"How did you find me anyway?" he said as she wiped away the crusted blood that had dried on his leg. "And what are you doing in Donetsk by yourself?"

Layla had been wondering when they'd have to talk about this stuff. She took a deep breath, reminding herself that this time, at least, neither one of them would be able to walk out on the other.

"Finding you was the easy part," she said. "The whole town is buzzing with stories about the gunfight you and Powell got into with the militia soldiers. I eavesdropped enough to figure out where it started, then followed your scent from there. I lost it for a while on the building where you and Powell split up."

"We didn't exactly split up." Jayson let out a harsh laugh. "The asshole thought we were about to be captured and decided he should kill me before that happened since I'm a shifter now."

She stopped working and looked up at him in shock. "Please tell me you're joking."

He snorted. "I wish I could. Son of a bitch tried to shoot me. I kicked him in the chest, then took off."

Layla felt her claws and fangs extend as the urge to track Powell down and tear him to shreds almost overwhelmed her. The only thing that kept her from standing up and leaving the dark basement right then was the fact that she was still bandaging Jayson's leg.

She took a deep breath, retracting her claws and focusing on Jayson's warm skin under her fingers as she tended to his wound. It took a while before she was finally able to look at Jayson without her fangs protruding past her lower lip.

"I guess I don't have to be concerned about your feelings when I tell you that I'm pretty sure Powell is dead," Layla said. "There was a lot of his blood on the roof as well as scuff marks where they dragged him away."

Jayson's jaw tightened. "I'm just sorry I didn't kill him myself. That guy was the biggest douchebag I've ever met—and I've met a lot."

She ran the cloth tenderly over the ragged part of the exit wound. "I just about freaked out when I realized you'd been shot."

He grimaced. "Getting shot wasn't exactly part of the plan, but at least I was over the river when I fell. If I'd slipped off that pipe two or three steps earlier… I don't like to think how bad it would have been."

Layla didn't like thinking about it either. "I'm just amazed you were able to swim all the way across that river. It must have been hard as hell."

She regretted the words as soon as they were out of her mouth, worried he'd think she was implying he was too injured to handle a physically demanding task like swimming. But instead he nodded and casually reached down to caress her hair.

"It was an ass kicker," he admitted. "But it wasn't like I had a lot of options. If I stayed on the other side of the river, the militia would have caught me at some point. Besides, the kids were on this side, so I had to make it."

The image of Jayson struggling to swim across the river in the dark, fighting to keep his head above water, made it hard to breathe. Tears filled her eyes and she was glad it was too dark for Jayson to see her face completely.

She finished wrapping the bandage around his leg in silence, then got to her feet. "There. I snugged it a little tighter to keep it from sliding down when you move, but you should stay off it for a while longer."

"I can do that. We've been waiting for it to calm down a little out there anyway." He frowned as he pulled up his jeans. "By the way, I didn't miss the fact that you never answered the second part of my question."

She'd hoped that with all the talk about Powell and the swim across that river, Jayson had forgotten that. Guess she wasn't that lucky. She busied herself with folding up the old bandage. "There was a second part?"

He bent his head so he could catch her eyes in the dim

light from the flashlight. "Uh-huh. The part about what you're doing in Donetsk by yourself."

Oh yeah, that had been the question she'd been ducking. She didn't know how to answer it without starting another argument. How could she tell him she'd been terrified he'd have some kind of horrible reaction to the hybrid serum or get hurt over here without him thinking she was questioning his abilities…or thought of him as nothing more than a cripple? God, she hated that word.

She tossed the strips of cloth in the corner and turned to meet his gaze. "I tried to call you a couple times when I was coming back from my mission, and when you didn't answer, I got worried. All I could think about was that fight we'd had and the things we had said to each other—and you saying you were seriously considering taking Dick's hybrid serum."

"I'm sorry about that," he said, his voice heavy with regret. "I never meant for any of that stuff to come out the way it did. Especially not right before you had to leave on your mission."

Layla nodded, believing that he really was sorry.

"I was worried when I got back to the complex and Kendra told me you'd taken the hybrid serum, then headed straight out the door on a mission with Powell," she continued. "I got this horrible feeling that something bad was going to happen and knew I had to come find you."

And now he'd think she believed he'd been duped into taking the drug. Or that he was too handicapped to take care of himself. *Great*.

But he surprised her. "I can't really say you were wrong, can I? Powell tried to kill me, I got shot and chased over half the city, and this is anything but the simple mission Dick said it was. So I'd have to say that your instincts were right. Though I am a little amazed John sent you over here by yourself. Your mission must have gone really well."

She couldn't keep from wincing. Unfortunately, Jayson saw.

"What happened?" he asked, concern in his blue eyes. "Did something go wrong in Glasgow?"

"It's not that," she said. "The mission went okay. I mean, the arms dealer, Kojot, got away, but that was only because he's a shifter and knew we were there before we even got close to him. I stopped some bad guys from getting away with a shipment of surface-to-air missiles. That felt good."

Jayson lifted an eyebrow. "But?"

She bit her lip. "When I told John that Dick sent you and Powell over here on a shoestring mission and that I wanted to come over to help, he said no. He said he'd reroute Clayne and Danica here instead. I tried to tell him that they'd probably be completely off the grid trying to catch up to Kojot, but he said it didn't matter, that I wasn't ready for a solo mission."

The expression on his face told her Jayson already knew where this was going. "But you came anyway?"

"Yeah. Kendra got me on the next plane out."

Jayson shook his head. "You're insane. Why would you do something like this?"

"Because you're the most important person in the world to me," she said. "I couldn't just wait around the DCO complex to see if you we're going to make it back okay. I had to do something."

She hadn't meant it to come out so sharply, but Jayson only smiled and pulled her into his arms. Not that she minded being there again, but she couldn't help being confused. A few days ago, he would have flipped out.

"You had to do something because you were worried about me and couldn't stand the idea of waiting around, hoping for the best, huh? Feeling powerless to protect the person you care about?"

Layla wasn't sure where he was going with this, but he was right. Powerless was exactly how she'd felt. "I know it probably doesn't make a lot of sense to you, but I had to come after you, no matter how insane it might seem."

Jayson pulled back a little and gently lifted her chin with his fingers. "Actually, it makes a lot of sense. I understand doing something totally insane—like taking an untested drug on the off chance it might heal your back. At least enough to get you back into the field again so you can be partners with the most important woman in your life."

Everything stopped then—except for her heart. It started thumping harder and harder until she was sure even Jayson could hear it.

"Wait a minute," she said. "Are you saying that you took the hybrid serum because Dick told you we could be partners?"

"If I proved myself in the field—yes." He must have seen the dubious look on her face because he shook his head. "I'm not stupid, Layla. I know you think he's manipulating me to get what he wants. Maybe he is. But that's okay because I'm using him to get what I want, too. I want to be healthy enough to go out and watch your back in the field."

She couldn't believe they were talking about this so calmly. Jayson had taken a drug that could have killed him just so he could be her partner? That was beyond insane. "How do you even know Dick will keep his word?"

"I don't, but I had to believe in something." Jayson cupped her face. "You remember how you felt when you found out that I had gone out with Powell? Well, I've been having those same feelings every minute of the day since you first told me that you were going to start field training. I laid awake at night thinking of you getting teamed up with a jackass who wouldn't even treat you like a human, much less a partner. That someone like Powell or Moore would shoot you in the back because the DCO has that stupid policy about not letting shifters get exposed."

She swallowed hard. "I'm sorry. I never knew you were worried about who my partner would be. Why didn't you ever talk to me about it?"

"What would we have talked about? You probably don't get a lot of say in who your partner is, and I get none at all. And until Dick offered me the hybrid serum, the idea of me being your partner was ludicrous."

Jayson slipped his hand into her hair and tilted her head back. In the dim light of the flashlight, she knew her irises were probably glowing green, but he didn't look away. Her eyes had never made him nervous, no more than her fangs and claws ever did.

"When Dick offered me the serum, I knew I had to risk it," he said. "For a chance to be strong enough to be your partner, to be at your side, to protect you and be with you—really be with you. That's more than I ever dreamed possible."

Layla cupped her scruffy jaw in her hand. "But you could have died, Jayson. When they initially gave you the serum or the first time your adrenaline started surging. That's part of the reason I felt I had to get here as fast as I could. I need to get you back to Zarina before it's too late."

He rested his forehead against hers, his scent washing over her and pushing every other smell far into the background. For a moment, it seemed almost possible to forget where there were and what they doing. All she wanted to do was breathe him in and let the rest of the world worry about itself for a while.

"I know I scared you, Layla, and I'm sorry about that," he whispered. "But I didn't die. The serum worked. My back isn't healed—not all the way—but the pain is bearable. I know I'll never have claws and fangs or be able to throw people around like Clayne or Declan or Tanner can do. I won't be able to jump off a three-story building or jump twenty feet, or sniff out a bad guy hidden in a closet, like you or Ivy, either. But I'm upright and mobile. I ran for a couple miles yesterday and leaped ten feet onto a small pipe, keeping my balance as I ran across it. Then I fell into the water from three stories up and swam for half a mile or more in a strong current. I could never have done any of those things before. The serum worked, at least well enough for me to be your partner and stand at your side."

They were too close for her to hide her tears. Layla tried to blink them away, but more took their place. In her heart, she knew Jayson wasn't simply talking about being her DCO partner or him physically standing at her side. He was saying he finally felt worthy of being with her. It made her furious knowing he'd thought that he wasn't before, but then she remembered what Danica had said about him needing purpose, a reason to keep going through all the crap he had to live with.

Tears ran down Layla's cheeks as she realized that Jayson had finally found his purpose—to be her partner and watch her back. Now she was the one who didn't feel worthy. Jayson had been willing to die for a chance to have this with her. What had she ever done to deserve that kind of devotion? Jayson might not have said the words, and maybe he wouldn't be able to for a long time to come, but he loved her. She knew it in her heart.

As amazing as the moment was, there was a little voice in the back of her mind urging her to tell Jayson about the antidote Zarina had given him. What if he went charging into a situation thinking his newfound hybrid abilities would save him? What if he found out that he was still an amazing former Special Forces soldier with a back that had been shredded by shrapnel? Didn't she have an obligation to tell him the truth?

As she stood there in his arms, breathing in his scent, his lips only inches from hers, she knew she couldn't do it. She could never destroy the slender poles of hope he'd used to prop up his life again.

In reality, she had no way of knowing if the serum helped. Even though she couldn't smell even a tiny trace of shifter or hybrid scent on him, there could be something buried way down deep. What if it had healed his back or taken away a part of his pain? Heck, what if the only thing the serum had done was make him believe in himself? Did she have a right to take any of those things away from him? Did she even want to?

She couldn't risk putting him into a tailspin, not when he'd just started to believe in himself. And not while they were all alone in the middle of a war-torn city with soldiers all around who would gladly kill them on sight if they caught them.

"We've both been running around worrying about the other person all along, risking our lives for each other," he said softly, as if he were hesitant to speak for fear of ruining the mood, "when what we should have been doing is talking."

Layla smiled through her tears. "If I'd known that all it would take to get us talking is a romantic getaway to a bombed-out part of Eastern Europe, I would have gotten Kendra to set it up a long time ago."

"Romantic, huh?" He smiled. "I like romantic."

Jayson bent his head and kissed her, his mouth moving over hers sweetly as his hands tightened in her hair. Layla moaned, her hand going to his belt. She was ready to strip off his clothes and make love to him right there in the middle of the devastated library when the sound of multiple feet coming their way caught her attention. Seconds later, footsteps descended the stairs. She and Jayson reluctantly pulled away from each other.

"So, when do you think you'll be strong enough to walk out of here?" she asked Jayson as the three teens came into the basement.

Two more flashlights turned on, illuminating the room better. Layla blinked. She'd been able to see in the dark for so long that she sometimes forgot what it was like to need lights to see.

"I could probably make it out of here by morning,"

Jayson said. "But we can't leave until we find Dylan's girlfriend."

She did a double take. "Girlfriend?"

"You didn't tell her about Anya?" Dylan's eyes narrowed. "What the hell were you two talking about all this time if it wasn't Anya?"

Layla had to resist the urge to flash her eyes at him. "Other things," she said. "Now, tell me about Anya and how she ended up missing."

Chapter 7

"LAYLA'S GOING TO BE OKAY."

Ivy wished she could be as sure of that as Landon. Despite how good her sister had looked in training, Layla wasn't ready to be in the field alone. Now, thanks to Jayson's selfish and irresponsible decision, she was in the middle of a war-torn country. If Jayson were there right then, Ivy would have decked him.

Okay, maybe not. But she was still mad as hell at him. If something happened to Layla...

"Come on," Landon said, interrupting her thoughts. Turning off the engine, he reached over to take her hand. "The faster we wrap this thing up with Thorn, the faster we can get over to Ukraine."

Fat chance of that, Ivy thought. Even if she hadn't smelled the unmistakable stench of death the moment she and Landon got out of the black SUV, all they had to do was follow the crime tape to the group of detectives and crime scene techs clustered together on the shore of the Potomac to know things with this investigation were only going to get messier. Braden Hayes was standing off to one side talking on his cell phone.

"Is it the shifter?" Landon asked as he fell into step beside her.

If they'd been anywhere else but at a crime scene, Ivy might have smiled. She'd had partners before Landon, and none of them would ever have considered asking that. Because no one before Landon had taken the time to learn and understand what she or any other shifter was capable of. It was one of the many reasons she loved him so much.

"No," she said softly. "The victim isn't female either."

She and Landon made their way through the crowd of onlookers there to gawk and flashed their Homeland Security badges at the uniformed officer guarding the crime scene. He glanced at the badges, then held up the tape so they could duck underneath.

Hayes's eyes narrowed when he saw them. Ending his call, he shoved his cell phone in his pocket and intercepted them before they got within ten feet of the body. "The DHS make it a habit of checking out every floater who washes up on the shore of the Potomac?"

Landon returned his gaze calmly. "Only those who seem to interest a very particular Metro PD burglary detective."

Hayes frowned. "You two following me or something?"

"Hardly," Ivy said. "Our computers flag certain things from the Internet, newspapers, TV, and radio— including the MPD police channel. When your name popped up saying you were headed to a crime scene with a dead body, we thought it might have something to do with the theft at Thorn's place."

Hayes stared at her in amazement. "That's either the most efficient use of government assets—or the creepiest. Either way, I think those conspiracy people out there worrying about Big Brother watching them might be onto something."

"What's the deal with the floater?" Landon asked, changing the subject.

Hayes hesitated, then motioned them forward with a jerk of his chin. She and Landon followed him over to the body lying on a plastic sheet ten feet from the edge of the river. Ivy knew from experience that the longer a body was in the water, the more its natural scent was washed away. Since she could still pick it up, that meant the guy hadn't been in the water for very long—three or four hours at the most.

The detective nodded to the medical examiner crouched down beside the body. "Give us a minute."

The woman eyed Ivy and Landon for a moment, then nodded and walked off, leaving them alone with Hayes.

"Joggers found him early this morning," Hayes explained. "The officers who responded thought it might be a mugging, but he still had his license and wallet on him. When his name popped up as a known fence of stolen jewels, they called me."

Ivy crouched down beside the dead man, wincing as she saw how badly he'd been beaten. Despite being in the water for hours, there was no mistaking the bruising, swelling, and abrasions on his face. Someone had worked him over good. She surreptitiously leaned in a bit closer, hoping to pick up a trace scent of whoever had beaten him up, but couldn't pick up anything. While the victim's scent still lingered, everything else had been washed away.

"Damn," Landon breathed. "It looks like someone went at his fingers with a meat cleaver."

Ivy looked at the man's hands—and wished she hadn't. Someone had hacked off his fingers with a sharp-bladed instrument. At first, she thought the killer had done it to hide the victim's identity, but that didn't make sense, since they hadn't taken his ID. They hadn't taken all his fingers either, but instead cut off one or two segments from each. Whoever had done it looked like they'd been trying to inflict as much pain as possible.

"Someone cut off his fingers to torture him," Hayes said as if reading her mind.

At the detective's soft words, Ivy looked up to see him regarding the dead man sadly.

"His name is Rory Keefe," he said. "He handled most of the high-end stolen merchandise in this town. Never could pin anything on him though. Or get him to flip on anyone either. I talked to him yesterday about the diamond stolen from Thorn. He claimed he didn't know anything about it, but I was in the process of putting a detail on him anyway. Guess I don't need to bother now."

Ivy was surprised to hear genuine regret in the detective's voice about a man who was a well-known criminal. Maybe Hayes was more complex than she'd given him credit for.

"Did you notice anyone following you when you stopped in to talk to Keefe?" Landon asked.

Hayes looked at him sharply. "What the hell is that supposed to mean?"

"Don't tell me you're naive enough to think that Keefe ending up dead little more than twelve hours after you questioned him is a coincidence," Landon said.

"Are you trying to say someone followed me to Keefe's place, then grabbed him and did this?" Hayes demanded. "Who the hell would do that?"

When Landon didn't answer, Hayes looked at Ivy.

"You're a detective," she said softly. "It shouldn't be that hard to figure out."

She and Landon had to make it look like they worked for Thorn, so they couldn't say anything that could get back to the former senator, but at the same time, they needed to warn Hayes.

Torturing Keefe and dumping his body where anyone could find it wasn't only reckless, but it also seemed completely out of character for the same Thomas Thorn who was behind the hybrids. That man was cold and calculating; this one seemed desperate. She didn't doubt he was responsible for Keefe's murder though. It only made her even more convinced the shifter had stolen something way more valuable than a diamond.

The detective looked around and lowered his voice. "Are you saying Thorn had his people do this just to get a family heirloom back?"

Ivy didn't say anything in answer to the detective's question. Neither did Landon. Their silence spoke volumes though.

"You might want to reconsider tracking down the thief," Landon suggested.

Hayes shook his head. "That's not something I can do."

"Then spend more time reading through old case files and less time laying a trail of breadcrumbs to every viable suspect in the city," Landon said. "Unless you like finding them dead."

"Of course I don't want anybody dead." Hayes clenched his jaw. "But you know it's not that simple. I work for people. They expect me to figure out who did this and bring them in—fast. The fact that Thorn is a former senator and a major MPD supporter only makes it worse. If Thorn's people are really out there grabbing any suspect they can get their hands on, the best thing I can do is catch the real thief as quickly as possible so I can protect them long enough for him to get his damn diamond back."

Landon glanced down at Keefe, then back at Hayes. "That's a risky way to play it. You could end up getting this thief tortured and killed if you don't move fast enough."

"Then I'll move fast enough," Hayes ground out. "I'm working through a list of the best second-story thieves in this city. If one of them did it, I'll know the moment I talk to them. In fact, I've questioned two of them already—one late last night, the other this morning."

Landon exchanged looks with Ivy. She knew exactly what he was thinking because she was thinking it too. While they might not have had plans to let Thorn get within a hundred miles of the shifter, Braden Hayes was in full bloodhound mode. He was going to lead Thorn right to her.

"Well, if that's the case, maybe you'd better check in on those other suspects you already talked to," Landon said, nodding at the corpse. "If they're not already in the river, that is."

⁓⁓⁓

Jayson leaned against the side of a stone building, his breath coming out in a fog in the early morning air. Dylan stood beside him, looking anxious. Layla, Mikhail, and Olek were across the street, chatting with a small group of Ukrainians. Mikhail and Olek were doing most of the talking, but with her dark hair and exotic looks, Layla could easily have passed for a local. He and

Dylan, on the other hand, not so much. Which was why they'd been relegated to security duty, instead of helping snoop for information on where Anya was being held.

He tensed as a trio of militia soldiers slowly walked past Layla and the others. The men didn't stop, though one of them eyeballed Layla openly. Jayson slid his hand behind his back to grip the pistol hidden under his jacket. If the soldier decided to cause trouble, he'd be across the street in a flash. But the man only let out a loud wolf whistle and continued on his way. A few moments later, he and his buddies disappeared around the next corner. Jayson relaxed, slouching against the brick building again.

Jayson looked around and noticed that he wasn't the only one who'd been tense when the soldiers had sauntered by. Everyone else on the street seemed to breathe a sigh of relief when they left too. It was kind of surreal in a way. On the surface, this city looked almost normal—if you overlooked all the damage caused by rocket warheads and artillery shells. People moved up and down the sidewalks, cars drove along the streets, businesses advertised their wares in bright window displays. But beneath the surface, the city was on edge. Every single person he saw seemed to have one eye looking over their shoulders, as if they expected trouble at any moment. And from the number of poorly concealed guns Jayson had seen as they walked around town, it was easy to see that Donetsk was a tinderbox waiting for the match to set it ablaze.

Jayson turned his attention to Layla and the two teens again. She'd tried to talk him into staying at the library and giving his leg a little more time to heal, but he'd nixed that the moment he heard her plan to come out here with the kids and help them track down Anya. Things may have seemed calm in the city right then, but it could change any moment. He'd finally gotten himself in position to be Layla's partner. He sure as hell wasn't going to sit on his ass and let her walk around Donetsk without protection—without him. If his leg started bleeding again, he'd deal with it.

Beside him, Dylan shifted a little against the wall, his frustration obvious. He wasn't thrilled to be stuck there with Jayson instead of helping find his girlfriend, but he hadn't fought them when they'd said it was too risky. The kid was smart enough to know that his accent alone would be enough to tell everyone within ten feet that he wasn't a local. He chafed at the short leash, but he dealt with it. He was a lot smarter and more mature than Jayson had ever been at his age.

"I miss being able to talk to Anya at night before going to bed," Dylan said suddenly. He'd taken a colorful scarf from the pocket of his jacket and was lovingly gliding his fingers along the silky material. "Back in Kiev, I'd hang out at her house until her parents chased me off at night. Then we'd talk on the phone for hours until we fell asleep. I hadn't realized how much of a routine that had turned into until she wasn't around for me to talk to. I haven't slept worth a crap since she was taken."

Jayson felt for the younger man. He was no stranger to sleepless nights himself. Up until last night, at least. Despite the soreness in his back caused by the thin piece of carpet scrap he laughingly called a mattress, he'd slept better than he had since he'd gotten injured. And it was all because Layla had been beside him. They'd laid together in his bed back in DC before, but it had always felt different, like they'd both been holding back and keeping each other at arm's length. But everything had changed last night, and whatever it was that had been between them was gone now. Jayson could feel it in the comfortable way they'd cuddled close without having to say anything, the way Layla's fingers had laced together with his when he'd pulled her against his chest, and the way she'd murmured sexily when his mouth had traced a good night kiss along the back of her neck as she fell asleep.

"How long have you and Anya been together?" Jayson asked Dylan, pulling himself back to the present. It felt wrong to think about how great things were going with Layla when Dylan didn't even know if Anya was alive.

Dylan smiled. "We've been dating pretty seriously for over a year. I've even talked to my dad about me staying in Kiev to go to one of the international colleges with her when he moves to his next state department posting. Dad's worried about me, but he gets that I couldn't do the long-distance relationship thing with her. Being away from her would kill me."

Jayson glanced at Layla. He could sympathize with that. "How did she get grabbed?"

"We were down near the RSA," he said, then added, "the regional state administrative building. It's the local militia headquarters these days. We planned on taking a few pictures and maybe talking to some people, but then antimilitia protestors showed up and started chanting. Everything was really chill and no one was causing any trouble. It didn't seem like that big of a deal, so Anya and Mikhail headed across the street to take videos for his blog."

Dylan paused, gazing off in the distance as some memory played through his head. He swallowed hard. "It went bad so fast," he said brokenly. "One second, there were less than twenty antimilitia protestors chanting peacefully. The next thing I knew, the whole street in front of the RSA was flooded with people shouting at the soldiers along the front of the building. I don't even know where they came from, but they got violent, and it wasn't long before they started throwing things at the building. That's when even more soldiers came out of the RSA and started hitting people with the butts of their rifles. Then it got really ugly. More protesters came running, then more soldiers."

"You couldn't reach Anya?" Jayson prompted when it became obvious that the teen was lost in his memories.

Dylan shook his head. "I tried. Olek did too. But there were too many people in the streets running around. By the time we got over there, Mikhail was in a fight with three militia soldiers who were trying to drag him away. Olek and I jumped in and got him free, but Anya was gone." He held up the scarf. "All that was left was this. It must have fallen out of her hair. She loves wearing colorful things in her hair. She says it makes her feel like a bohemian."

"Did Mikhail see her get grabbed?" Jayson asked.

Dylan nodded. "Mikhail said she was one of the first people the soldiers took, like they'd known all along that she was ethnic Ukrainian."

"What does the militia usually do with people they arrest, especially ones they think are pro-Ukrainian?"

Dylan's fingers tightened reflexively on the scarf. "Anything they want. There's no one around here with the authority or power to stand up to them. They answer to no one but themselves. It's the reason we came here in the first place, so people could see how out of control they are. They could lock her in prison for a year or ten years, or they could execute her. All without a trial or anything."

He smacked the stone wall with the palm of his hand. "I should have been with her, dammit! But I let her talk me into staying in the background with Olek. She was worried that if the militia soldiers saw me, they'd know I was American and arrest me for being a spy. It's my fault they grabbed her. If I'd been there—"

"Those soldiers might have killed you," Jayson said softly as an older couple walking down the street turned to look in their direction. "And Anya would have no one looking for her."

Dylan's jaw flexed, but he didn't say anything.

"So, how do you know Olek and Mikhail?" Jayson asked. Time to change the subject again before Dylan got upset and attracted too much attention.

Dylan didn't say anything for so long, Jayson thought he might have to repeat the question.

"I've known Olek since my dad and I first moved to Kiev three years ago. He was actually the one who introduced me to Anya. They've known each other since they were little kids. They're more like brother and sister than friends." Dylan shook his head. "What happened to her is as hard on him as it is on me."

"And Mikhail?" Jayson asked. "What's his story?"

Dylan shrugged. "I never even talked to him in

person until we got here, just knew him by reputation. He's a hacker and a blogger and has definitely pissed off a lot of the militia leaders by taking videos of them roughing up the local shopkeepers for money and beating people for no reason. If he's ever caught, he'll probably disappear even faster than a pro-Ukrainian sympathizer. And I can guarantee you that his body would never be seen again."

He fell silent and they both stood watching Layla, Mikhail, and Olek for a while.

"Anya is the whole reason we came here, you know," Dylan said quietly, fingering the scarf again. "It's not that I was oblivious to all the horrible things going on here with the militia and what they're doing, but it was Anya who got me to do something more than just write a blog about it. That's the kind of person she is. When everyone else is moaning and groaning about how bad things are, she's coming up with a way to try to make it better. She's the one who found Mikhail and got him involved, using his blog to get people back in Kiev to stop talking and start doing things. She knew how dangerous it was to come here, but she came anyway because she knew it was the only way to get people to really understand what was going on in their own backyard. More of our friends wanted to come with us, but she didn't want to expose them to the risk, so we left in the middle of the night. Olek figured it out, of course, and followed." He wiped his eyes with the heel of his hand. "She was so worried about everyone else getting hurt, and she's the one who got grabbed."

"We're going to get her back, Dylan. I promise," Jayson told him. "We're not leaving here without her."

"If we can even find her."

"We'll find her. Like I said, Layla is very good at tracking people. All we have to do is get her close, and she'll lead us the rest of the way to Anya."

Dylan gave him a sidelong glance. "Layla is special, isn't she?"

Besides the growls and the iridescent-green eyes, Layla had put two of the kids on their asses like it was nothing last night. Dylan would have to be completely clueless not to suspect there was something unusual about her.

"Yes," Jayson said. "She's very special."

"Are you guys a couple?"

Jayson grinned. "Yeah, I guess we are."

"I figured," Dylan said. "You seem completely different when you're with her—more alive."

Damn. When he was Dylan's age, he was oblivious to anything that didn't come up and smack him across the face, but the kid was completely right. He did feel more alive when he was with Layla.

"Are you guys getting married?" Dylan asked.

Jayson couldn't help but laugh. The kid definitely didn't beat around the bush, did he? One thing was for sure: he was going to make a hell of a journalist someday—if he lived through this.

"We haven't really discussed that yet. To be honest with you, last night was the first time we had a chance to really talk about what we mean to each other."

"But she knows how you feel about her, right? The most important thing is that she knows you love her," Dylan said. "My dad is divorced, but that's one of the things he said his relationship with my mom taught

him—don't assume you have tomorrow to say something that would be better said today. Because tomorrow
might not get here."

Okay, that was sort of profound. Like fortune-cookie
profound. And true too. Jayson had learned that all too
well when his parents had died in the fire four years ago.
One of the biggest regrets in his life was never having
had a chance to sit down and tell his parents how much
he really loved them. They'd been close, but his father
had been a soldier, so sharing emotions simply wasn't
something his family had done very well. And now it
was too late.

While he and Layla had talked a lot last night, Jayson
hadn't said the one thing that was most important. The
one thing he knew Layla really needed to hear—and that
he really needed to say. But that was going to change.
As soon they had some privacy, he was going to tell her
exactly what she meant to him and that he was completely and hopelessly in love with her. As Dylan had
said, tomorrow wasn't a given, especially in the middle
of a dangerous mission in war-torn Ukraine.

Jayson was still thinking about how he might get
Layla alone for a little while after they got back to the
library when she and the two teens walked over to them.
Jayson couldn't tell from the looks on their face whether
they had good news or bad.

"Everyone we've talked to has said the same thing,"
Layla said without preamble. "All political prisoners are
being held in the makeshift holding cells that the militia
has constructed in the basement of the RSA building.
If Anya is still in the city, that's where she's probably
being held."

Dylan nodded enthusiastically. "Excellent! So when do we slip in and get her out?"

"You don't." Jayson appreciated the teen's desire to help his girlfriend, and while he had no desire to get into it with Dylan—especially here—he had to make the kid see he had no part to play in this kind of mission. "The RSA building is going to be heavily guarded and getting in there is going to be tricky. You're not going in. None of you are."

"But we can help," Mikhail protested.

"If you want to help, stay outside and provide lookout for us," Jayson told him.

"We—" Olek started, but Dylan caught his arm.

"Jayson's right," he said. "We'd only get in the way if we went in with him and Layla."

Mikhail and Olek grumbled something under their breaths but fell silent at the pointed look Dylan gave them.

Shit.

"I'm serious, Dylan," Jayson said firmly. "I know what you're planning on doing, but slipping into that building after we go in isn't going to help Anya at all. You might be okay with risking your life, but are you okay with risking hers too?"

The immediate look of guilt on the teen's face told Jayson he'd been spot-on. Dylan let out a breath and shook his head. "Okay, I'll stay outside. But you have to promise that you'll get her out safely."

"If she's in there, we'll get her out," Jayson said, praying God didn't make a liar out of him.

Chapter 8

"MAYBE YOU COULD HAVE PICKED SOMETHING A LITTLE easier for our first official mission together?" Layla said in a teasing whisper as the two militia soldiers rounded the southeast corner of the big, stone RSA building and disappeared from sight.

Jayson chuckled softly as he poked his head out of the alcove they were hiding in and looked around. "Where's your sense of adventure? Besides, how hard can it be? We're just going to take a little stroll through the building and break out a political prisoner. We'll be on our way to Kiev before the sun comes up. Should be a piece of cake."

She shook her head. They'd been there since midnight trying to get a sense of the guards' patrol schedule. If the soldiers stayed to their routine, the street that ran along the east side of the building would be empty for another twelve minutes.

Layla was doing her best to hide it, but she was more than a little worried. She was ecstatic to find Jayson alive and well, and learn that the hybrid serum hadn't caused any serious damage she could see. Maybe it wasn't a big deal in the grand scheme of things, but she was also thrilled with how things were going between her and Jayson. It wasn't like either of them had come out and confessed their undying love and devotion for one another yet, but they'd both finally admitted how much they cared about each other. The fact that both of them had been willing to risk their lives for the other had changed everything.

Romance aside though, this mission had her freaked. Dick had violated every rule in the DCO playbook by sending an inexperienced team like Jayson and Powell out on a mission with little intel, no equipment, no backup, and no plan. It was part of the reason Layla had been so worried about Jayson in the first place.

Yet here she and Jayson were. An inexperienced team on a mission with little to no intel, no equipment, no backup, and no plan. What little they did know about the layout of the four-story RSA building they'd gotten from Mikhail. As far as gear, they were limited to the small amount of stuff they'd had on them—two 9mm pistols, a few clips of ammo each, her lock pick set, and her phone. Their backup was three teenage kids armed with cell phones. And as far as a plan? Well, Jayson had just laid it out in its entirety—slip in, find Anya, get out, then run for pro-Ukrainian territory. They were making up everything else as they went.

She couldn't even count the number of ways this whole thing could go wrong.

"Smell anything?" Jayson asked softly.

Layla pushed her negative thoughts aside, closed her eyes, and let her sense of smell kick into high gear.

People with normal senses never realized how *noisy* the world really was when it came to all the external stimuli that existed around them every day. But shifters knew, and if they didn't figure out how to deal with that stimuli, it was easy to become overwhelmed with all of the sights, sounds, and smells out there. For people like her, a walk through a quiet park could seem like a commute through Times Square during rush hour. And the actual Times Square? That was more like a walk through hell. A really loud, bright, and smelly hell.

So learning how to dial down the sensitivity of their external senses like vision, hearing, and smell was something every shifter—and hybrid too, she supposed—had to do early on after they went through their change. Unless they enjoyed living with their heads in a sight, sound, and smell kaleidoscope, of course. Layla didn't. Fortunately, she had a sister to learn from, which had made it a lot easier and faster for her.

Layla had always thought of it like putting on a motorcycle helmet, one that would blunt the worst of the incoming sights, sounds, and smells. At times, when she needed to use her abilities to their fullest, she envisioned lifting the visor of the helmet. Like now.

Thousands of scents immediately came rushing in, almost knocking her on her butt. She gripped the edge of the wall as they all hit her nose at once, fighting to be sorted, identified, and catalogued.

"You okay?" Jayson asked, putting his hand on her shoulder to steady her.

She nodded. "Yeah. There are just a lot of smells to take in. I'm good now."

Giving him a reassuring smile, she stepped out of the alcove and inhaled deeply. She immediately picked up the scent of the two soldiers who had just walked past, as well as trace smells of dozens of other people who had recently moved down this street, not to mention car exhaust, gas, oil, explosives, gunpowder, burned wood, crushed stone, sweat, and blood—lots of blood. This part of Donetsk had obviously seen a lot of violence.

On the upside, there definitely weren't any other people heading their way, which was the one thing she'd actually been sniffing for.

"We're clear," she said softly.

Jayson gave her hand a squeeze, then led the way to a Dumpster near the twelve-foot-high wall surrounding the building. According to Mikhail, there was a loading dock on this side of the RSA with a big roll-up door used for deliveries, as well as a standard door for the workers. Layla prayed one of them had been left open. Ivy had trained her a little on picking locks, but she wasn't very good at it.

When they got to the Dumpster, Jayson stopped and waited for her to do her thing. Layla hopped up onto the edge, nearly gagging at the stench coming from the trash. She wrinkled her nose. Focusing on who or what might be on the far side of the wall was difficult with the odors bombarding her.

Jayson climbed up beside her as if he hadn't even noticed the stench. A benefit of not having a super-smeller, she guessed.

"All clear?" he asked.

Layla sniffed the air, but it was no use. All she could smell was garbage. She closed her eyes, shut down her nose, and depended on her ears instead. It took a few moments to tune out everything else around her, but once she did, it didn't take long to confirm that there was no one on the other side of the wall.

She opened her eyes and looked at Jayson. "Clear."

From where they stood on the edge of the Dumpster,

the wall was only four feet above them and about five feet away. While it wasn't far, Jayson still let out a small grunt as he made the leap. She frowned as he favored his right leg, ready to jump in and help, but he got both hands on the top of the wall and pushed himself up and over.

Layla followed, leaping across the gap between Dumpster and the wall, landing on the top feetfirst. She'd considered using her hands and pulling herself up like Jayson had, but decided against it. He'd know she was holding back on his account and wouldn't appreciate it. If they were going to be a team, there were going to be some physical things she could do that he couldn't, even without the back injuries. He knew that.

She dropped lightly to the ground on the other side of the wall and found him waiting for her with his pistol out. She reached for hers but stopped as she picked up the scent of Jayson's blood. She looked down at his thigh, but it was hard to tell if any fresh blood was coming through his jeans because he was already heading across the courtyard toward the door on the loading dock. She didn't need to see blood to know it was there though. Damn, he'd torn open the bullet wound in his thigh making that jump.

Unfortunately, this wasn't the time or place to check the wound again.

Layla pulled her cell phone from her pocket as she ran and tapped out a quick message to Dylan and the others to tell them that she and Jayson were in. The three teens had positioned themselves around the front of the RSA building so they could warn her and Jayson if they saw anything—like militia soldiers showing up unannounced.

She put her phone away, slowing when she neared the truck backed up to the loading dock. Big and white, with tarp-covered sides, it was used to transport troops around the city. Her nose told her there was no one inside it, but she stepped up on the running board to check the interior anyway. She was about to jump down when she saw the keys swinging from the ignition. *Huh.* The militia soldiers were obviously the trusting type—or stupid. But then again, she doubted there was anyone around here crazy enough to steal a truck from them.

Jayson was waiting for her when she reached the top of the loading dock. "The door's locked. How are your breaking-and-entering skills?"

Layla bit back a groan as she slipped her lock pick tools out of her back pocket and dropped to one knee in front of the door. Jayson moved closer to her, keeping an eye on the northeast corner and the main entrance. If someone came back here, that'd be the direction they'd come from.

She slipped her tension wrench and pick into the lock, closing her eyes and letting her ears tell her when she'd disengaged each pin. It was a little hard concentrating with Jayson standing so close to her. The tangy odor of blood had taken a backseat to his masculine pheromones, and they were driving her crazy. She'd always had a thing for the scent he naturally put off, but since they'd gotten over a few of their relationship hurdles last night, it seemed like she was even more aware of him.

Fortunately, he didn't try and rush her. Instead, he simply kept an eye out for trouble and let her work. She felt another pin move aside. That meant there was only one left. She wiggled her tools again. A moment later, she felt the last pin give way. She smiled. Maybe she was better at this lock picking stuff than she thought.

Putting her tools away, she opened the door just enough to take a sniff and sighed with relief. She and Jayson had been lucky so far. Sooner or later, they were going to run into the patrolling militia soldiers. The thought of a confrontation with them made her tense up all over.

"You know," Jayson said as she got to her feet, "I think women who can pick locks are hot."

Layla whipped her head around to give him a startled look—along with a reminder about where they were—only to smile as he teasingly waggled his eyebrows at her. Jayson had known she was nervous and cracked a joke to calm her down. It worked.

Giving her a nod, he opened the door and slipped inside, taking point. Layla drew her pistol and followed. Of course, if they ended up having to shoot somebody in there, the rescue mission was going to be cut way short. One gunshot would probably bring twenty soldiers running. It would be damn near impossible to save Anya if they were busy trying to save themselves.

They crossed through a big open area filled with pallets. Most held office supplies, but there were also boxes of bottled water, military rations, and small arms ammunition. Because obviously, everyone in Donetsk stored their food and ammo together.

From there, they headed down a long, central corridor, looking for the stairs to the basement. Even though she and Jayson had never trained together, they moved well as a team. They covered each other smoothly as they slipped past each intersection, not having to say a single word to communicate what they were doing. Another indication of how in tune they were with each other. She'd never been in such perfect sync with anyone like she was with him.

They had to duck into offices twice to avoid roaming soldiers, but luckily, Layla could hear when they were coming, so she and Jayson never came close to getting caught. He never hesitated or questioned her judgement, which was nice. Not that she thought he would, but her sister had told her horror stories about her former partners who hadn't respected her shifter abilities at all.

Just to be on the safe side, she and Jayson avoided the main staircase in the center of the building as well as the elevator and kept searching until they found a set of steps leading to the basement in the far corner of the building. It turned out that there were actually three floors beneath the main one. They passed by first two and headed to the very bottom.

"If they're keeping people prisoner in here, they'd want to keep them as far away from everyone else as possible," Jayson said.

Layla silently agreed.

When they got to the door at the bottom of the stairwell, she opened it a crack to take a peek and quickly closed it again. *Crap.*

"There are two soldiers in the hallway," she told Jayson softly.

He cursed. "How far away?"

"About fifteen feet maybe. They're standing side by side, one a little closer to us than the other."

"They're standing guard," Jayson murmured. "That has to be where they're holding Anya."

"How are we going to deal with them without bringing everyone else down here?" she whispered. "One gunshot and we're done."

Jayson didn't say anything right away; then his mouth curved up as an idea came to him.

"What?" she prompted.

"Do you think you can distract them for a little while?" he asked.

She frowned. "How?"

He chucked softly. "These are guys we're talking about here. If you do this right, you won't need to say a word. Trust me."

Layla resisted the urge to roll her eyes as she figured out what her part in the plan was. She supposed she couldn't fault his logic. They each brought a certain set of skills to the team, and using her feminine wiles to distract a guy—or two—was definitely in her wheelhouse.

She went up on tiptoe and gave Jayson a kiss. "Don't do anything crazy."

"You either," he said. "Be careful. And don't worry— I've got you covered."

─⁓─

The urge to follow Layla when she opened the door and walked out of the stairwell a few moments later was nearly overwhelming. Layla might have some special weapons of her own—namely claws, fangs, and strength way beyond a person of her size—but she'd be the first to admit she didn't have a lot of experience with hand-to-hand combat.

She moved so silently that she was almost upon the soldiers before they even realized she was there. They both jumped, clearly startled by her presence.

"*Kak dyela?*" she said in the sexiest Russian accent he'd ever heard.

Jayson didn't know what she'd said, but whatever it was, the soldiers relaxed. One of them said something in reply, making his buddy chuckle. Layla laughed too, moving around in front of them so the soldier closest to Jayson had to turn his back to the stairwell to look at her.

Jayson was out the door and moving down the hallway fast, pistol at the ready. Layla was smiling at the two soldiers, nodding at something they were saying. The men were playing it cool, their rifles still slung over their shoulders. Jayson couldn't see their faces, but he had no doubt they had big grins pasted on them. And Layla had been worried she wouldn't be able to distract them. What a joke. She had them eating out of the palm of her hand.

The soldier closest to Jayson must have sensed him coming at the last second because he turned his head to look over his shoulder. It was too late for the guy to do anything by then though. Jayson transferred his pistol to his left hand and quickly laid the man out with a single blow of his fist to the side of the temple.

The other guard muttered something in Russian and reached for his weapon, but Layla grabbed him by the front of his tactical harness and shoved him back against the wall so hard the man's head bounced.

Jayson looked around, praying the noise wouldn't bring the rest of the soldiers in the RSA down on them. He didn't hear anything but waited while Layla closed her eyes and listened. When she opened them and showed off that beautiful, green glow her eyes got when she was really in the zone, she gave a quick shake of her head.

"We're good," she said.

He handed her pistol back to her, then opened the door the soldiers had been guarding, ready to take out any others they might find on the other side. But there weren't any. There were cells filled with prisoners though—a hell of a lot of them. The people in them stared at him and Layla in surprise. Layla threw him a look, then hurried over to the first cell while he focused on dragging the two unconscious soldiers out of the hallway and into the room where the prisoners were being kept. Undoing the laces on their boots, he used them to tie the men up, then grabbed one of the assault rifles and all the ammo he could find on them, as well as the two hand grenades they were carrying just in case he needed the extra firepower on the way out.

By the time he got to his feet, Layla had already found the keys to the cells and was unlocking them. She called Anya's name over and over as she opened each door, but no one answered. Jayson didn't know if it was because they were too scared to talk or simply too weak. These people hadn't simply been imprisoned but beaten as well. While there were a half dozen women in the group, none were young enough to be Dylan's girlfriend.

"Anya isn't here," Layla said. "There aren't any teenaged girls at all."

"All young girls taken away two days ago," an old man said in broken English. Tall and skinny, he had a nasty bruise covering half his face. "The guard come and take them. Not tell us where they go."

"Shit," Jayson muttered. Dylan was going to be devastated. What the hell were they going to do now?

"You help us?" the old man asked, looking up at Jayson and Layla with hope in his watery eyes.

Jayson looked around at the collection of battered and bruised prisoners. There was no way in hell he and Layla could leave them to escape on their own. Getting them out wasn't going to be easy, though.

He looked at Layla. "We may be able to get them up the stairs, and if we're lucky, we'll get them through the building without being seen, but there's no way in hell we're getting them over that wall in the courtyard."

"Crap, you're right," she said. "Wait a minute! That big truck we saw at the loading dock has the keys in it. We can use that."

Jayson grinned. He'd never figured Layla would be so crazy. He liked it.

"You might want to text the guys and let them know about the change in plans," he said, then added, "but don't mention anything about Anya, or Dylan will probably come charging in here to look for her himself."

Getting all twenty-two of the former prisoners upstairs and to the rear of the building was a job and a half, especially since he and Layla had to practically carry some of them up the stairs. His back didn't enjoy the workout, that was for sure, but that was the least of his problems. Halfway to the loading dock, Layla's head snapped up. Handing off the older woman she'd been helping to a younger guy with wild hair, she spun around to face the way they'd come, her eyes locked on something behind him. The man Jayson was assisting must have sensed something was wrong because he nodded and hobbled toward freedom on his own. Jayson turned in time to see two militia soldiers round the corner at the end of the hallway. The men stood frozen for about half a second before going for the rifles slung across their shoulders.

Jayson pulled his P-96 and put two rounds through the center of the first soldier's chest. He was just about to do the same to the second one when that guy went down thanks to a single round Layla fired.

"Get everyone to the truck!" he shouted at her, not caring about anyone hearing him now. "I'll give you time, but move fast."

Layla hesitated for a moment, and he thought for sure she was going to argue, but then she nodded and started herding the freed people down the hallway.

Jayson put his pistol away and pulled the AK-74 off his shoulder. He'd grabbed it praying he wouldn't need it but was glad as hell now that he had it. He'd barely flipped down the safety lever when three more soldiers came around the corner. They took one look at their friends on the floor, then at him, and immediately dived for cover. Jayson popped a few rounds in their direction anyway, just to keep their heads down. Weapon trained on the now-empty hallway, he backed slowly toward the loading dock, keeping one eye on the progress Layla was making with the captives and the other out for more soldiers coming his way.

He did everything he could to slow down the ones who came running to investigate all the shooting. He hit a couple of them but was damn lucky not to get hit himself. There were too many shooting at him now.

"We're in!" Layla yelled from behind him. "Let's go!"

He fired off the rest of the magazine at the remaining soldiers, pitched a hand grenade down the hall, then turned and hauled ass. The grenade slowed the bad guys down a little bit, but the moment the frag stopped falling, they were up and coming at him like a bunch of berserkers.

Jayson reached the big storeroom just inside the loading dock before they did, but they were mere seconds behind him. If he jumped in the truck with that many people on his ass, they'd blaze away at the canvas-sided vehicle like it was a game at the carnival. He and Layla might make it, but anyone in the back of the truck would be as good as dead. He needed to slow them down. Tossing the other grenade at them would do it—at least for a couple seconds—but as he ran through the storage room, he got a better idea.

Skidding to a stop beside a pallet of small arms ammo, he shoved the boxes around until he created a hole in the middle of the stack.

"Let's go!" Layla called over the racing engine of the big truck.

"Coming, dear!"

Yanking the pin on the grenade, he stuffed it into the hole he'd made, then ran as fast as he could for the door, ignoring the soldiers shooting at him from the hallway, the pain in his back and leg, and the knowledge that he probably only had about four seconds to reach the truck before the whole storage room and loading dock area turned into one big Fourth of July demonstration.

"Go!" he shouted to Layla as he jumped in the front seat.

She took off, working the gears on the truck like a

pro. They made it ten feet from the dock before the grenade went off. It was followed by hundreds of smaller
pops as the pallet of rifle rounds caught on fire and
started to go off like popcorn on crack.

Layla had the big truck doing almost thirty miles
an hour by the time she steered it around the northeast
corner of the building. Flooring it, she smashed through
the heavy gates, then turned east and headed away from
the RSA building.

Jayson chuckled, unable to help himself. He'd almost
forgotten how much fun shit like this could be.

Layla tossed him her cell phone. "Think you can stop
laughing long enough to get Mikhail on the line? See
if he knows a place we can ditch the truck and get the
prisoners some help."

Still grinning, Jayson poked the buttons on the phone
as Layla drove the big truck through the nearly deserted
streets. As he waited for Mikhail to answer, his thoughts
turned to Dylan and what the hell he was going to tell
him. That put a crimp in his good mood damn fast.

Chapter 9

DREYA DOWNED HER SECOND SHOT OF TEQUILA SINCE commandeering a stool in the mostly deserted bar in the heart of Foggy Bottom. She wasn't surprised it was so empty. It might be a weekend, but it was also after three in the morning. Technically, the place was supposed to be closed, but there were still a few diehard partiers hanging around, and the guy who ran the place—Kincaid—certainly wasn't going to kick anyone out. Not while he was still making money. At least until the cops showed up and made him.

That was okay with her. She certainly wasn't going anywhere. Why go home when she knew there was no way in hell she'd be able to sleep? Hell, after what had happened tonight, she might never sleep again.

She'd gotten a call four hours ago from Stacy Ellerby, Rory's assistant at the jewelry shop, saying Rory had been murdered. Worse, according to someone Stacy knew in the police department, it appeared that Rory had been tortured before he'd been killed.

Dreya had refused to believe Rory was dead, even going so far as jumping on her motorcycle and riding over to the jewelry store, then his apartment. Rory hadn't been at either place, but the cops had. Lots and lots of cops. She'd sped away with tears in her eyes only to pull over and stop barely a mile down the road. Then she'd just sat there on her bike and lost it.

She couldn't remember ever having cried that hard. But then again, she'd never lost anyone like Rory. He wasn't just a friend. He was her confidante, her mentor, the only person who really knew her and accepted her. There wasn't anyone else like him in the world, and now he was gone.

When she'd gotten it together enough not to be a danger on the road, she'd cranked up her bike and driven around town for a long time before she'd finally ended up stopping at the bar where she and Rory had always gone—the same trendy little place where Rory had told her about Thorn and that damn diamond of his. It seemed somehow fitting—and tragic—to come here.

"Thorn killed him, you know," Kincaid said from the other side of the bar as he fixed her another drink. Big and barrel-chested with graying hair pulled back in a ponytail, he had tattoos on his forearms that would have made Popeye jealous. "Or at least had someone do it for him. The word is all over the streets. Thorn has his people out looking for that big-ass diamond of his, and he's willing to kill to get it back."

Mouth tight, Kincaid slid her a shot. Tequila, in honor of Rory. It was the third one tonight.

Dreya knew she shouldn't be drinking at a time like this—not that alcohol had ever affected her. But she didn't know what else to do. Without Rory around to serve as her anchor and her compass, she felt as if she was floating away, like a balloon without a string in a windstorm.

Of course, Dreya didn't need Kincaid to tell her Thorn was behind Rory's death. Her best friend had as much as told her it was going to happen, that Thorn wasn't a man to be screwed with. But she'd ignored him and now he was dead. Not just dead, but tortured. Because he wouldn't give up her name.

Rory hadn't looked like a tough guy and certainly didn't come off that way when he talked, but Dreya knew he'd had a quiet strength about him that no one would ever crack. There was nothing Thorn's goons could have done to make him talk. If giving up her name would have saved his life, she would have been the first to beg him to do it, but men like Thorn and the people who worked for him didn't let people live after thumping the hell out of them. Rory would have known that as well as she did, which was another reason he wouldn't have talked.

"Rory was targeted because everyone knew he was the most connected fence in the DC area," Kincaid continued. "If any thief in this town was going to try to move a rock like the one Thorn had, Rory would be the one he'd go to."

Dreya picked up her glass and took a healthy swallow, feeling the harsh, agave-based alcohol burn as it rolled down her throat. The funny thing was, she hated tequila. She'd always drunk it because Rory had liked it. Now she couldn't imagine drinking anything else.

She didn't say anything in response to Kincaid's comment because there really wasn't anything worth saying. Kincaid fancied himself a fence of sorts, but even he knew he hadn't been in Rory's league.

Kincaid leaned forward conspiratorially, resting his forearms on the bar. "Do you know if Rory was working with someone to fence Thorn's rock?"

Dreya looked up, meeting Kincaid's eyes and staring

at him intently. His heart immediately began beating faster and the acrid scent of sweat wafted off him in waves. That particular kind of sweat tended to leak out of people when they were really nervous—or lying. She locked eyes with him a moment longer, then casually looked away. The tight, little world she, Rory, and Kincaid lived in had been buzzing since yesterday with talk of Thorn's people spreading money around and promising even more for the person who gave up the name of the thief who had broken into the former senator's mansion.

Dreya had always thought Kincaid was a stand-up guy, but she guessed Thorn was offering a lot of money. Enough to make even a stand-up guy turn his back on his friends. No honor among thieves and all that.

"Not that I know of," she said softly. "But then again, Rory rarely ever told me about the other people he worked with."

Kincaid straightened. "I figured. Can't imagine there are that many second-story men in the DC area with balls big enough to go after somebody like Thorn."

"True," Dreya agreed, knowing the bartender was still fishing.

Kincaid turned and headed for the other end of the bar and a group of well-dressed political staffers who had stumbled in looking for one more drink for the night. One of them gave Dreya a drunken smile but blanched and looked away when she gave him a glare that told him he was wasting his time. She rarely had time to play games with wannabe Romeos, tonight even less so than usual.

Kincaid didn't come back over, and outwardly at

least, it seemed like he'd dropped the subject of Thorn's diamond. His elevated heart rate told her he was still thinking evil thoughts behind those beady, little eyes of his though. He'd sell her out in a second flat if he had the chance.

Dreya tipped her head back and finished off her tequila, the burn reminding her pleasantly of the last time she and Rory had almost polished off that bottle of El Tesoro.

Damn, she was going to miss him like crazy.

She was about pick up her motorcycle helmet and head back to her place—even if that wasn't the best idea in the world right now—when her cell phone rang. She considered ignoring it, but with all the crap hitting the fan so hard lately, it would probably be a good idea to answer the damn thing.

She pulled it out, cursing when she saw the name on the screen. *Oh God, what now?*

Dreya thumbed the green button and put the phone to her ear. "Stacy, what's wrong?"

Rory's assistant hadn't been deeply involved in the darker side of Rory's jewelry business, and as far as Dreya knew, Stacy had only a limited knowledge of the part Dreya played in Rory's day-to-day life. Stacy might have guessed Dreya was a thief, but she didn't know.

Stacy didn't bother with any pleasantries either. "One of Rory's associates is dead. They found him in his apartment a couple hours ago. The guy's name was Melvin Whittaker. Apparently, he'd been worked over just as badly as Rory."

Crap. Melvin was another second-story person like her. He wasn't as good as Dreya—and his best days were certainly behind him—but he was smart and had still handled jobs for Rory every now and then. The older man had even taught Dreya a few tricks of the trade. Damn Thorn to hell in a little red wagon.

If Melvin was dead, it confirmed that Rory hadn't broken and Thorn's men were going after every thief they could find. It also meant they were willing to track down and torture every single thief in the DC area if that was what it took to get their boss's crap back.

"Where are you now?" she asked Stacy. "You're not at your apartment, are you?"

"Hell no," Stacy said. In the background, Dreya heard the distinct sound of a loudspeaker calling out operating hours of the TSA security checkpoints. "I'm sitting in a coffee shop at Reagan National. I'm going through security the second they open; then I'm going to disappear for a while. I know you were good friends with Rory, so I thought I should call and suggest that you do the same."

"You have a little something set aside for a situation like this?" Dreya asked softly.

She and Stacy weren't exactly friends, but she knew Rory had thought highly of the woman, which counted for something in Dreya's book. If she needed money, Dreya would gladly give her some.

"Yeah. Rory had something set up for me just in case," Stacy said. "I'll be fine, more than fine in fact, but I don't think I'm going to be coming back to DC for a while. Rory told me once that you had your own rainy day plans made. It might be a good time to buy an umbrella and take a vacation."

Dreya thanked Stacy and hung up, then shoved her

phone in her pocket. Jumping on a plane and getting the hell out of DC sounded like a rational idea, but she didn't have the luxury of doing that. If Stacy left town, Thorn's people would barely notice. But if Dreya, who was known in some circles as a top-level thief, suddenly disappeared, people would definitely notice, especially those who knew about her connection to Rory. Splitting town would be the equivalent of ringing a bell and announcing she was guilty, and Thorn's goons would come running like Pavlov's dogs. She was slippery and could probably stay ahead of them, but then she'd be looking over her shoulder for the rest of her life.

Besides, she really didn't want to leave her family. She wasn't close with her parents and siblings, but they were still family. And now that Rory was gone, they were all she had left. She also wasn't too keen on the idea of leaving her jewelry business behind. While she definitely didn't need the money, she enjoyed the legitimate business she'd built.

If she was going to stay, she needed a plan. Unfortunately, she didn't have one at the moment.

As she threw a twenty-dollar bill on the bar and picked up her helmet, she knew one thing for sure. She definitely couldn't go back to her apartment or her shop—not until she figured out how to get off Thorn's radar.

Chapter 10

Layla lay on the floor of the library watching as sunlight slipped through the cracks in the rubble above her and highlighted the dust motes floating through the air. At her side, Jayson was asleep, his breathing deep and relaxed. This had to be one of the most perfect mornings ever.

She wiggled over to Jayson, practically purring with pleasure as he wrapped his arm around her in his sleep and pulled her close. They fit together perfectly, like two spoons in a drawer. When she was in his arms, she could almost forget they were in a hostile, foreign city that was crawling with soldiers who would kill them on the spot, all while looking for a young woman no one had seen in days.

Hopefully, that last part would soon change.

Things hadn't turned out as well as they'd hoped last night. If they had, she probably would have woken up this morning in a nice, soft hotel bed in Kiev beside Jayson with plane tickets for the States sitting on the nightstand. Dylan and his friends would have been back with their families, and Mikhail would no longer have a death sentence hanging over his head. Other than the fact that she had Jayson at her side and they'd discovered that they made an awesome team in the field, nothing else had gone according to the vague plan they'd been following.

Shortly after leaving the RSA building in their rear-view mirror, Mikhail had given them directions to a warehouse large enough to hide the truck in. By the time the Russian teen and the others had gotten there, most of the more mobile prisoners she and Jayson had rescued were long gone. That had left them with those people too weak to walk on their own and the seriously wounded. Mikhail had come through for them again, knowing people who would not only take the injured locals in, but also help them get medical aid. That Russian kid was starting to impress the crap out of her.

Of course, Dylan had been devastated when he'd been told that Anya wasn't in the RSA building. Like Jayson predicted, the diplomat's son had wanted to immediately turn around and go back, sure they had missed her somehow.

Luckily, Mikhail had brought over the old man who had spoken to them in broken English back at the RSA. The man had wanted to tell them how grateful he was for what Layla and Jayson had done for him and the other prisoners. She couldn't help but be curious about how a sweet, old man like him could have ended up locked in one of those cells, so she had asked.

"I would not give food in my store to the militia soldiers for free," he said. "When I stood up to them and said they must pay, they beat me and took me away. They tell me they would release me if I promise to give them what they want, but I say no."

"How long were you in there?" Jayson asked.

The old man shrugged. "Eight months or so." That had shocked Layla even more than the reason they'd arrested him. "I am a stubborn old man who does not fear death. I would die before backing down from those pigs!"

"Did you see a Ukrainian girl named Anya in the cells?" Dylan had asked urgently. "It would have been about four days ago. She's tall, with dark hair, and was wearing a bright red shirt when she was taken."

The old man thought a moment. "I think maybe... yes. Over the last week, they bring several young girls in. One of them was wearing a red shirt. I remember because very few people wear red now. It draws too much attention. But she was only in the cells for a little while. Then the soldiers came and took her some-where else."

"Do you know where?" Mikhail asked.

But the old man hadn't.

It had taken over an hour to get the old man and the last few prisoners somewhere they would be safe. By then, Layla and everyone else had been exhausted— and worried.

"I know a guy who might be able to help us find Anya," Mikhail had said when they'd gotten back to the library. "He's a cop, or at least he was before the militia came in and took over. He was a soldier in the Russian army before he was a cop, and has worked in this city for something like forty years, so he knows everything that goes on here. If there is anyone who would be able to tell us why the militia grabbed Anya and those other girls and where they took them, it would be him."

"Why the hell didn't you mention him before?" Dylan demanded angrily.

Mikhail shrugged and gave him a sheepish look. "I'm not exactly on the best of terms with the guy. He arrested me a few times. I would not willingly go to see him, but we have nowhere else to turn."

Jayson had wanted to meet with the guy right away, but Mikhail had said no. "This man doesn't like outsiders. I'll take Olek and go talk to him first, convince him that you are really here to help. If I tell him what you did tonight, he might be willing to talk to you."

"I'm going with you too," Dylan had said firmly. "Anya is my girlfriend. We need to make him understand how important this is."

Layla had heard him and the other teens leave thirty minutes ago.

She'd had been leery of letting them go alone, but it wasn't really like they were asking for her permission. Besides, Jayson had pointed out that they had very little choice. If they wanted to find Anya before it was too late, they were going to have to take some chances. Jayson trusted their instincts to bail if anything felt off. Hopefully, they'd be back in a couple hours with information about where Anya was being held.

Layla sighed. Knowing where Anya was being held was only the first step. Getting her out of wherever that was would come next, and something told Layla the next rescue was going to be a lot harder than the on-the-fly mission into the RSA building.

An operation like that would normally have called for a larger, more experienced DCO team, like the one she'd been part of in Glasgow. But they didn't have a larger, more experienced DCO team. They had three teenagers, a former Special Forces soldier with a back full of shrapnel, and her—a barely trained shifter not qualified to be in the field on her own. Even considering how well she and Jayson had performed last night, their odds of rescuing Anya and getting out of this alive didn't seem good.

Layla had called Kendra last night after getting back to the safety of the library, hoping for news on their backup. Since they still weren't sure Clayne and Danica had received the order to divert to Donetsk, John had reached out to coyote shifter Trevor Maxwell and his industrial espionage team, telling them to drop what they were doing and get to Eastern Europe ASAP. But Trevor's team was in Buenos Aires, and it would take at least thirty-six hours for them to reach the Ukraine, maybe longer.

"This is all probably going to be over well before they get here," Layla had explained to Kendra. "Whatever the militia is grabbing these girls for, it can't be anything good, and Jayson is going to want to move as soon as we figure out where they are."

Not that she blamed Jayson. She was just as eager to rescue Anya and the other girls as he was. Layla shuddered to imagine what might be happening to a handful of missing young women.

Kendra had sighed. "Look, I know this isn't the mission either of you went over there to do, but it's the one that needs doing right now. And with Powell gone, you two are on your own. I know it seems impossible, but you're going to have to find a way to make it work."

Layla lay there listening to Jayson's steady heartbeat now, trying to imagine how they could possibly *make it work*. Especially when they still didn't know exactly what was going on with the hybrid serum Jayson had taken. She was still agonizing over whether to tell him about the antidote Zarina had given him.

After what she had seen last night, it seemed obvious that the serum hadn't turned Jayson into any kind of hybrid as she thought of them, but beyond that, she honestly had no idea.

Had it healed his back? Increased his pain threshold? Sped up his reflexes? All she could say was…maybe.

She'd already been impressed as hell with what he had done since arriving in Donetsk, then last night, she'd watched him hump those injured people up three flights of stairs and survive a running gunfight with at least a dozen militia soldiers. Maybe the hybrid serum had done something to him. Then again, maybe it hadn't and he was just being insanely reckless because he thought he was something he wasn't.

That was the biggest reason she needed to tell Jayson about the antidote. What if he went into this next rescue mission—assuming they could find out where Anya was—and did something insane because he thought he had hybrid abilities that he really didn't? Just the thought of him doing something crazy—and getting hurt—made her heart freeze into a solid block of ice in her chest.

Then again, telling him that he was essentially no more than the battle-scared vet he previously believed himself to be could prove just as deadly for him. There was a good possibility that everything Jayson had been able to accomplish up to this point was because he simply believed he could. If she took that confidence away from him, what would he have left?

Layla closed her eyes and let out a long, slow breath. As a psychologist, she should know what the hell to do in a situation like this, but when it came to Jayson, she didn't have a clue. Her heart was simply too involved.

She was still contemplating what she should do when she picked up on the fact that Jayson's breathing pattern had changed while she'd been lost in thought. She opened her eyes to find him wide-awake beside her, his head cradled in one hand and a smile on his lips.

"What?" she said, suddenly self-conscious. "Was I drooling?"

He chuckled. "No."

That was a relief. "Then is my hair a tangled mess?"

"No," he said, reaching out to smooth his hand over it. "It's perfect, like the rest of you. I was just lying here watching you and thinking about how beautiful you are."

Layla made a face. "Right. I've been sleeping on the floor of an abandoned building for the last two nights. I'm pretty sure I look the opposite of beautiful right now."

"I disagree," Jayson insisted.

She laughed and would have said something about him needing glasses, but he rolled her onto her back and kissed her. His fingers threaded their way into her hair as his mouth roamed over hers, taking everything she had to offer.

Layla wrapped a leg around him, pulling him closer and letting out a little shiver at the feel of his hard-on pressing against her body. He grabbed her thigh, running his hand up and down her jean-clad leg, making her warm all over. What she wouldn't give for the two of them to be nestled in a pile of warm, soft blankets back home in her apartment with nothing to do but make love all day.

Suddenly, Jayson pulled back. She chased him,

extending the kiss and letting him know that she was more than ready to keep going if he was. Dylan and the others would be out for a while. They might as well make good use of the time. But the serious look on Jayson's face was enough to make her back off.

"What's wrong?" she asked, rolling onto her side as he did the same. "Are you okay?"

"I'm fine—better than fine." He gently caressed her bottom lip with his thumb. "It just occurred to me that I've never told you how beautiful you are until now, which has to make me either the slowest or dumbest man in the world."

She opened her mouth to tell him he was being silly, but he stopped her with a gentle finger on the lips.

"And since we're on the topic of me telling you things that I should have said a long time ago," he continued, "I also need to tell you I know how incredibly lucky I am to have you in my life, even if I haven't always shown it. I'm sorry about that. But I want you to know that you're the most important thing in the world to me."

"You don't have anything to apologize for, Jayson," she said softly. "Not after everything you've had to go through."

Jayson smiled wryly. "That's where you're wrong, Layla. Last year may have been total shit, and there were times when the pain became so unbearable and the future so hopeless that I thought about giving up and just ending it, but I still had no right to treat you the way I did. I was hurting and couldn't see my world ever getting better, so I lashed out at the only person who cared enough about me to put up with it. I need you to know how incredibly sorry I am for putting you through all that."

Tears filled Layla's eyes. Suddenly, she had a hard time breathing. Part of her had always known that suicide was something Jayson had considered. Still, it was hard for her to hear him say it out loud. But having him apologize for things he had said and done when he'd been in that deep, dark place was tough too. Worse, it was scaring her. It was like he was trying to get stuff off his chest before they went on this rescue mission, like he thought he might not have a chance to say it later.

"Why are you telling me this all of a sudden?" she asked. "You're not going to do anything stupid are you?"

He frowned in confusion, but apparently figured it out because he shook his head again. "No, I'm not going to do anything stupid. If I scared you, I'm sorry about that too. All I'm trying to say is that I was in a bad place for a long time, and I did some things then that I'm not very proud of. But I'm not in that bad place now, and it's all because of you."

Her heart squeezed. "I didn't do anything."

"Yes, you did," he said firmly. "You had no way of knowing this, but when I first met you at Landon and Ivy's wedding, I was at my lowest point. The Army Medical Review Board had just told me that my request to be allowed back on active duty had been denied. I'd known it was a long shot, but I'd still invested a lot of hope in that chance, and I was seriously down. I almost didn't go to the wedding, but I figured Landon would harass the hell out of me if I didn't. I planned to show up and say congrats, then bail. But I met you and everything changed."

Layla smiled, remembering the first time she'd seen Jayson. He'd looked so handsome in his suit, though she could tell he'd been in pain even back then. She barely remembered any of the reception because she'd spent the whole evening with him.

"From the moment we met, there was something about you—a spark," he said. "While we were hanging out together at the reception, I forgot I was a wounded warrior. I was just a guy attracted to a beautiful woman."

"The attraction was mutual," she assured him, leaning in for a kiss. "I can assure you of that."

It was just a short, playful tangling of the tongues, but it was enough to make her body start to heat up again. When Jayson pulled back, the serious expression was still there.

"But that evening was just the beginning," he continued. "When you started coming to see me at Walter Reed, I found myself getting out of bed a little earlier in the morning on the chance you might show up. And when I was transitioned to outpatient status, you were the one who helped me find a place to live."

Now she was getting seriously embarrassed from all the praise and adoration. "Anyone could have done that."

"Anyone could have, but you were the one who did it. You were the one who put up with the grouchy, medically chaptered army guy."

"You weren't grouchy," she protested.

He lifted a brow.

Layla laughed. "Okay, maybe you were a little bit grouchy."

"I was way more than that," he corrected. "I was a total ass on more than one occasion, but you hung in there and never walked away, no matter how much I pushed."

She caressed his stubble-covered jaw. "There was nothing you could ever do that would make me walk away. My only fear was that you would be the one to leave without ever giving me a say in the matter."

He caught her hand and pressed his lips to her palm, his breath warm on her skin. "Thank God I was never stupid enough to do that. If I had been, I wouldn't be where I am right now."

She laughed and kissed him. "You mean in a bombed-out library in Donetsk?"

"No," he whispered. "I mean lying in the arms of the most beautiful woman in the world, telling her how important she is to me and how much I love her."

Layla almost missed the significance of what Jayson had just said, but then his words sank in. "Did you just say…?"

He grinned. "That I love you? Yeah, I said it. I love you, and I have from the first moment I met you. It just took me a while to figure it out. Though I have to admit, I envisioned it coming out completely differently— more romantic, you know?"

"I think it was perfectly romantic just the way it was," she said, her voice a little husky because her throat was tightening up again as emotions began to pour through her.

She realized now that some part of her had become convinced that she'd never hear those words from Jayson, and that she was okay with it. She'd come to accept that it would be enough to love him, but she'd been lying to herself. She'd needed to hear those words. The joy of hearing them now, having never expected them, nearly overwhelmed her.

She wrapped her arm around his shoulders, pulling him close and burying her face in his neck. As she breathed in his amazing scent, tears filled her eyes. She needed the tears as much as she'd needed to hear that he loved her. She'd been holding her emotions in check for so long, it felt good to finally let it all go.

Jayson held her close, his hand gently caressing her hair. "I didn't mean to make you cry. I'm sorry it took me so long to get to a place where I could say I love you, but to be truthful, I couldn't imagine ever being good enough for you. I've realized that I had to tell you though. Or risk losing you. I couldn't live with that. I'd die rather than live without you."

Layla pulled her face away to blink at him. "You're never going to have worry about being without me because I love you too. I have since the day I saw you at the wedding. I'll always love you, and I'm not going anywhere."

Jayson tenderly brushed a tear from her cheek with his finger, then leaned forward and kissed her. His lips were warm and sweet, and her mouth opened of its own accord to give him an all-access pass. His tongue slipped in to tangle with hers, making her moan. He tasted like the chocolate bar they'd had before going to bed last night mixed with something else that was intrinsically his and more delicious than any candy.

He rolled onto his back, pulling her with him. Layla slowly slid atop him, cautiously straddling his hips. She was very careful not to put too much weight on him, worried she could hurt him. But the position didn't seem to bother him at all, and as his hands slid down to her hips to tug her down a little harder, she couldn't help noticing the impressive erection he had in his jeans.

She dragged her mouth away from his and looked down at him with amusement. "It seems there's someone down there that loves me too."

He groaned. "Yeah, that would be true. He's definitely in love and has been from the moment we met."

His words made her think of all the times they'd gotten close to making love but never had. Those make-out sessions on the couch or in bed had been seriously hot, and she'd felt him get hard every time. Now that she knew he'd been into her from the start, she wondered why things had never gone any further.

She straightened up, sitting back on his thighs. "Can I ask you something?" When he nodded, she continued. "Why didn't you ever make love to me?"

The pain that flashed in his eyes took her breath away. "I wanted to—a lot of times—but then doubt would creep in. I was never sure if I would be physically capable—not just of making love to you, but pleasing you."

Layla was taken aback by his honesty—and his stupidity. "That is the absolutely sweetest and dumbest thing anyone has ever said to me. Trust me, that hard-on tells me you're completely capable, and as far as pleasing me, something tells me you could do that in your sleep."

He chuckled. "You think so, huh?"

She wiggled against him. "Only one way to find out for sure, I guess."

His beautiful blue eyes widened. "Um…you serious? Not that I'm complaining, but aren't you worried about Dylan and the others coming back?"

She gave him a lazy smile. "I'll keep my ears open for them."

"You can do that?" he asked. "Make love and listen at the same time?"

"Of course." She smiled wider. "I'm a woman, which means I can multitask."

Deciding that they'd talked enough, Layla leaned forward and kissed him again. Jayson's hands slid up her thighs and cupped her ass, massaging her firmly through the material of her jeans. She remembered him squeezing her bottom like this when she'd first gotten here and couldn't help wondering if Jayson had a thing for her butt. She hoped so, since she was very fond of having his big, strong hands there.

Sighing, she let her mouth move across his scruff-roughened jaw to his ear. Jayson groaned as she nibbled on the lobe, gripping her derrière even harder. Heat flooded her midsection, and she nipped his ear before slowly kissing her way down his neck.

His pulse beat under her lips, and she ran her tongue over it. She was so caught up in how scrumptious his skin tasted that she didn't realize Jayson had started undoing the buckle on her belt until she felt her jeans being tugged open. A moment later, she felt him push her jeans and panties down over her hips just enough for him to get a grip on her bare bottom. *Mmm*, if she thought those hands had felt good before, it was nothing compared to how they felt now.

Layla closed her eyes and buried her face in the curve of his neck with a sound that was close to a purr. She'd never had a guy pay so much attention to her ass. If they were back at her place, she could have him worship that part of her body for hours on end. But sadly, they were in the middle of a bombed-out library where three teenagers could walk in on them at any moment.

She sat up with a groan. "If we were anywhere but here right now, I'd let you do that all day. But since we don't know when Dylan and the other guys will be back, we'd better move this along."

He looked as reluctant to stop playing with her ass, but he didn't protest as she pulled up her panties and jeans, then swung her leg off him and stood up. She knew she was taking a risk getting completely naked, but there was no way in hell she was going to let her first time with Jayson be a half-dressed quickie like she was a teenager in the back of a car.

If the heated look Jayson gave her as she stripped off her T-shirt was any indication, he definitely approved. Gaze locked with his, she reached around and unhooked her bra, letting it fall to the floor. His blue eyes turned the color of a midnight sky as they caressed her breasts. Her nipples tingled under their intensity and it was all she could do not to give them a squeeze. Kicking off her shoes, she shimmied out of her jeans and panties.

Jayson stared, his expression one of awe as he took in her totally nude body. Layla had to admit there was something extremely arousing about being naked in front of him while he was still completely dressed. She'd always been a little shy in front of guys, but the way he was devouring her with his eyes right then, she felt anything but shy. In fact, his gaze made her feel more confident than she'd ever been.

He sat up, one hand gliding up her bare thigh and making her quiver. "I spent so many sleepless nights picturing you like this, but you're even more beautiful than I imagined."

Layla blushed despite herself. Not trusting herself to speak, she took his hand and urged him to his feet, then kissed him. Her hands went to the bottom of his T-shirt, finding their way underneath and pushing it up. Being the only one without any clothes might have been a serious turn-on, but she needed him naked too. Jayson took the hint, breaking the kiss to yank his shirt over his head.

Since time was of the essence, Layla should have immediately reached for his belt, but all she could do was stare. When it came to seeing his body up close, it was something she simply couldn't rush. It was like unwrapping a Christmas present. She always did that slowly too, preferring to savor the moment.

Jayson didn't seem to mind as she ran her hands over his chest and shoulders. She'd seen him with his shirt off of course, but those had just been glimpses. She'd never been able to really explore. He had a beautifully muscled chest, his pecs straddling the line between bulky and wiry. His shoulders and arms were the same—thick but built more for fast movement than lifting weights.

His abs were just as spectacular. She ran the tips of her curved claws down his chest and traced them along each and every curve and twist of those muscles, then back up again.

As she did so, she couldn't help noticing the tiny, barely visible scars where some of the frag that had entered his back had come out the front. It made her heart thud in her chest to imagine how badly those had hurt and how much damage they'd done. It was difficult to think about and a part of her wanted to stop looking, but Jayson's scars were a part of him. They had made him the man he was today. If she wanted to be in his life, she had to accept all of him—even the scars. So she lovingly trailed her fingers over those marks, memorizing each and every one of them.

Those included the ones on his back.

Pressing a kiss to his lips, she walked around behind him. Jayson tensed, and for a moment, she thought he might stop her, but then he relaxed again.

When they'd first started dating, she'd frequently massaged his back to help ease the soreness there, but he'd always kept his shirt on. Now that they'd declared their love for each other, she refused let him hide his scars from her any longer.

Jayson's upper back was unmarked and laden with glorious muscles that rippled as he turned his head to watch her out of the corner of his eye. The scars started at the middle of his back, running in ragged crisscross patterns all the way down to his belt line. She knew from the small glimpse she'd gotten when she'd given him massages that they continued another few inches lower. If not for the occasional markings left from his stitches, it would have looked like Jayson had been whipped.

Blinking back tears, she kissed the skin at the base of his neck as she glided her fingers down his back. Even though they were as healed as they were likely to ever get, the scars there were rougher than those on his abs. She traced each of them, silently letting him know that she loved them as much as she loved the rest of him.

To emphasize her point, she kissed his shoulders while she caressed him, alternating between soft licks and harder love bites. He shuddered and shivered under her ministrations, letting out an appreciative groan as she wrapped her arms around him and pressed her breasts against his back.

Jayson reached around and rested his big hand on her hip, his fingers grazing her ass. Layla ran her hands down his abs and unbuckled his belt, then unzipped his jeans. She slowly worked them over his hips to midthigh before turning her attention to his erection. She couldn't see anything standing behind him, but when she wrapped her hand around his shaft, she knew she was going to like what she saw.

Jayson's hard cock pulsed in her hand, and he let out a husky sound of appreciation when she gave him a gentle squeeze. She sighed her own gratitude. The mere thought of what he was going to feel like inside her had heat pooling between her thighs.

She rubbed his cock up and down, smiling as her fingers got a little sticky when she reached the tip. He was as excited as she was.

Releasing him, she sauntered around front and saw that her fingers had failed to do him justice.

She lifted her gaze to his. "You are the perfect one."

Then, without giving him a chance to answer, Layla wrapped her hand around his cock and went up on her toes to kiss him again. Jayson let her play for a while, but when she ran her thumb up and down the sensitive part of his shaft right below the head for the umpteenth time, he dragged his mouth away from hers with what sounded suspiciously like a growl.

"Hold that thought," he said hoarsely.

She'd rather hold on to something else, but Jayson obviously had other ideas. She tried hard not to laugh at how cute he looked trying to get his jeans off as fast as he could. She failed of course.

Jayson chuckled too. "Hey, this is harder than it looks."

Kicking his pants aside, he caught her hand and gave it a tug, pulling her down with him onto the makeshift bed they'd slept in last night. Layla threw her leg over his hips and straddled his lap again, but instead of his hard-on trapped beneath a layer of clothing like before, it was wedged nice and comfy between her legs.

"We don't have any protection." Jayson rested his hands loosely on her hips. "Are you okay with that?"

Layla nodded. Based on her cycle, she was in her least-fertile time of the month and would be for about another week. But she wasn't going to get into all that with Jayson.

"I'm very okay with that," she said. "If you are."

He grinned. "We both already know we're in this together forever, so I'm not scared about whatever the future holds, even if it happens to be kids."

She leaned forward and kissed him, loving him more with each minute. "Well, there's not much chance of that happening right now, but it's nice to know you're okay with kids since I want us to have a very large family."

Jayson probably would have replied, but she interrupted him by reaching down between her legs and wrapping her hands around his shaft. He was still hard as a rock—even with all the talk about kids and large families—and he inhaled sharply as she lined up the tip of his cock with her pussy and slowly slid down on his length.

Layla gasped. She had never been more ready to be with a man, but she'd also never been with anyone quite as big as Jayson. Feeling him fill her took her breath away. He was touching her in places she'd never known existed.

Jayson tugged her down until she was firmly seated on him. "You don't know how often I dreamed of doing this with you."

She made a sound that was half-laugh, half-moan. "I think I might. I've been dreaming of the same thing."

"Ride me," he rasped, his hands on her bottom urging her to obey.

Layla placed her hands on his chest and rotated her hips the slightest bit. Even that tiny wiggle was enough to send sparks pinging all over her body, not to mention make Jayson groan.

"Like this?" she teased softly.

"Just like that," he said. "Don't stop."

She gyrated a little more, slowly moving up and down. His hands slid from her butt, up her sides, and around front, to cup her breasts. He brushed his thumbs over her nipples, making it difficult to think straight.

Luckily, she didn't need to think right then. All she needed to do was feel.

The urge to ride him fast and hard was almost impossible to resist, but she did. This first time was going to be slow and gentle. In addition to being worried about hurting Jayson's back, she was also concerned someone might hear them and come investigate if they were too loud.

But slow and gentle was just as pleasurable. The combination of Jayson's hands on her breasts while she took him deep with each rocking motion of her hips was absolutely heavenly, and she let out a whimper.

Jayson gave her a lazy smile. "Do you like that?"

"Mmm," she sighed.

"What about this?" he asked, taking her sensitive nipples in his fingers and treating them to a firm squeeze.

She jumped a little, which only made Jayson chuckle and tweak them again before he took her hand and pulled her down on top of him. She caught her breath as her nipples came into contact with the hard muscles of his chest, but the sound was lost as he captured her mouth with his. One hand found its way into her hair while the other immediately settled on her butt. Oh yeah, he definitely had a thing for her ass.

She undulated her hips, falling into an easy rhythm that Jayson quickly matched. The tip of his cock caused little zaps of lightning to course through her every time he plunged deep, and despite how slowly they were moving, that little trick soon had her breathing hard and quivering all over. She dragged her mouth away from his with a groan and buried her face in the curve of his neck, sliding both hands up to grasp his shoulders.

She was so caught up in how wonderful he felt in her pussy that she almost missed the tingling in her clit. Having that kind of orgasm while in this position was something she'd never been able to do. Until now. She and Jayson fit together so perfectly that every time she moved, her clit ground against the base of his cock, resulting in the most exquisite sensations.

Layla lifted her head just as her orgasm began to peak so she could gaze into his eyes when she climaxed. Jayson tightened his hold on her bottom, taking control of her body and yanking her down even harder, then holding her there. The move ground her clit against him perfectly, pushing her over the edge, and she had to bite her lip to keep from screaming as her orgasm washed over her.

She was still quivering from aftershocks, so she was a little fuzzy about how he did it, but the next thing she knew, she was on her back and Jayson was between her legs. He thrust fast and hard, taking the climax that had been just about over and ramping it up again.

Layla might have screamed a little then, but it wasn't her fault. There was no way she could be expected to stay quiet when Jayson was making her come that hard.

Above her, Jayson suddenly tensed, and she knew he was coming too. She wrapped her arms and legs around him, holding on to him tightly as he buried his face in her hair and groaned his release.

They stayed entwined like that for a long time, him nuzzling her neck while she purred with pleasure in the afterglow of their lovemaking. They had gotten a little more intense than she'd intended, but if it bothered Jayson's back, he gave no indication of it. She sighed and ran her tongue over her lips. That was when she realized her fangs were out and fully extended. *Crap*. They must have come out when she'd orgasmed. That had never happened before. Then again, no one had ever made love to her like Jayson.

Layla was still marveling at that when he lifted his head and kissed her, fangs and all. She was worried she'd nick him with their sharp tips, but he navigated them as expertly as he had the rest of her body.

"In the event that you still had some doubts," she said softly, "I think you can rest easy when it comes to the question of whether you can please me in bed—or out of it. That was ah-mazing."

He chuckled, the sound deep and sexy. "That was nothing. Wait until I get you back home. I promise we're going to make up for all the time we wasted…on every piece of furniture in your apartment."

She pulled him down for another kiss, loving the sound of that. First, they had to get a diplomat's son, his girlfriend, and their friends back to Kiev in one piece. Then they could worry about getting home.

Chapter 11

IVY HAD REALLY BEEN HOPING SHE WAS WRONG, BUT THE moment she and Landon got out of the SUV, the scent of death wafting into the street from the alley told her that the world didn't care what she wanted. Unfortunately, there wasn't a river nearby to help mask the smell this time. There was still the requisite group of gawkers, however, and she and Landon had to push their way through the crowd trying to get a glimpse of the crime scene from the end of the alley.

"Before you ask, it's not our shifter," she whispered to Landon.

That didn't mean she still didn't hate this case. People were being tortured and murdered, and the body count was only going to rise until Thorn got back what the shifter had stolen from him.

Beside Ivy, Landon's face darkened. He was just as frustrated as she was. They'd been trying for days to identify the female shifter who had broken into Thorn's place so they could figure out what she'd taken, then get it back to the former senator without her or anyone else getting killed. So far, they were doing pretty crappy on all counts. Last night, two other well-known thieves Braden Hayes had questioned had been beaten to death. Assuming this latest victim was also someone he'd questioned, that meant every single suspect Hayes had talked to about the robbery had ended up dead.

If that wasn't enough, she and Landon still had no idea who the feline shifter was.

John didn't want them using DCO resources because he was worried Thorn had moles inside the organization, so he'd asked the mysterious shifter Adam for help. He had an amazing network of people who had a knack for finding shifters, but unfortunately, they didn't have any leads either. Whoever this feline shifter was, she was damn good at hiding her tracks.

The uniformed officer guarding the crime scene glanced at their badges, then lifted the yellow tape and motioned them through without a word.

Hayes was standing beside the Dumpster with a body bag on the ground beside it. He didn't look surprised to see them.

"Another suspect on your list, Detective?" Landon asked drily.

Hayes's mouth tightened, but he only gave them a curt nod.

Ivy jabbed Landon with her elbow. She knew he was pissed, but taking it out on Hayes was a waste of time and energy.

They watched in silence as the people from the medical examiner's office lifted the body out of the Dumpster and placed it in the body bag. Ivy made a face. Crap, this guy was in even worse shape than the previous ones. Thorn's men were obviously getting more vicious—and impatient.

"The victim's name is Kevin Greene," Hayes said softly, referring to his notepad for this one. "He's pretty new in the DC area, but has a long line of B and E, car theft, and larceny. Even though he has the skills, hitting a target like Thorn would have been a big step up for Greene. I thought he might have tried it in an effort to upgrade his reputation, so I talked to him this morning."

"Was that before or after you tried to convince your bosses at headquarters that Thorn is the one behind all these dead bodies suddenly showing up all over town?" Landon asked.

Hayes looked like he wanted to punch Landon. Jaw tight, he motioned them to the side. They moved away from the gathering of ME personnel, crime scene techs, and cops, finding a quiet spot near the back of the alley. This wasn't something they should be talking about in front of people—and Landon knew that. Or he would have if he hadn't been so pissed off at that moment.

"For your information, I talked to Greene an hour before bringing my suspicions to the brass," Hayes said. "As soon as I realized he had a solid alibi, I warned him about Thorn and told him that he needed to get out of town for a while. He said he'd take off as soon as I left." The detective shook his head. "Dammit, I warned him this would happen if he stuck around. I should have put him on a bus myself."

Beside her, Landon's expression softened as he finally figured out what she'd known all along—Hayes was doing the best he could in a crappy situation. Hayes was a cop. It was his job to solve crimes not deal with people like Thorn. Hell, she and Landon were trained to deal with people like Thorn and they still were having a hard time.

"What happened when you talked to your boss?" Landon asked quietly.

Hayes had brought up the idea of telling his

supervisors about Thorn after finding the third dead thief last night. She and Landon had told him it was a mistake, that no one was going to take on Thorn, especially when he had absolutely zero evidence to back up his accusations.

Hayes had disagreed. "If Homeland Security considers this is a legitimate possibility, it has to count for something."

"Say we do," Ivy had said. "What is that going to get us, even if we convince your boss we're right? No way are you going to find a judge somewhere crazy enough to sign a warrant to search Thorn's mansion. Or maybe you'll just drag him downtown for questioning? Either way, it will be a waste of time. There's no evidence in his home, and he'll have a hundred lawyers on you and the MPD before you can even ask your first question. In the end, all you'll do is let Thorn know that you're onto him."

"We've worked too hard getting close to him to waste it on a Hail Mary," Landon had added.

But Hayes had refused to admit they were in a no-win situation. He'd insisted that if he talked to his boss, the guy would back him up. From the look on his face now, Ivy guessed things hadn't worked out the way he'd hoped.

"Both my division and bureau commanders looked at me like I was insane," Hayes admitted. "They threatened to toss me out of Criminal Investigations Division if I even breathed a word about Thorn to another human being. I talked to a couple detectives in homicide I knew too. They said the same thing, that nobody in their right mind would go after Thorn without rock-solid evidence."

No surprise there. People who made it to the upper levels of any police department were all smart enough to know their careers would end the second they went after somebody like Thorn. Hayes was lucky he'd gotten off with just a warning. He could have easily been shuffled off to patrol duty for something like this.

"What are you going to do now?" Ivy asked. Hayes was one driven cop. She doubted he was going to give up simply because his job was on the line.

The detective frowned as he watched the crime scene techs finish taking close-up pictures of Greene's hands before the ME's people took the body away. "What the hell can I do? If I keep talking to the suspects on my list, they'll likely end up dead long before I solve this crime."

Landon glanced at her. "There is another way," he said to Hayes.

"Yeah?" Hayes said. "What's that?"

"Trust us enough to show us your list of suspects."

Hayes narrowed his eyes at them, immediately suspicious. "What the hell can you two do with a list of suspects that I can't? Put them in the Federal Witness Protection Program?"

"This is the part where the trust comes in," Landon said. "We have a plan to take down Thorn, but it's complicated, and it starts by getting the diamond back."

Hayes stared at them for so long that Ivy thought he was going to tell them to go to hell and storm off, but instead he sighed and reached into his leather jacket to pull out a carefully folded piece of paper.

"I put this list together a couple hours after I left Thorn's mansion back when this all started," he said as he handed it to Ivy. "The list isn't scientific or based on

any detailed FBI profile. It's based purely on my knowledge of the criminals who live and work in this area and
which ones I think have the ability to pull off this kind
of crime. None of these names appear in my official case
notes or the files at headquarters. I was worried Thorn
would get his hands on them if I did."

Ivy glanced at the list. "There aren't many people
on here."

"There aren't a lot of people in the area who meet my
criteria for this kind of job," Hayes said. "It requires a very
unique skill set, specifically an ability to work high off the
ground and a pair of brass ones that would let them go
after a person like Thorn. Those two things alone disqualify
about ninety-five percent of the B and E types in this town."

Ivy glanced at the list again. Besides Rory Keefe,
there were only five other names on it, and three of
those names were crossed out. That left one man and
one woman—Dreya Clark. Ivy listened with half an ear
as Hayes gave them the rundown on the man, waiting
impatiently for him to get to the woman.

"I've picked up Ms. Clark for questioning on at least
eight different occasions, but I never came close to
making anything stick," he finally said. "Technically,
she doesn't even have a record since I've never been
able to get a DA to file charges against her."

"Then why is she on your list?" Landon asked.

Hayes's mouth curved into a wry smile. "Gut instinct.
Every time I've picked her up, it was like she knew I'd
be questioning her. She also strikes me as someone
who's completely fearless and good at hiding secrets.
There's also the interesting fact that she is—or was—
close friends with Rory Keefe."

"What's so interesting about that?" Ivy said. "If she's a thief, wouldn't she have a relationship with her fence?"

"Yeah, except she's not a thief. At least not full-time. She makes high-end jewelry for people with lots and lots of money. She even comes from money and is always hobnobbing with the jet-set crowd. Maintaining a relationship with a known criminal isn't something you would expect from someone who moves in that world."

Unless you're a shifter who gets bored easily and entertains yourself by stealing from the same people you sell your jewelry to, Ivy mused. She glanced at Landon and saw he was thinking the same thing. This was their thief.

"I think it would be a good idea if Ivy and I are the ones who go to talk to these two," Landon said to Hayes. "Thorn's men seem to be following you, not us."

Hayes blew out a breath. "As much as I hate the idea of turning something like this over to you, I'd agree, but unfortunately, I think it might already be too late for that. Word on the street this morning is that there are criminals ratting each other out left and right for a payoff from Thorn. Sooner or later, someone is going to slip his men these two names."

"Then we don't go talk to them," Ivy said. "We bring them in for their own protection. At least until we can get that diamond back. I'll go talk to Dreya Clark. You two take the guy."

Hayes frowned. "You can't go off alone. I just told you that Thorn's men might already know about Dreya Clark. They could be after her right now."

"Ivy knows how to take care of herself," Landon said. "The faster we find our suspect, the faster we can help her. Are those addresses on the paper still good?"

Hayes snorted. "Yeah, but these two have to know Thorn is onto them by now. They're likely holed up somewhere that'll make them hard to find."

"Then let's get moving," Ivy said.

She appreciated how smoothly Landon had gotten Hayes off her back so she could focus on finding the shifter on her own. Now she just had to hope she could do it before Thorn's goons found her first.

"Be careful out there," Landon whispered, lightly running his fingers down her arm when Hayes wasn't looking.

She nodded, reaching up to finger the engagement and wedding rings she kept on the necklace she wore underneath her blouse. It was just one of the ways she and Landon communicated their love for each other while working in an organization that forbid partners from dating, much less marrying.

"You guys be careful too," she said. "Thorn probably knows by now that you tried to come for him, Hayes. He isn't going to take that well."

Hayes looked surprised. "You think he'd be ballsy enough to try to take out a cop?"

"Yeah, I do."

Giving them a nod and another reminder to be careful, Ivy took the keys Landon held out and quickly hurried to the SUV, dialing John on the way. Now that they had a name, Adam would be able to find the shifter even if she'd gone into hiding. Ivy was sure of it.

———

Layla was surprisingly relaxed as she and Jayson walked slowly up the sidewalk toward the small, carefully maintained home in front of them. The place was a one-floor ranch house with flower boxes on either side of the porch and a beautifully painted exterior. She could easily picture this house sitting in the middle of almost any small town in America. That in itself reminded her once again that Donetsk used to be a normal place before all the politics, militias, and fighting had taken center stage.

She probably should have been more uptight than she was, considering they were walking unarmed into the home of a man who might help them find Anya or might turn them over to the militia for all the reward money that was being offered for them. But it was difficult to be tense after having multiple orgasms, even when the local militia was offering a hundred thousand Ukrainian hryvnia for information on the foreigners who had broken into the RSA building and vandalized the place. Fortunately, the only people who knew about their involvement in the *vandalism* at the militia headquarters were the prisoners they had helped escape, and Layla was pretty sure they weren't going to say anything.

Three dark-haired men were waiting for them on the porch. They came down the steps as she and Jayson approached. Mikhail had told them that the former Donetsk police officer Victor Garin would have men there to search them for weapons before letting them inside.

"You're friends of Mikhail?" the tallest of the three men asked.

"Yes," Jayson said.

"He said you'd be unarmed, but you will understand if we want to see for ourselves."

The man didn't wait for an answer but simply nodded to his buddies, who quickly and expertly patted her and Jayson down for weapons. When the first man gave her and Jayson a nod, Jayson placed his big, warm hand on her back as they followed the men up the steps and into the house. She liked the feel of his hand there. It reminded her of how he'd held her waist when they'd made love a few hours ago and the fierce way he'd gripped her hips as he gave her more pleasure than she'd ever felt in her life. If someone had told her that she and Jayson would take their relationship to the next level in a half-demolished library in the middle of Donetsk, she would have said they were crazy. She'd been madly in love with him for so long and knowing that he felt the same about her meant more than she could have imagined.

Layla expected at least one of the men to follow them into the house, but they all stayed outside, leaving her and Jayson with Victor Garin. Layla would have pegged the man standing in front of the fireplace for a former soldier-turned-cop even if Mikhail hadn't told them what Victor had done for a living. At least sixty years old, with more salt in his hair than pepper, he still stood like he was at attention, his muscular shoulders filling out the crisp button-down shirt he wore, his blue eyes sharp.

"I expected you to be older," he said in heavily accented English. Giving them a nod, he gestured to the floral-upholstered couch and matching chairs. "Sit, please."

She and Jayson did as he asked, taking a seat on the sofa. The inside of the home was as neat and quaint as the outside. There were lots of framed photographs of soldiers and police officers in uniform, as well as pictures of Victor with a pretty, dark-haired woman his age that Layla assumed was his wife. There was also a big Russian flag pinned up to the wall on one side of the fireplace and another flag for the Donetsk People's Republic on the other.

Victor sat down in a wingback chair across the coffee table from them just as his wife came into the room with a tray filled with ceramic cups and a teapot. She set the tray on the table and poured tea into each of the cups, then looked at Layla and Jayson.

"Cream and sugar?" she asked.

Layla nodded. Beside her, Jayson did as well.

Sitting down in a matching chair beside Victor, the dark-haired woman fixed their tea in silence, handing their cups to them when she was done. Then she added sugar to one of the remaining cups and milk to the other, giving the sweetened one to her husband and taking the other for herself.

"Mikhail tells me that you two are American CIA," Victor said. "Is this true?"

Jayson answered for both of them. "We're from an organization very much like the CIA, but you've never heard of it. Very few people in the world have."

The answer seemed to satisfy the former police officer because he moved to his next question. "Did you come here to spy on the DPR?"

"No," Jayson said. "We came to rescue the American boy, Dylan. He followed his girlfriend here, and his father at the embassy in Kiev wanted us to bring him back. Quietly."

"You have the boy," Victor pointed out. "Why are you still here?"

"Because Dylan's girlfriend, Anya, is from Kiev," Jayson told him. "She was grabbed by militia soldiers outside the RSA building almost a week ago. We're not leaving until we get her back."

Victor's wife regarded them thoughtfully. "Why do
you care about the girl if she is not American?"

"Because Dylan cares about her," Layla said. "He
won't leave without her, and we won't leave without
him. When we learned that there were other girls about
the same age as Anya who were captured, we realized
we couldn't leave without rescuing them too."

The woman considered that for a long time, then
turned to give her husband a nod. Victor asked how they
had broken into the RSA building and how they managed to free all the prisoners held there on their own.

Jayson and Layla answered each question honestly,
not leaving anything out. Well, except for the part about
her being a shifter.

"And what will you do if you find out where the girls
are located?" Victor asked.

"Get them out," Jayson said simply.

"No matter where they are?" his wife pressed.

"No matter where they are," Jayson affirmed.

The woman exchanged looks with her husband, then
nodded. Victor set his cup down on the table and stood.

"Come with me," he said. "I have something to
show you."

Layla and Jayson put their cups down on the table
as well and followed him into a modest kitchen. She
thought at first that he was going to take them outside,
but instead, Victor shoved aside a set of shelves along
one wall to reveal a hidden door.

He led them down a set of old, wooden steps into a
darkened basement, yanking a chain dangling from the
ceiling as he went. Layla blinked as light flooded the room.
Now she saw what all the secrecy was about. Half of one

wall was covered with dozens of surveillance photos of militia soldiers. The other half was filled with pictures of eleven teenaged girls. And in the middle was a poster-size print of a dark-haired man wearing the same uniform as the militia. Big and muscular with cold eyes that seemed to bore right through you even in a photograph, he didn't look like someone you'd want to mess with.

"I am a loyal Russian citizen of the DPR, but what is happening now with the militia is not the Russian way. Something must be done to stop them." The words seemed hard for Victor to say, but he took a deep breath and straightened his spine, then pointed at the picture in the center of the wall. "This is Colonel Grigori Zolnerov. He's the senior commander of most of the militia forces on this side of Donetsk. He has been responsible for the fighting that has gone on here. He is the one who has kidnapped these girls." The old man swallowed hard as he lovingly touched a photo of a smiling girl with dark, curly hair and big dimples. "This is my granddaughter Larissa. My wife and I raised her since her parents were killed. She was one of the first taken."

"How do you know Zolnerov grabbed them?" Jayson asked.

"I've talked to several witnesses who saw some of the girls get abducted," Victor said. "In each case, it was Zolnerov's personal bodyguards who either kidnapped them or picked them up from another holding facility."

"What is he doing with them?" Layla asked, almost afraid of the answer.

Victor shook his head. "I don't know. The only thing I can say with certainty is that Zolnerov's personal guards have all left the city and are now in a dacha—forgive me, a luxury home—north of the city that the colonel took over shortly after he arrived here. They've been on nearly constant alert since then."

Victor took a photo off the wall. With all the other pictures, Layla had completely missed this one. It was of a huge brick house surrounded by a high wall. Even in the limited view offered by the picture, Layla could count six heavily armed guards. Her stomach clenched. She tried to think of some other reason a man like Zolnerov would keep a dozen girls captive in that house, but her imagination failed to come up with anything that wasn't depraved.

Victor handed the picture to Jayson. "The dacha is about thirty miles outside of town, due west. The address is on the back, and I will let you use one of my trucks to get there. Mikhail will know the way. He is a smart kid, never afraid to stand up to people when it is necessary. Try not to get him killed."

Jayson regarded the Russian thoughtfully. "If you've known where your granddaughter is all this time, why haven't you tried to rescue her? Those men out there who searched us look capable enough."

Layla wondered the same thing.

Victor didn't say anything for a long time. "We tried," he finally said in a sad voice. "But they are police officers, not soldiers. The team of men I sent in four days ago were killed before they even made it through the front gate. They never had a chance." His gaze went from Jayson to her. "I am praying you two can do better because there's no one else who can stand up to Zolnerov and his guards, and I fear what he has planned for my granddaughter and those other girls."

Jayson leaned over a table in one of the few areas of the library that hadn't been bombed to pieces watching as Layla and Olek added details to the map they were drawing of the large estate where Victor believed the girls were being held.

When they had come back from their meeting with Victor, Layla had immediately called Kendra and asked if she could find out anything about the layout of the house as well as dig into Zolnerov's background. It had taken a few hours, but Kendra emailed a ton of information. And none of the intel on the colonel was good.

The man had been booted out of the Russian army two years ago for corruption and had taken over leadership of the militia forces in the area when the more senior officers had died during a supposed terrorist attack. No one thought the senior officers' deaths had been a coincidence and most doubted that pro-Ukrainian loyalists had been responsible.

Since then, Zolnerov had developed a reputation as an ambitious man willing to do whatever it took to gain more money and power. He'd been leaning on many of the local businesses and charging them protection fees while doing as little actual fighting along the regional borders as he could get away with. According to Kendra, it looked like he was positioning himself for a run at president of the DPR if and when it became an independent country. While there were quite a few other political figures in the race ahead of him, Jayson doubted they'd be around long enough to claim it. People who stood up to Zolnerov seemed to disappear.

"I wish I could get you guys some more help, but it looks like you're on your own for a while longer," Kendra had said before hanging up. "I still haven't heard a peep out of Clayne and Danica. And Trevor and his team had a hell of a time getting out of South America. It could take them another twenty-four hours to reach you."

The thought of waiting around another twenty-four hours didn't sit right with Jayson. His gut told him they needed to get to those girls sooner rather than later. To do that, they needed a solid plan. That was why Layla and Olek were transferring the drawings of the house Zolnerov had commandeered from Layla's iPhone to a large sheet of paper. Jayson needed the layout of the place before they tried to slip in there. He had no desire for this rescue mission to end up like the one Victor had attempted.

While Layla and Olek were doing that, Dylan and Mikhail were out trying to find more ammunition for the pistols he and Layla carried, as well as the AK-74 assault rifle he still had from the raid on the RSA building. Jayson felt a twinge of guilt about sending them out to hunt up ammo, but Dylan and Mikhail had a better chance of getting the task done than if Jayson attempted it

He scanned the map, paying special attention to the perimeter walls around the house as he tried to develop a feasible assault plan. Not that he was used to coming up with plans for breaking into a heavily guarded residential estate, taking on anywhere from fifteen to twenty soldiers, and saving a group of kidnapped girls from who knew what kind of fate, all with only two armed DCO operatives and three teenaged boys. He should have been freaking out at the thought of such an impossible task, but he felt more alive than he had in a long time. Most of it had to do with the fact that he and Layla were finally truly together.

Jayson smiled as he watched her work. When she concentrated really hard on something, she had this adorable way of sticking out her tongue. It was all he could do not to walk around the other side of the table and kiss her. Of course, he couldn't do that because kissing would definitely lead to other things, and they didn't have time for that right now.

It was hard to believe it had been twelve hours since they'd made love on the floor a few feet away in the other room. For the first time in his life, Jayson actually understood the difference between sex and making love. Because there was no way in hell he would ever describe what had gone on between them this morning as a simple roll in the hay. It had been epic, mind-blowing, and powerful. He supposed that was what sex was like when you were completely head over heels in love with the other person.

They had lain naked together on the floor for nearly an hour afterward, her head on his chest, her hair splayed out, her body warmly wrapped around his. They'd talked about their respective pasts and collective future. Jayson found himself talking about dreams he'd long since given up and some he'd never known he had.

Layla wanted to travel the American Southwest with him, while he wanted to see France with her. She wanted to go snorkeling with him along the Great Barrier Reef, and he wanted to lay on the beach with her in Hawaii. When she talked about wanting to learn how to hang glide, he suddenly felt the urge to learn with her. She made him want to do things he'd never even thought about doing.

They'd even talked about having kids. Layla hadn't been sure of what he would think about that since he'd been an only child, but he couldn't imagine anything better than a whole house full of kids with Layla's big, dark eyes and silky, black hair running around. Hopefully they wouldn't look too much like him. He wouldn't wish his mug on any kid.

That was when Layla had brought up subjects that were a lot harder to talk about, like Dick and all the stuff that had happened at the DCO before he'd gotten there. She told him about what had happened to Ivy, Tanner, Kendra, Declan, and Minka, and how Dick and some guy on the Committee named Thomas Thorn had been behind all of it. By the time Layla was done telling him about all the manipulative shit Dick had done, it wasn't hard to see how the man had been able to sucker him into being a voluntary test subject for the hybrid program. It turned out that Dick was a total asshole and really good at getting people to do what he wanted.

"But as much as we'd both like to put all of the blame on Dick, we'd be lying to ourselves if we did," Jayson told her. "He was only able to convince me to take the hybrid drug because I was so desperate. Yeah, he saw me coming, but I was the one who took the bait hook, line, and sinker."

Layla kissed him hard before pulling back to look at him, her eyes flashing green. "None of that matters now. You survived—that's what's important. Just remember that Dick will always try to twist every situation to his advantage. He's going to try to convince you that you *owe* him for what he's done for you and that you need to do one more thing for him. If you go down that road, it's never going to end."

He caressed her hair. "Dick can say anything he wants. It doesn't mean I'll believe him. The only thing that matters is that we're together and that we're partners."

She bit her lip. "And what if Dick—or other people at the DCO—try to get in the way of that? We're not like Ivy and Landon. We can't hide our relationship because everyone already knows we're together. What if they say we can't be partners?"

Jayson hadn't even thought about that. "Then we're both out," he said. "I don't know what we'll do after that, but I can promise you that we'll do it together."

Layla smiled. "We stay together," she said fiercely. "In the DCO or out."

Then she'd given him a kiss that was well on its way to leading to lots of other distracting activities when Dylan and the others returned. The teens were too excited about the possibility that Victor might know where Anya was being held to notice that he and Layla had barely finished getting dressed before they'd bounded down the stairs.

Jayson stifled a groan as he tried to get the sexy image of a half-naked Layla wiggling into her jeans out of his head. He leaned forward, pretending to look at a detail on Layla's side of the drawing, hoping the move would hide the bulge in his jeans. While it did that, it also reminded him how tight his left hamstring was. Making love to Layla had been incredible, and having her draped over his chest afterward had been heavenly too, but it had also hurt like a son of a bitch. His back was throbbing, his left leg was numb all the way down to the knee, and his butt felt like one big muscle cramp.

He was finally starting to realize that while the aches and pains were a nuisance, they weren't anything he couldn't deal with. That was a serious epiphany in itself, but the bigger one involved the fact that he'd come to the conclusion that Dick's hybrid serum treatment had been a bust.

When he'd first gotten to Donetsk, he told himself it was the serum that allowed him to run all over the place when the militia soldiers had been chasing him. That his new hybrid abilities had allowed him to make the leap onto the steel pipe and run across it after Powell had tried to kill him. That he never could have swum across that river without the help of a magic cure-all drug.

Hell, for a time, he'd even convinced himself it was the serum that allowed him to be a man worthy of Layla.

Looking back, he realized none of those things had been true. He'd run all over Donetsk because he was being chased by men trying to shoot him and the teens, and he hadn't been willing to let either of those things happen. He'd made the leap to that pipe out of necessity because not making it would have meant falling to the ground with a loud and painful *splat*. Likewise, he'd swum across the river because the idea of drowning had scared the hell out of him.

And as far as the serum making him good enough for Layla, he knew now that was bullshit. He'd always been good enough for her. He'd just needed to get to a place in his head where he could see and believe that.

If the serum had made any changes to his body, they

weren't monumental. It definitely hadn't healed all his injuries, and it certainly hadn't turned him into some kind of lean, mean animal machine. But that was okay. Because he didn't need a magical hybrid drug to let him do the things he needed to do to feel alive—he just needed Layla.

Jayson turned his attention back to the drawing and was just starting come up with a plan for breaking into Zolnerov's estate when Dylan and Mikhail jogged down the rubble-filled steps. The two teens reached into the gray sports duffel that Mikhail had been carrying and came out with three boxes of 9x18mm ammo for their pistols, and two boxes of 5.45mm cartridges for his AK-74. Two thirty-round boxes of ammo for an automatic weapon wasn't much, but then again, if he ended up having to shoot that many rounds, it meant they were in deep shit and were probably screwed anyway. With what he already had, it should be enough.

Mikhail dumped the boxes on the desk to the side of Olek and Layla's drawing, then pulled out three battered and abused-looking Makarov pistols and placed them on the table too.

"What are those?" Jayson asked as he saw Layla look at the weapons from the corner of her eye.

"Those are Makarov pistols," Mikhail said.

Jayson arched a brow, wondering if the Russian kid was trying to be a smart-ass or if he were just clueless. "No shit. The question is why do you have them? I sent you out for ammo, not more weapons."

Dylan was the one who answered. "They pretty much came with the ammo. This might be a big town, but word gets around. People have heard about what we're trying to do, and when we talked to one of Victor's friends about needing ammo, he gave us the weapons too."

"He said he knows one of the missing girls." Mikhail shrugged. "He just wanted to help."

Jayson opened his mouth to tell them to ditch the weapons, but Dylan interrupted. "Look, I know you don't want us getting involved in any shooting, but we may not have a choice. What we're doing is going to be dangerous, no matter how much you try to protect us."

Jayson glanced at Layla to see her regarding him with a questioning look. Clearly, she was going to leave this up to him. The ultimate in *go ask your father*, he supposed.

His gut was shouting at him to leave the kids out of this, that they weren't old enough to risk their lives in a shoot-out, but he didn't have the right to make that decision for them. Dylan was going to do whatever was necessary to get Anya back, and Olek was going to help. As for Mikhail, he'd been risking his life against these people for a long time now. Jayson couldn't change the circumstances or the danger the three teens were in. The best he could do was try to manage the situation and reduce the risk to the lowest level possible. But no matter what he did, things could still go wrong. If it did, these kids had to be able to defend themselves.

"Okay," he said. "You keep the weapons. But you fire them only as a last resort. Understood?"

All three of them nodded in return.

"What's the plan?" Dylan asked. "How are we going to get Anya and the other girls out?"

Jayson readjusted the flashlight until it shone fully on the drawing of Zolnerov's residence. The main house seemed like a cross between a Tuscan villa and an American ranch with a multifloor structure in the middle and single-floor wings spreading out to either side. If Layla's drawing was to scale—and Jayson had no reason to think it wasn't—the place was easily ten thousand square feet. And that wasn't counting the outlying buildings or the smaller structures set at various places along the perimeter wall that served as guard shacks.

"Dylan, you'll be out on the road in front of the villa with Mikhail and Olek. When I give the signal, I need the three of you to draw the attention of the militia soldiers in that direction. I'm not sure how you're going to do that, but I need as many guards heading that way as possible. You just need to keep them occupied for a few minutes. Then I want the three of you to bail." Jayson pointed at an intersection on the map about a quarter mile from the gate. "Fall back to this road junction here and hide."

Dylan glanced at Mikhail and Olek. It was obvious that none of them liked the idea of hiding, but after a moment, they nodded.

"I might know some other people who can help us," Mikhail said. "We'll be the distraction you need. What are you and Layla going to do once we get the soldiers moving our way?"

"Layla and I will be going in over the perimeter wall in the back of the property," Jayson said. "We'll find Anya and the other girls, then get them out over that same wall."

Mikhail frowned. "That is a very big house. How will you be able to find Anya in time? Even with a distraction, you probably won't have more than five or ten minutes."

Jayson didn't point out that Mikhail was probably being optimistic with how much time they'd have. "That's Layla's department. But to find Anya, she's going to need that scarf you've been carrying around, Dylan."

Dylan looked as confused as the other two teens, but he reached inside his coat and pulled the piece of colorful material out, handing to Layla. "I don't understand why you need this, but please bring it back. It's Anya's favorite. It's pretty important to me too."

Layla nodded solemnly. "We will. I promise."

Jayson looked at the tense and worried faces around the table. "I won't lie and say this is going to be easy. Or that it's not dangerous. But I promise, if we all stick together and have faith in each other, we're going to find Anya and those other girls, and we're going to get them out alive."

At his words, everyone at the table stood up a little straighter. Jayson was stunned at the trust and belief in their eyes—Layla's as much as any of the others. He only hoped he was able to live up to that kind of trust. They might have survived the short raid on the RSA building, but his previous attempt at leading a combat mission had ended in disaster.

"All right, let's get moving." He rolled up the map Layla and Olek had made. "It's going to take us a while to get out there, and I need time to check the place out in person before we go in."

The teens immediately headed for the stairs, but Layla hung back with him. Jayson clicked off the flashlight, plunging the old library into darkness. Layla could still see of course, and she reached out to take his hand.

"We're going to do this," she whispered softly. "Together."

He squeezed her hand. "Together."

Chapter 12

DREYA HAD ALWAYS THOUGHT THAT THE APARTMENT she maintained over in Columbia Heights was a tremendous waste of money. Not only did she already have a beautiful place in Foggy Bottom, but Rory had insisted she keep the lease paid up a year in advance—in cash. He'd been of the opinion she needed to have a place to hide out that was completely off the radar and where everything was under a fake name. According to him, cash made all that easier.

She'd humored him because, well…Rory knew a lot more about this business than she did. At the same time, she hated the idea of spending that kind of money on a place she rarely ever slept in. Of course, with so many of her fellow thieves showing up dead all over town, she'd changed her mind on the subject completely. As far as she was concerned now, Rory had been brilliant beyond belief.

The only problem was that she hadn't kept the place stocked with food. If Rory were there, he would have been pissed. If he were there, she also liked to think he would have been proud to know she was taking his advice. Not that she had much of a choice.

With all the groceries she had in the trunk of the hatchback she'd borrowed from Zipcar, she'd be set for at least a week, maybe more. She'd hide out for a while, eat Cap'n Crunch out of the box while reading a few romance books and let things cool down. By then, hopefully she would figure out a way of getting Thorn's crap back to him in manner that didn't equal her ending up dead.

She parked the car along the curb four blocks down and two blocks over from her apartment complex. She didn't know for sure, but she'd hazard a guess that Zipcar had GPS chips in their cars, and while the apartment was listed under a false name, her Zipcar account wasn't. She didn't want anyone tracing the car to her safe house.

She went around to the back of the car and opened the trunk, reaching in to pull out the first half-dozen bags. Crap, it was going to take her at least two trips to get all this food into the apartment. What a pain in the butt.

Fortunately, it wouldn't be physically strenuous. Yet another fringe benefit of her freaky side. She could have carried all the bags at one time, but a woman her size doing that would have attracted a load of attention. That was something she definitely didn't want.

Dreya had just turned and was walking down the sidewalk when she felt a strange prickling sensation run up her back. Dropping her bags, she spun around, her claws extending as she prepared to defend herself. Instead of someone charging at her with a butcher knife, a roaring chain saw or even a machine gun, the street was empty. Well, not exactly empty. There were a few cars passing by on the street, and a little farther away, there was a tiny, old lady walking her pug. The pug might have been eyeballing Dreya with an expression of major confusion, but there was definitely nothing around that looked threatening.

She glanced up at the nearby apartment windows and

balconies, but there was nothing there either. The skin at the base of her neck was still tingling like mad, though. She couldn't shake the feeling that something was seriously wrong.

Dreya was used to her freaky side telling her things. Like when cars got too close to her motorcycle. Weird crap like that had been happening to her for over a decade now. But this was different. This felt like her head was sitting right in the middle of a sniper's crosshairs.

She doubted that was the case, but she couldn't stand out there in the street all day, her groceries lying at her feet like she had lost her marbles. She looked around one more time. She was probably just freaking out because she'd been under so much stress. With her only real friend in the world dead, a multimillion-dollar diamond hidden in her apartment, and Thorn's goons ready to beat her to a pulp the moment they caught her, how could she not be stressed out?

Dreya collected her bags and hurried down the sidewalk toward her apartment again. The prickling sensation immediately began to fade, but she still ducked down a side street that ran along the back of the nearest apartment complex anyway. Instinct told her to get off the main street and out of sight With no one watching, she was able to pick up her pace without worrying about someone wondering how she was able to jog while carrying six heavy grocery bags.

She ran for three blocks, staying behind the long line of multifloor apartments, figuring she'd turn left at the next alley, then cross over Fourteenth Street. Then it would just be a short run up the stairs and she'd be in her apartment. Maybe she'd hang out there for a couple hours before she came down for the rest of her stuff.

But as she approached the alley, the feeling of dread she'd been experiencing earlier subsided almost to the point that she wasn't sure if it had ever been there. Maybe she was just losing her freaky mind.

She turned and was halfway down the alley when she saw the black SUV turned sideways across it. The tingling sensation lit a fire along her back again, even hotter than before.

Dreya dropped her bags, her claws and fangs coming out this time as she focused on the heavily tinted windows of the vehicle blocking her path. There was no way in hell that thing parked there was a coincidence. Someone *had* been watching her out on the main street earlier. They'd somehow figured out where she was heading and had gotten in front of her.

The seconds ticked by, but no one in the SUV moved. She was about to abandon her groceries altogether and sprint past the vehicle, but the electric tingles along her spine were so painful now she wanted to scream.

She spun around and saw two big men in dark suits wearing sunglasses standing in the middle of the alley behind her, cutting off her escape in that direction. Her first instinct was to turn and run. She knew for a fact that there was no one on the planet who could keep up with her when she really cut loose and ran hard.

Then she saw the weapons both men held. She knew nothing about guns, but the things they were holding didn't look like any revolver or automatic she'd ever seen. Instead of the typical gun barrel, the front of the weapons were closed off with a bright-green square of plastic. If she didn't know better, she'd think they were toys. She knew she wasn't that lucky.

The two men smiled menacingly at her, their eyes hidden behind their dark glasses as they shifted their weapons just enough so that they were pointed straight at her. She might be fast, but something told her she couldn't outrun whatever was going to come out the end of those guns, though.

Time froze for a moment as she tensed, ready to spring to the side the second it seemed like the two men were about to fire. The grins on their faces broadened, as if they knew exactly what she was going to do and that it wouldn't help.

Suddenly, a roar so loud filled the air it seemed to shake the walls of the buildings on either side of the alley and vibrate through her chest like thunder. Dreya barely caught movement out of the corner of her eye before a blur slammed into both gunmen. The two guys who'd been about to shoot her were big, but this new guy completely dwarfed them, and when he slammed into them, they both went flying. One hit the far wall of the alley and crumpled to the ground, unmoving. The other hit the ground and rolled, somehow coming up with his weapon pointed in the general direction of her savior.

There was a pop, then a zipping sound. Dreya's eyes widened as they followed the movement of the multiple electrode wires that sprang from the gun and closed the distance between the man on the ground and his attacker. Two electrodes struck the big bull of a man in the chest, and the air was suddenly alive with the sizzle and ozone stench of electricity. *Crap.* Those weapons were some kind of Taser guns.

Dreya expected the big man to fall to the ground and start flopping—like they did in the movies. But the guy just stood there with a pissed-off look on his face as he casually ripped the wires away from his chest. Then he roared again and charged. If Dreya thought he moved fast before, it was nothing compared to how quick he was now.

The shooter's eyes widened as he tried to get out of the way, but it was too late. The big man grabbed him off the ground and tossed him across the alley, slamming him into the same wall his partner had just bounced off. The man in the dark suit and sunglasses who'd likely been planning to torture and kill her flopped boneless to the ground. Dreya was pretty sure he wasn't ever getting up. That was okay with her.

The huge man turned and looked at Dreya with eyes that were glowing the brightest green she'd ever seen. Gaze locked on her, he took a step in her direction.

That was enough for her. She knew he'd just saved her life, but she was scared and he was freaking terrifying. She turned and took off running, her feet barely hitting the hood of the black SUV blocking the alley as she hurtled over the top of it.

Dreya knew it was stupid to go back to her apartment instead of the safe house, but she had to get a few things, including her emergency stash of cash and Thorn's diamond. Then she was getting the hell out of town.

The thunder of artillery fire rumbled in the distance, accompanied by dim flashes of light that filtered through the low cloud cover like fireworks on a rainy

Fourth of July. Layla had only been in Donetsk a few days, but already the thump and crack of exploding artillery and rocket shells was becoming like background noise for her.

Background noise or not, the ominous rumbling sound combined with the misting rain that had started a short time ago seemed to cast a subduing blanket over all of them, most especially the three teens. Dylan and his friends had grown quieter the closer they'd gotten to Zolnerov's estate as the weight of what they were about to do began to bear down on them. Now that they were there outside the huge house, the three teens silently regarded the dwelling with somber expressions. Layla couldn't miss the anxiety that sped up their heart rates and made them as tense as bow strings. She wanted to tell them that everything was going to be okay, and that everyone was going to make it out of this okay. But she knew she couldn't because there was a good chance she'd be wrong.

"I didn't think the place would be so big," Dylan said softly.

Even though it was dark, the teens hung back in the trees as if they were worried that one of the many guards roaming the property would see them.

"Dylan's right. How are you two ever going to find Anya in that place?" Mikhail asked. "It's huge. And creepy."

The Russian kid was right. In the darkness, the brick home that she and Jayson had first seen in Victor's photo now looked more like something out of a Dracula movie. Layla couldn't begin to imagine how many rooms there were. There had to be forty at least, and that wasn't counting the equally large outbuildings. Some of those looked big enough by themselves to hide a hundred kidnapped girls. If she and Jayson had been planning to search this whole place room by room, Dylan and his friends would have been right to worry. Thankfully, they didn't have to do that. They just had to follow her nose.

"Don't worry about that," Jayson said to the Russian teen. "The three of you need to be focused on pulling off the distraction we talked about. You do that, and Layla and I will find Anya."

Mikhail took a deep breath and nodded, like he was absorbing some of Jayson's confidence. Layla could easily believe that was possible. Jayson was in his element out here, leading their small team into danger. There'd been no hesitation or doubt in anything he'd said or done during the drive out here in the truck Victor had loaned them, or after they'd parked and moved the rest of the way in on foot. Even though she was the only one who could see in the dark, it was Jayson who had confidently led them through the last mile of woodland as they approached Zolnerov's estate. He'd moved through the forest as if he could see as well as she could, and the teens had followed his lead.

Layla imagined this was what Jayson had been like back in the army, when he was doing things that were insanely dangerous and important. She understood now more than ever why it had been so devastating when his injuries had taken all of it away from him.

The change she'd seen in him over the past few days was dramatic. It wasn't that he was a different person or anything, but there was a calm fire in his eyes that hadn't been there when he'd been sitting behind a desk at the DCO or even standing on the weapons range. That was because Jayson's life finally had a purpose again. Layla knew she was a big part of that purpose, but being in the field and doing the work he loved was critical, too.

Which was why Layla had spent almost as much time on the way out here worrying about their future in the DCO as she had wondering how they could possibly make it through this rescue mission alive and unhurt.

Would Dick and everyone else at the DCO really let them stay together as partners? Once Dick realized he wasn't going to get what he wanted out of Jayson anymore, the deputy director would probably break them up just for the fun of it. Heck, once everyone figured out that Jayson hadn't picked up any obvious hybrid abilities, she wasn't sure anyone at the DCO would let him go back into the field with or without her for a partner. She loved Jayson more than she could put into words and the thought of him losing something so important to him—again—was more than she was willing to accept.

She was still thinking about that when a curious voice suddenly jarred her out of her scheming thoughts.

"How do you even shoot this gun?"

Layla turned her head to see Olek staring down at the Makarov in his hand, a confused look on his face. It was hard to believe that one simple question could carry so much weight, but with those few words, Olek reminded her once again how young these three guys were, and how much she and Jayson were asking of them.

Crap.

Layla was about to tell Jayson this was never going to work and that they needed to come up with a new plan, but before she could open her mouth, Jayson stepped forward and gently took the battered Russian pistol out of the kid's hand. Then he dropped to one knee and motioned for them to join him.

"Have any of you guys ever fired a weapon before?" he asked softly.

Layla couldn't help but notice that there wasn't a trace of concern in Jayson's voice. How the hell did he do that? It was like he was asking them if they'd driven a car or kissed a girl.

Dylan shook his head, but Mikhail nodded. "Yes, but not one like this. It was an old AK-47 that my father had. I've never fired anything but that."

Jayson shook his head in the dark. "No problem. You may not have known it, but you picked a good weapon for you three to use right out of the box."

"I did?" Mikhail asked, surprise clear in his voice.

"Yeah," Jayson told him. "The Makarov is a simple, rugged, fixed-barrel, blowback-operated automatic. It's never going to win any marksmanship awards, but at short distances—which is the only distance I want you three shooting at—it's as accurate as you need it to be."

"Is it hard to shoot?" Dylan asked.

"Not once you get the hang of it." Jayson held up the weapon so the glow coming from the lights outside the house shone on it a little. "Nothing fancy, though. I'll just cover the stuff you have to know right now, okay?"

They all nodded.

"First thing's first. This is the safety." He pointed at the flip switch on the rear of the slide. "Push it down to fire. Remember—down is dead. Say it."

"Down is dead," the three teens said in unison.

"Good."

Layla stood there and watched as Jayson showed them how to unload the weapon, slip bullets in the ammo clip, then reload the weapon and chamber a round. He talked slowly, letting them see what he was doing. Then he had them do it. Maybe it was the Special Forces training in him coming out, but in five minutes, he had them handling the 9mm pistols like they'd been doing it for years.

"Nothing fancy with the shooting, either," he added as they each chambered a round and put their weapons on safe. "If you have to do it, square up on your target, wrap both hands around the gun like I showed you, and shoot for the center of the chest, then get the hell out of there."

Dylan said something in reply, but Layla completely missed it as a very distracting scent suddenly wafted past her. Even as her head started shuffling through memories to identify it, she found herself instinctively spinning around, reaching behind her back to pull out her 9mm as she did.

Jayson was at her side in a flash, his assault rifle on his shoulder and aimed into the deeper forest behind them. The teens were right there with him, chambering rounds in their weapons as they moved.

Half a second later, her nose finally figured what the heck she was smelling—or whom to be more precise. She opened her mouth to tell Jayson and the kids that everything was fine when a gruff voice drifted to them through the forest. If she hadn't known who it was, the disembodied growl coming out of the rain-misted forest would have been kind of freaky. Okay, even knowing who it was, it was still a little disconcerting.

"Good to see they finally let you off the range, Jayson. Although I gotta say, the DCO must be getting desperate for field agents if they're sending out kids now."

Just then, a pair of glowing, yellow eyes appeared from behind a tree and started moving toward them.

"What the hell?" Mikhail said, his voice filled with alarm as he lifted his pistol higher and took a step forward.

Jayson lowered his weapon and put a hand on the Russian kid's shoulder. "Relax, Mikhail. It's our backup."

"Yeah, relax, Mikhail." The words were more of a growl than anything. "I know Jayson just got finished teaching you how to use that weapon, but I can promise you it won't work nearly as well after I shove it sideways up your ass."

"That's enough, Clayne," Danica said as she slipped out from behind his very large shadow and moved up to stand beside him.

Mikhail gave Jayson an uneasy look but lowered his gun. Beside him, Dylan and Olek did the same.

"I'm glad you guys finally got here," Jayson said. "Did Kendra fill you in on our plan to hit Zolnerov's place?"

The wolf shifter exchanged confused looks with Danica, then turned his gaze back to them. They looked at Jayson like he was speaking a foreign language.

"What the hell are you talking about?" Clayne demanded. "Were you two going to hit Zolnerov's place on your own with three kids for backup?"

All three teens opened their mouths to say something, but Clayne cut them off with a growl and a glare that made them take a step back.

"Wait a minute," Clayne said to Jayson. "Before you answer that, how did you guys even know Kojot was here? Danica and I were too busy trying to keep up with him to ever get a chance to call the DCO and tell them the piece of shit was on his way to the Ukraine."

Layla's jaw dropped. "Kojot is here? Right here—in Zolnerov's house?"

Clayne looked so exasperated that Layla thought he might go into full wolf mode. "Yeah. Isn't that why the two of you—make that the five of you—are here? To take down Kojot and stop Zolnerov from getting the weapons the arms dealer is bringing in?"

"No." Now Jayson was the one who looked confused. "We're here to rescue Anya and the other girls. Didn't Kendra tell you guys anything?"

"Who the hell is Anya?" Clayne asked.

Jayson—who looked like he was on the edge of losing it too—started to answer, but Layla interrupted. "Look, we don't have time for this. But if the two of you insist on talking it out, maybe we should pull back into the woods a little in case one of Zolnerov's guards comes this way?"

"Agreed," Danica said, taking Clayne's hand and pulling him back into the forest.

Layla did the same with Jayson, leaving Dylan and the other two teens to follow. Once they'd gone a few dozen yards into the woods, they all stopped. Jayson immediately began to explain who Anya was and why they were breaking into Zolnerov's estate to get her, but Clayne stopped him before he could get very far.

"Hold on," Clayne said. "You and Powell came here to rescue Dylan, but now you and Layla are rescuing Dylan's girlfriend. Why the hell would John send you here with a jackass like Powell, and where the hell is that walking asshat of a so-called DCO agent now that the shit is about to hit the fan?"

Jayson looked at Layla as if to say, *You wanna help me out with this?*

Layla quickly brought them up to speed.

"How did you get involved?" Danica asked.

"I was worried about Jayson, so I convinced Kendra to send me here to help," Layla said. "John doesn't know, of course, and will probably have a cow when he finds out."

She paused, trying to see if she'd left anything out, then decided she'd hit most of the high points. "So now we're going in to get Anya and the other girls Zolnerov kidnapped. We don't know what he wants with them, other than the typical creepy reasons why a man like Zolnerov would hold a group of teenaged girls captive."

Layla braced herself for another barrage of questions, especially about the hybrid drug Jayson had taken. As much as she didn't want to get into that in front of Dylan and his friends, she was going to have to tell Clayne and Danica enough to satisfy them. Maybe she and Jayson could talk around the subject and still get the critical details across.

"So, Powell's dead, huh?" Clayne said conversationally. "Couldn't happen to a nicer guy."

"Clayne," Danica rebuked sharply.

Layla knew how she felt. It was like men had no filter at all between their heads and their mouths.

"What?" the wolf shifter growled. "The guy was a total dickweed. The only reason no one capped him before now is because he was usually smart enough to keep his ass out of the field. Serves him right for trying to off Jayson."

Danica just shook her head. "I think we can help you fill in the blanks on why Zolnerov kidnapped Anya and the other girls."

"You can?" Dylan stepped closer. "Why?"

"They're payment," Clayne said.

Layla got a sinking feeling in the pit of her stomach.

"Payment for what?" Dylan asked.

"For the weapons Kojot is giving him," Clayne said, then added, "Kojot will take just about anything as payment as long as it's valuable. In this case, it seems he's okay with taking those girls."

Jayson frowned. "That doesn't make any sense. What kind of weapons could Kojot offer that Zolnerov doesn't already have? We're in a frigging war zone. There are more weapons here than he could ever shoot."

Clayne shook his head. "Not like this he doesn't. We just followed Kojot in from the Kurgan region of southern Russia. He left there on a private cargo aircraft with a large shipment of crates delivered to him from a Russian military facility called Shchuch'ye. He loaded the crates on a big truck and came straight here."

"Shit," Jayson muttered.

"What is it?" Layla asked. She didn't know where the Kurgan region even was, much less want kind of weapons the Shchuch'ye facility made.

"Russia has been destroying their stockpile of chemical agents for years, but the Shchuch'ye depot still stores plenty of it," Jayson explained. "I don't have a clue what kind of delivery platform we're talking about— rocket warheads, artillery rounds, who knows?—but if he brought a shipment of weapons from there, you can pretty much guarantee it's some kind of toxic crap."

"Oh God," Mikhail murmured. "The colonel is going to use chemicals on the pro-Ukrainian forces to try to end the fighting all at once."

"Maybe," Danica agreed. "But based on what we know about Zolnerov, we're thinking his plan is a little more twisted. It's possible that he could use the weapons somewhere here in Donetsk against his own people, then blame the pro-Ukrainian forces for it."

"That actually makes sense," Layla said. "There's still a lot of fighting going on right now, but the borders have essentially stabilized. If Zolnerov is able to convince everyone the Ukrainians used chemical weapons on them, all that will change. It would rip the top off this whole region and destroy any possibility of a negotiated peace settlement. As one of the most senior military leaders in the area, people would naturally look to him to take charge."

"We have to stop him," Mikhail said urgently.

Clayne regarded the Russian teen for a moment before turning his attention back to her and Jayson.

"Kojot's cargo truck with the weapons is in one of those outlying buildings on the south side of the compound," the wolf shifter said. "If I know him, he's going to be close to his weapons until he gets his payment. Since it seems like he's getting paid in human cargo, I'm guessing he'll use that same truck to get the girls out of here. Danica and I didn't have enough intel to come up with a plan, other than killing Kojot in the most violent method I can think of. If you two have a better idea, we're listening."

Layla blinked in surprise. Clayne had always struck her as the make-it-up-as-you-go type. She never thought he'd be willing to go along with someone else's plan. Then again, Ivy had told her that Danica was a good influence on the wolf shifter.

She and Jayson quickly outlined their plan to Clayne and Danica, from the teens creating a distraction to her tracking down Anya. Since Dylan and the others were there, Jayson avoided any mention of using Anya's scent on the scarf to find the girl, but Clayne and Danica were experienced enough to read between the lines.

"What kind of distraction do you have planned?" Clayne asked Mikhail.

"I have some friends bringing in a car that we're going to ram into the gate and blow up remotely. The trunk is full of old ammo, so the guards are going to go flip out when the vehicle catches on fire."

Clayne looked impressed. "That should do it." He looked at her and Jayson. "The plan sounds good. You two rescue the girls. Danica and I will target Kojot and those chemical weapons."

"Whoever gets their part done first goes and helps the other," Jayson added.

Clayne nodded. "Agreed. Be careful in there. With Kojot here, there are probably even more soldiers around than normal."

A soft buzzing sound came from Mikhail's back pocket. He pulled out his cell phone and looked at the display.

"My friends are here," he said. "We need to meet them around front. It should only take us about ten minutes to get everything set up and ready."

Dylan looked at Jayson. "You want us to text you before we're ready to let the car go?"

Jayson shook his head. "No. We'll go when we hear the boom."

"Those kids are pretty ballsy," Clayne remarked softly as the teens disappeared into the woods.

"Yeah," Jayson agreed. "Hopefully they don't do anything too ballsy and get themselves killed."

Layla silently agreed.

"We're going to move around to the south," Clayne said. "We'll go over the wall at the boom, too."

"I'll call you on the satellite phone if we need you," Layla said.

Danica arched a brow in her fiancé's direction. "I'd say that'd be great, but Clayne smashed the sat phone to pieces three days ago."

He shot her a glare in the dark. "It kept ringing all the time."

"Phones have been known to do that on occasion," she said. "Some people have even been known to put the crazy things on vibrate or silence them altogether. But you decided to slam it into a brick wall, then throw it in the river for good measure. Both approaches work I guess."

Clayne growled.

Danica shook her head. "If you need us, yell really loud. Clayne will hear and we'll come running."

A few moments later, the other two DCO agents were gone, leaving Layla and Jayson alone in the forest with the occasional thud of artillery in the distance to keep them company.

"We're going to have to figure out a quiet way to get

over the wall," Jayson said. "Maybe you can show me how to do one of those shifter jumps of yours so I can see if I have it in me."

Layla bit back a groan. *Crap.* She couldn't put off telling Jayson about Zarina's antidote any longer. He seriously thought he might have the ability to jump up and grab the top of a fourteen-foot-high wall. She had to tell him the truth. She couldn't let him go in thinking he had some kind of miraculous abilities he didn't. She had to tell him, no matter how much it hurt him to hear it.

"Before we go over that wall, there's something important you need to know," she said.

He grinned. "I already know you love me—remember?"

She couldn't help smiling in return, even if her heart was thudding so hard in her chest it was almost painful. "I do love you, but this is something different. Something I should have told you long before now."

He must have picked up on the urgency in her tone because the smile left his face. "What is it?"

She took a deep breath, wishing she could come up with a better way—a better time—to say it. But there was no better time or place. There was just now, only minutes before Dylan and the others created a distraction and kicked off the mission. She had to trust that Jayson's love for her was enough to get them through this.

"Jayson, do you remember Zarina giving you a shot before Dick's doctors injected you with the hybrid serum?"

He looked confused for a moment, then nodded. "Yeah. It was a gamma globulin. She said it would boost my immune system."

Layla shook her head. "It wasn't a shot to boost your immune system. It was an antidote that Zarina had developed for Tanner in the hope that it could change him back into a regular person. She wasn't planning to give it to you, but she had no choice. She was terrified you'd end up like all the dead hybrids the DCO has found, so she gave you the antidote hoping to save your life."

Jayson looked stunned. "What are you saying?"

She knew her eyes were now glowing vivid green, reminding him of exactly what she was—and what he wasn't.

"I'm saying you're not a hybrid and you're not indestructible. You need to know that before we go over that wall."

Chapter 13

Ivy was sitting in a comfortable chair in Dreya Clark's living room waiting for the feline shifter to come home when she heard footsteps heading down the hallway. She breathed a sigh of relief as she picked up the other shifter's scent. After seeing what had happened in Columbia Heights with Thorn's goons, she wasn't sure Dreya would come back to her apartment in Foggy Bottom. There had been an equally good chance she'd bolt and find another place to hide. Hell, there was still a chance the shifter would bail when she smelled Ivy and realized there was someone in her apartment. Ivy hoped not. The woman was scared enough already and chasing her wouldn't help.

Ivy drew her SIG 9mm and rested it on the table beside the chair, keeping her hand on the grip. She hated the idea of having the gun out in plain sight when Dreya walked through the door, but Ivy wasn't sure how this meeting was going to go down or if the other shifter had a weapon.

Once they'd gotten Dreya's name, Adam's people had been able to track her down within a couple hours. Ivy had swung by the thief's jewelry shop first, but it had been locked up tight. She'd been heading to her apartment next when she got a call from a man with a deep voice who told her that Dreya Clark had a safe house under another name in Columbia Heights and that was where Ivy would find her.

Ivy had gotten there just in time to see Thorn's men corner Dreya in the alley. Ivy had been about to jump in when a huge guy charged in like a bull and crushed both of them. Even though she couldn't pick up his scent, the man was too big and fast to be anything other than a shifter. She suspected he was one of Adam's people but didn't have a chance to confirm it. She couldn't let Dreya get away. She only hoped Dreya would let her talk before the inevitable fight-or-flight instinct kicked in.

Dreya opened the door and was ten steps into the living room before catching sight of Ivy. The blond shifter stopped short, eyeing Ivy—and the gun— suspiciously. Her blue eyes darted around the room, as if calculating the odds of reaching cover before Ivy could shoot her.

She must have decided her chances weren't that good because she didn't move. Dreya was nervous, no doubt. Two men had just tried to Taser and kidnap her.

"Are you the one who's been torturing and killing all my friends?" Dreya asked.

"No." Ivy stood, then slowly picked up her gun and made a show of putting it back in its holster. If Dreya had a weapon, she would have pulled it out already. "That would be Thorn's personal security, a man named Douglas Frasier. Those two men who cornered you in that alley in Columbia Heights worked for him, too."

Dreya's eyes narrowed. "I don't know anyone named Thorn. I think you've made a mistake."

Ivy almost smiled. She didn't know why, but she liked Dreya. Maybe because she reminded her of Layla—whom, according to Kendra, had found Jayson and would be on her way home soon. Dreya seemed to have that same kind of clever innocence about her that Layla possessed. Too bad she'd gotten herself involved with stuff that put her on Thorn's bad side.

"I know you have absolutely no reason to believe this, but I'm here to help you," Ivy said. "You stole something from a very powerful person and if we can't figure out a way to get him off your trail, you're going to end up dead like your friends."

Dreya folded her arms and lifted her chin. "It wasn't me. I've never stolen anything. Like I said, you have the wrong person."

"Wrong person, huh?" Ivy snorted. "That wasn't you who broke into Thomas Thorn's mansion over near Embassy Row a few nights ago? It wasn't you who came over the back wall and climbed the side of the three-story structure like it was nothing? Or ran along the ridgeline of the roof, somehow walking on those terracotta tiles without breaking any of them, then slipping in through a third-story window?"

Ivy went on to describe exactly how Dreya had moved around Thorn's library, right down to where she'd walked and what she'd touched.

Dreya blanched. "You were outside Thorn's place that night, weren't you? You were the one I smelled as I was climbing on my bike. Why didn't you stop me then? Or come after me?"

"I couldn't care less that you stole something from the man, but now Thorn is after you and I can't stand around and do nothing while he tries to kill you."

Dreya chewed on her lower lip, considering that. "So what are you doing here if you don't work for Thorn? You want a cut or something?"

"No, I don't want a cut," Ivy said. "I want to help you get away."

Dreya regarded her warily. "Why would you want to help me? You don't even know me."

Ivy shrugged. "Let's just say we have a lot in common, not the least of which is a great dislike of Thomas Thorn and the way he does things. I have no interest in seeing someone like Thorn and his goons get away with killing you. And that's what will happen if he doesn't get back what belongs to him."

Dreya's eyes darted to the window.

"If you make a run for it, I won't try to stop you," Ivy said. "We both know you'll survive the fall easily enough, even from this high up. Sure, with all the trash cans, AC units, and bikes down there, you'll almost certainly break a few bones, but I don't imagine it will hurt as badly as what Thorn's men will do to you when they catch you. You know as well as I do that the only reason you got away in that alley earlier is because you had a guardian angel out there watching over you. He killed those men and Thorn will never have a clue what happened to them or where they went. But that big guy won't be there every time, especially not if you go on the run. Thorn will come after you. And he's not going to stop until he gets what he's after. Be smart and give me what you stole from Thorn."

"How do I know you won't just kill me the moment you get what you want?"

"Because I give you my word."

That was the best Ivy could do.

Dreya stared at her for a long time, then let out a sigh. Shaking her head, she walked into the kitchen. Ivy had thought a thief like Dreya would hide the diamond and whatever else she'd stolen from Thorn somewhere better than her refrigerator.

But Dreya didn't open the fridge. Instead, she pulled it smoothly out of the cubby in the wall, then slipped behind it and slid a piece of paneling aside to reveal the front of a combination safe. The woodwork had been done so seamlessly that Ivy would have had a hard time finding it on her own, even with her shifter senses.

Dreya flipped through the combination quickly, then yanked open the door and reached inside. Ivy had about a half second to wonder if the other shifter was going to come out with a gun, but when Dreya turned around, all she held was a big, beautiful diamond on a long, gold chain. Dreya tossed it across the room, forcing Ivy to snatch it out of the air before it smashed against the wall.

"You've got what you came here for," the shifter said. "Now you can leave."

"Not until you give me what else you stole."

Dreya swallowed hard. "I don't know what you're talking about."

Ivy tightened her grip on the diamond. She didn't want to get in a staring contest, but the longer they hung around, the more likely Thorn's people would find out where Dreya was and come looking for her.

"I don't know what else you took when you grabbed that diamond, but whatever it is, it has Thorn behaving more viciously than I've ever see him. And trust me, I've seen him be really frigging nasty," Ivy said. "I know you have family in town, and as soon as Thorn figures out exactly who you are, he won't have a problem going after the people closest to you. Is that what you want?"

Dreya's eyes filled with pain. Turning back to the safe, she reached inside and took out a small, black, rectangular-shaped box. For a moment, Ivy thought it was a jewelry box, but when the other shifter walked over and handed it to her, she realized it was too heavy and solid for that. There wasn't a hinge or any way to open it, either. There was only some kind of recessed, multipin connector on one side and an irregular hole like something a key would fit into on the other.

"What is it?" Ivy asked.

Dreya shrugged. "Beats me. I thought it was some kind of hard drive, but if it is, it's not like anything I've ever seen and I don't know how to get it open."

Ivy stared at the thing in her hand. "If you didn't know what it was, why did you take it?"

The blond shifter smiled. "It was in a fancy safe with a fancy diamond. I figured it must be valuable. Plus, I figured it would piss off the rich asshole if I took it. It's one of the benefits of my chosen career path—pissing off rich people."

"Until you piss off the wrong one," Ivy said.

Dreya snorted. "So you're just going to give this stuff back to Thorn, and that's it—he leaves me alone?"

"I wish," Ivy said. "No. For this to work, I'm going to have to make sure that the person who took this stuff is dead."

Dreya's eyes widened.

Ivy laughed. "Good thing you're not the person who took it."

Dreya visibly relaxed. "So…what do I do?"

"Get out of town for a while, at least until everything is cleaned up," Ivy suggested. "And when you come back, you might want to think about staying away from men like Thorn."

Pocketing the diamond and the little black box, she turned and headed for the door.

"Hey!" Dreya called. "That's it? You're just going to walk out without even telling me your name?"

Ivy stopped at the door and turned back to look at the feline shifter. "I don't think we have to worry about that. I get the feeling we're going to meet again soon. I'll tell you my name then. Take my advice and get out of town, okay?"

Dreya nodded.

Without another word, she turned and walked out, closing the door softly behind her. On the way down the stairs, she called Landon and let him know that she'd found Dreya and had Thorn's stuff.

"What the hell did she have besides the diamond?" Landon asked.

Ivy climbed into the SUV and cranked the engine. "I think it's some kind of electronic storage media, like a hard drive. I'm going to show it to the techs at the complex. If it's some kind of storage drive, they'll know how to get the info off it."

"If you're right about that being some kind of hard drive, you know what this means, don't you?"

She laughed as she pulled out of the parking lot and headed for the beltway. "It means we have Thorn by the balls and all we have to do is twist. Make sure Hayes stays away from Dreya Clark, then get your sexy butt down to the complex. This is all coming together fast."

"I'm on it." Landon chuckled. "Holy shit, I'm on it."

Jayson felt like he was sinking in quicksand. He'd already told himself that the hybrid serum hadn't worked and that he'd gained little if anything from taking it. He'd been okay with that and had come to accept that what he'd done since arriving in Donetsk was more about the power of his will and his commitment to Layla than some crazy miracle drug. Finding out that the serum hadn't even had a chance to work because Zarina had dosed him with something that kept it from ever being a possibility made him angry as hell. He felt betrayed…cheated.

Shit.

They didn't have time for this. Dylan, Mikhail, Olek, and their friends were going to be ramming that car into the gate any minute now. But Jayson had to know.

"Why would Zarina inject me with something like that without telling me?" he asked softly.

Layla closed her eyes. When she opened them again, the green glow was gone. All that was left in the darkness was overwhelming sadness. She hadn't wanted to tell him about this, he realized. If he hadn't made that crack about trying to leap up on the wall like a shifter, she probably never would have.

"Zarina knew that serum would almost certainly kill you—or worse, turn you into a monster that even you wouldn't recognize," Layla said. "She used the only thing she had that might stop it. Considering the fact that you were willing to die for a chance at having a normal life again, she didn't see much point in telling you about the antidote in advance."

"Did you know she was going to do it?" he asked.

Layla shook her head. "No. When you walked in with Dick all ready to take the drug, she didn't have time to call me and ask what she should do. She had to act. But if I had been there, or if she'd been able to reach me, I would have told her to give you the antidote. Even if you hated me for it later, I would have told her to do it. Because while you needed more from your life than you had, all I needed was you. And if it means that I'm selfish for wanting you alive, then so be it."

Jayson started to say that it wasn't her decision to make, but the words died in his throat. Suddenly, he felt like he was the one being selfish, not to mention frigging stupid. Layla was completely right. He'd been willing to die rather than keep living with the injuries he'd sustained in Afghanistan because he thought those injuries were keeping him from living the life he wanted. But since coming on this mission, he discovered it had always been within his power to decide what kind of life he ended up living. It had just taken him time—and Layla's love—to figure that out.

In return for this wonderful gift, all Layla had ever asked was that he simply not give up, that he stay here in the world with her whether he was whole or not. And here he was making her feel like there was something wrong with that. Of all the people who had done things wrong in this situation, Layla wasn't one of them.

Tears stung his eyes and he blinked them back. He wrapped his arms around her, pulling her against him.

"There's nothing selfish about not wanting me to take a drug that could have killed me, or being happy Zarina gave me something that kept me safe," he said hoarsely. "And if I made you feel any differently, I'm sorry. I got stupid there for a second, thinking about what could have been instead of what I already have. Again—I'm sorry."

Layla tipped her head back and stood up on her tiptoes to kiss him. Time stopped for a moment as their lips touched, and he was reminded once again that he had already gained the only thing of any real value that could have come from taking that serum—Layla.

"What you've accomplished on your own is far more impressive than anything you could have done with hybrid abilities," Layla said. "I couldn't be prouder of my partner—or the man I love."

At those words, Jayson felt a surge of pride unlike anything else he'd ever experienced. He kissed her again, then pulled back. "Let's go get those girls and bring them home."

As if on cue, an explosion from the front of the estate shook the ground beneath them and a big, red fireball rolled up through the night sky. Seconds later, the popping sound of small arms fire filled the air like someone was hosing down the front of the estate with a half-dozen machine guns.

Shit. If they blew this because he was too busy throwing a pity party for himself to stay focused on the mission, he was going to be pissed.

"Go!" Jayson urged.

Trusting the teens' distraction would get everyone's attention turned the other way, Layla took off running for the back of the house, Jayson at her side. Dropping to one knee, he put his back to the rough stone and cupped his hands in front of him. He tensed, knowing it was going to hurt, but doing it anyway. Layla read his mind, launching herself at him, her booted foot thumping into his outstretched hands on the fly. He shoved up at the same time she jumped, propelling her to the top of the wall.

She stretched out on her stomach, then threw one of her legs over the top and reached down with her free hand. Jayson didn't know how the hell a woman her size could hold his weight even if she was a shifter, but he leaped up and grabbed her outstretched hand anyway. The moment their palms clapped together, she gripped tightly, pulling him up as he kicked with his legs. Considering they hadn't practiced this particular move, they executed it amazingly smoothly, and within a few seconds, they were both dropping down to the far side of the high wall and were inside the estate.

Jayson pulled the AK-74 off his back as Layla drew her pistol. He waited while she tested the air inside the compound with her nose and ears to make sure there weren't any guards hanging around back there.

After a moment, Layla gave him the all-clear signal.

"Let's head for the main section of the house, then hope that you pick up Anya's scent from there," Jayson said.

Layla nodded and took point. Jayson followed her across the property as she tried to stay in the deep shadows as much as possible. They moved fast but carefully, too. It wouldn't do Anya or anyone any good if they ran into a group of armed guards.

As they ran past a big swimming pool artfully surrounded by raised flower beds made of stacked stone and shaped concrete, Jayson had a hard time not gawking.

The place looked more like something you'd see on a private island getaway in the Mediterranean than an estate in Ukraine.

He followed Layla around the loungers and outdoor bar as she led the way to the large french doors that led into the main house. Jayson expected the gunfire from the front of the house to start to taper off—surely there couldn't have been that many rounds of ammunition in the trunk of a car—but as he and Layla reached the heavy glass doors, the sound of weapons fire actually got heavier.

"Dylan and the others better not be out there in a gun-fight with the guards," he whispered to Layla. "If they are and they live through this, I'm going to kill them."

"A concept only a man could understand because yeah, that makes sense," Layla muttered as she opened one of the french doors.

They slipped inside a large space that looked less like a living room and more like a rest area if you got tired going from the west side of the estate to the east side. A central hallway branched off left and right, toward the two separate wings of the huge home, while ahead of them a monstrously large sectional couch made out of some kind of dark wood and marble sat in front of an equally large brick fireplace. Just past that, Jayson saw another hallway that looked like it led to another living room.

Layla took Anya's scarf out of her jacket pocket, pressed the fabric to her nose, and breathed deeply. Eyes closed, she sniffed the air, searching for the scent. A moment later, her eyes flew open, revealing that they were greener than Jayson had ever seen them.

"I have her," she announced.

Stuffing the scarf back in her pocket, she turned and ran toward the east wing.

Now that Layla had the scent, she moved fast, and it was all Jayson could do to keep up with her and provide some kind of cover. Running that fast through a house when you didn't know if there were bad guys around every corner was reckless as hell, but he was still damn glad he had Layla and her nose leading him. They ran past more rooms, doorways, and corridors than he bothered counting. If he'd had to go down every hallway, open every door, and search every room to see if the girls were there, he'd have been there until tomorrow.

"Anya's scent is strong, which means she was in this hallway recently," Layla said. "I can smell the other girls, too."

Layla picked up speed, forcing him to keep up. The gunfire from outside was getting even worse and from the sounds of it, there was now shooting coming from the outlying buildings where Clayne and Danica had gone. Jayson cursed, looking for other exit doors in case he and Layla ran into problems and couldn't get out the way they'd come. Because this plan seemed to be going wrong fast.

He was so focused on developing an alternate escape route that he almost ran over Layla when she suddenly hit the brakes and came to a sliding stop. "What's wrong?"

She backtracked a few dozen steps until she came to a marble-lined arch that opened up onto a set of spiraling stairs leading downward. Then she leaned out over the railing and sniffed.

"The girls are down there somewhere," she whispered.

"There are three men, too. Do you think we can get away with me distracting them like I did at the RSA building?"

Jayson shook his head as he slipped his rifle over his back and took out his pistol. "Those guys are going to be tense as hell from all the shooting going on. If you pop down there and say hi, they'll likely put a bullet in you."

"So what do we do?"

"We put a bullet in them first," he said. "Depending on where they're standing, I can probably take down two of them before they return fire, but three would be pushing my luck. Can you handle one of them yourself?"

She didn't hesitate. "Yes. If you asked me a week ago, I'm not so sure what I would have said, but if it means saving Anya and those other girls, I can do it."

He gave her a nod. "We'll slip down and get as close as we can before we step out. Before we do, try to use your nose and ears to help me understand where the men are positioned. No talking—just finger and hand signals."

Layla nodded and descended the stairs. Halfway down, she stopped cold, testing the air again with her nose.

"What is it?" he whispered in her ear.

She turned to him, her eyes wide. "I smell Powell. He's not down there now, but he was down there recently. I can smell his blood. He didn't die up on that roof. Zolnerov has him."

Shit. Now they had someone else to rescue.

Ivy headed straight for John's office the moment she walked into the operations building at the DCO training

complex, but Kendra intercepted her before she got
more than ten feet.

"Dick hasn't been around since he sent Jayson and
Powell to Donetsk, but John doesn't want him showing up out of the blue and figuring out that we're onto
something with Thorn," Kendra said, taking Ivy's arm
and turning her back around. "Come with me."

"Are Layla and Jayson on their way back yet?" Ivy
asked as they crossed the central quad area of the complex and headed toward the building where the DCO's
tech wizards maintained all the servers and databases
the covert organization depended on for intelligence
gathering operations.

"Not quite." Kendra gave her a sidelong glance.
"The diplomat's son was in Donetsk with his girlfriend.
Long story short, she got kidnapped along with some
other girls and is being held by one of the militia leaders. Layla and Jayson are going in to rescue them." She
glanced at her watch. "In fact, with the time difference,
they should be hitting the place right now."

Ivy halted in midstep. "What?"

Kendra stopped too, turning to face her. "Layla is
going to be fine. She's more like you than you think.
Besides, Jayson loves her like crazy. He would never let
anything happen to her. They're going to be an amazing team. I think they can handle a little pervert warlord
who's kidnapping girls so he can build his own harem."

Ivy sighed. She didn't like the idea of Layla going
up against a militia leader, but at least her sister was
with a partner who would watch her back. "You're right.
And while Powell is a jackass, at least he's there to back
them up. That has to count for something."

Kendra turned and started across the quad again, walking faster than before. Ivy followed. Her friend's heart rate was spiking and it had nothing to do with the vigorous exercise.

"What aren't you telling me?" Ivy asked sharply.

Kendra didn't answer. Ivy thought she might have to circle around in front of her friend and get in her path when Kendra stopped abruptly and turned to look at her.

"Powell isn't going to be helping them on the rescue mission because he's dead," Kendra said. "He and Jayson got into a gunfight with the local militia shortly after they arrived in Donetsk. Powell apparently decided that he needed to off Jayson to keep the locals from getting their hands on a hybrid, and Jayson didn't go along with the idea."

Ivy stood there stunned. "Jayson killed him?"

"I don't have all the details," Kendra said. "It's more likely that the local militia killed Powell, but I got the feeling that Jayson played a part in it. The important thing I'm trying to tell you isn't that Jayson had anything to do with Powell's death—that jerk tried to kill Jayson in cold blood and got exactly what he deserved—it's that Layla and Jayson are a real team out there, and they're good enough to get this done."

Kendra turned and started walking again. Ivy fell into step beside her. As they crossed the quad, Kendra brought her up to speed on everything she knew about what had happened over in Donetsk. "Jayson jumped off a three-story building and swam across a river at least half a mile wide. Does that sound like something the Jayson we know could do?"

"No," Ivy admitted, a little shocked.

If Powell tried to kill Jayson, that meant the serum must have worked. The idea that Layla was out there on the mission with another shifter—or hybrid or whatever Jayson was—made Ivy feel a lot better about the danger her sister was in. That said, she still wouldn't sleep until they were both back home.

When she and Kendra got to the IT building, her friend led her through the maze of cubicles that filled the front half of the building and into a big room. All four walls were lined with computer servers while worktables filled the center of the room.

John was waiting for them, along with Evan Lloyd, an analyst from the intel branch Ivy had worked with several times, as well as two techies she didn't recognize. One was a woman in her midthirties with her black hair pulled back into a very businesslike bun, while the guy looked like he'd just graduated from college the week before. John introduced them as Lisa Marino and Karl Thomas.

"So what do you have?" John asked her.

Ivy reached into her coat pocket and pulled out both the diamond and the strange black box, setting them on the nearest table. Lisa immediately snatched up the box and examined it with Karl, leaving the rest of them alone with the diamond.

"This is absolutely spectacular." Kendra picked it up by the chain, watching the light bounce off the facets of the gem. "Can I keep it? I promise to take good care of it, take it out on walks every night, and clean up behind it when it makes a mess."

Ivy laughed. "I don't think even you would be able to clean up the kind of mess that follows something like this thing around. I think we'd better just send it back home."

Kendra looked disappointed but set the diamond down on the table again. "Yeah, I guess so. Besides, I have nothing that would go with it. I'd have to buy a whole new wardrobe."

"I don't know," Ivy said. "I'm pretty sure Declan would be okay if you walked around the house wearing nothing but that."

John let out a polite cough, gesturing to Evan, then himself. "Two men standing right here."

Ivy opened her mouth to tease John, but Lisa cut her off.

"It's a solid state drive, but it's way more advanced than anything either of us have ever seen."

"So it's a hard drive?" John clarified, his eyes lighting up.

Ivy shared his excitement. Considering the fact that this thing had been locked up in Thorn's private safe, it had to have some really juicy stuff on it. Ivy doubted it was just his taxes.

"This is so much more than a hard drive," Karl said. "It's one big, solid silicon-based integrated chip. There's no moving disk like a normal hard drive."

He and Lisa started babbling about nonvolatile NAND flash memory, unpowered storage, fully integrated circuit design, and seamless controller chips, completely oblivious to the fact that no one else in the room understood a single word they were saying.

"There are plenty of solid state drives out there right now, of course," Karl added, as if everyone knew that. "Price has kept them mostly on the fringes though, so they're mostly in toys. This thing looks to be light-years ahead of anything I've ever heard of. It would have cost a small fortune to make, but the storage capability must be insane."

"What kind of storage are we talking about?" John asked. "How much information could be stored on here?"

Lisa exchanged looks with Karl, who shrugged.

"Well, it's all just theory at this point since this seems like a prototype, you know?" Karl said.

"How much information?" John asked again, firmer this time. "Five terabytes or something?"

The woman shook her head. "Definitely not. If all he wanted to do was store five terabytes, he could have used a normal hard drive. Heck, he could have used a flash drive for that. No, this thing is probably in the pet-abyte range, maybe a lot more."

"I have no idea what that means," John said in exas-peration. "Is that a lot?"

Karl held up the black box. "A lot. As in the Library of Congress kind of a lot."

John grinned. "How long will it take to download the data?"

Lisa studied the back end of the black box and gri-maced. "I suppose I could come up with a transfer cable that would work. It might take a few days, though, not to mention a lot of trial and error because we don't have a clue what kind of data transfer protocols this thing uses. The real problem is that we don't have the key."

"Key?" John repeated, the smile disappearing from his face.

Karl pointed at the irregular slot in the front of the box. "That's a security key slot, like we use to switch on our classified phones. Without having that, it could take months to hack into this thing."

"Even longer if the data is encrypted, which it almost certainly is," Lisa added.

"Encrypted?" John said.

Karl nodded. "Like the encryption code on the wireless router in your home. Except we have no idea how long of a code it might be. These days, it could easily be sixteen digits. Unless whoever designed this thing was working for a paranoid type. Then it could be anything—twenty-four or thirty-two characters even. Regardless, the chances of stumbling over that code by accident is almost nil."

John cursed. "You're telling me that we likely have every piece of data that we need right here in this box, but we can't get it out?"

Lisa shook her head. "We can get the data out. It will just take time. Maybe a few days to come up with an interface cable, then a few weeks to bypass the key interrupt. After that, it's just a matter of working out the encryption code."

"How long will it take to break the code?" John asked.

Lisa exchanged looks with Karl again. "We know a lot about Thorn, so that helps. Maybe if we get lucky, we could do it in a few months."

John's eyes widened. "Months?"

"That's if it's on the lower end of the security scale," Karl said. "If the code really is thirty-two digits long, it will take longer."

Ivy frowned. "John, we can't wait that long. I told the shifter who stole this to get out of town for a while, but if we haven't done something soon, it won't matter what we do. Thorn will figure out her identity sooner or later and once he does, she's dead. I promised her I wouldn't let Thorn get to her. We're going to have to give the box and the diamond back to him."

John was silent for a long time. Finally, he nodded. "You're right."

Ivy blinked. She'd expected him to fight her a little more. While he had no desire to see Thorn get his hands on Dreya any more than Ivy did, he'd been after Thorn for a long time.

John looked at the two techs. "If you test this thing with mass spec or X-ray or whatever you people use, could you make a realistic model of it?"

Lisa looked confused. "Well, yeah, the material technology is well-known. It's just a silicon crystal structure. Like a regular computer chip, but a lot bigger, with a few thousand layers of boron and phosphorus to form the semiconductor paths. Throw in a circuit card or two to handle the security key and the encryption code, and you're done. But it won't work and the data certainly won't be there."

John shook his head. "I don't need it to work or for the data to be there because when you get done with it, you're going to smash it."

The two techs looked baffled beyond belief. "What?" they said in unison.

"Smash it, make it look like a building fell on it or a steamroller drove over it, whatever," John said. "I want it recognizable as what it used to be, but that's all. You have two hours to make that happen. No one outside this room knows what you're doing and why. No details of what you've done will ever be written down or disclosed to anyone. Is that clear?"

Lisa and Karl nodded, still clearly confused but ready to do whatever their boss asked of them. They moved over to another table and started pulling out tools, calipers, and notepads from the drawers underneath.

John turned to Kendra and Evan. "This is going to sound crazy, but we need a building we can set on fire and a fresh dead body to put inside it. It has to be someone we can create a detailed criminal record for, so if the guy already has a criminal past, that would be good. Burglary, safe cracking, explosives, the works—the record you create needs to be a perfect match for a criminal who would pull off the theft at Thorn's place, and it needs to be bulletproof. Can you do that?"

Ivy didn't have to ask what John was planning because she already knew. He was going to make it look like the thief who'd stolen the hard drive had died in the fire and that the little black box had been destroyed. It was brilliant.

Kendra looked at Evan, then nodded. "We can do that."

While Evan pulled out his cell phone and started dialing, Ivy turned to Kendra, saying, "I'm going to go find Landon and let him know what's happening. We'll be ready to go as soon as you get the body in place. In the meantime, let me know the moment you hear anything from Layla. I need to know she's okay."

John frowned. "What do you mean 'hear from Layla'? Where is she?"

Kendra looked extremely uncomfortable as her boss moved his gaze back and forth between the two of them.

"Kendra, I want you to look me in the eyes and tell

me that Layla isn't over in Ukraine trying to find Jayson and Powell," John said.

Kendra looked over quickly at Ivy, then turned back to their boss. "Layla isn't over in Ukraine looking for Powell."

John's scowl deepened. "Kendra."

Ivy gave Kendra a quick wave, then hurried to the door, never so happy to have silent feline shifter footsteps as she was right then.

Chapter 14

LAYLA LED JAYSON DOWN THE TIGHT SPIRAL STAIRCASE, her 9mm pistol clenched firmly in a hand that had suddenly become very moist with sweat. Shooting the man in the RSA building was completely different than what she was about to do in the next few minutes. He'd had a weapon pointed in their direction and been about to shoot them. This time it wouldn't be in self-defense.

She knew she was being stupid and that there was no reason to be squeamish about it. It wasn't like they could walk in and politely ask Zolnerov's men to simply release the girls. Something told her the men would certainly have no problem putting a bullet in both her and Jayson without another thought.

Layla didn't realize she'd been holding her breath until she reached the bottom of the steps. She glanced at Jayson over her shoulder, pointed down the hallway, then followed her nose to an arched doorway. She stopped just outside the door, but instead of peeking inside, she used her shifter senses to tell her what was happening in the room.

The sour, acrid scent of fear wafted out, making her nose wrinkle up and tingle, like she wanted to sneeze. But she could also sense hope in the room as well. The girls had heard all the shooting and probably assumed it was a rescue party. They were murmuring excitedly to each other in Russian.

"Quiet!" a man ordered harshly in Russian. "No talking."

The girls immediately fell silent.

Layla forced herself to ignore the girls and what they were feeling and focused on the men. Once she had them, she turned to Jayson and traced a square outline of the room with her fingers on the wall in front of her. Then she stabbed her forefinger at three locations in that square—one in each of the far back corners and the third in the center of the room.

Jayson nodded and pointed at himself, then the two farthest targets. He touched the center spot and motioned to her, lifting a brow in question. He'd take the two harder targets and leave the easier shot for her. That meant he was leaving himself wide-open to the shooter closest to them while he took out the other men in the room. If she didn't make the shot—or she hesitated— Jayson would be the one paying the price.

Layla took a deep breath and nodded.

Jayson moved to her right shoulder and held up three fingers, then started counting them down before she had a chance to wonder how many different ways she could screw this up.

When he got to zero, they both entered the room. It was a small home theater, complete with comfortable lounge chairs, a ceiling-mounted projector, and a wide, white screen mounted on the far wall. All twelve girls were sitting in the front of the room. They looked exhausted, scared, and more than one of them bore visible cuts and bruises. The signs of abuse sharpened Layla's focus and she snapped her attention to the man in the center of the room, the one who was already spinning around in their direction, an assault rifle coming off his shoulder.

She distantly heard Jayson's pistol going off to her right, but she ignored it as she aimed for the center of her target's chest and squeezed the trigger. The weapon bucked once in her hand, then again as she fired again to make sure he went down.

The man forgot about the rifle in his hand, letting it hang loose as he looked down in shock at the blood seeping through the front of his shirt. A moment later, he dropped to the floor.

Layla spun to the left and right, looking to see if she needed to help Jayson with his targets. She didn't. Both men were already dead.

She turned her attention to the girls on the floor to find them staring up at her and Jayson, concern and worry warring with hope on their faces.

"Anya Zelenko?" Jayson called out.

At her name, all other eleven prisoners in the room looked at a tall, dark-haired girl in the back of the theater. She had a bruise on her right cheek and fire in her eyes.

"That's me," she said in English as she got to her feet.

Layla smiled, hoping to reassure the girl that they were the good guys; however, as she got closer, she realized Anya was anything but terrified. Instead, she was brimming with bold defiance. No doubt she'd gotten that bruise on her cheek for getting in one of her captor's faces and telling him exactly what she thought of him. Layla decided she liked the girl before ever exchanging a word to her.

"It's time to go," Layla said in English. "Dylan and your other friends are waiting outside for you."

Anya's eyes lit up with a different kind of fire at the mention of her boyfriend's name. "Dylan is here?"

Layla nodded. "Yes. Neither of us speak Russian as well as you do, so if you can help us get the other girls moving, we can get out of here."

Anya looked like she had a thousand questions to ask, not the least of which was who the hell she and Jayson were and how Dylan had gotten them involved, but the Ukrainian girl focused on what they'd asked her to do. Scooping up the rifle from the man Layla had shot, she turned and urged all the other girls up. Layla led the way out of the room, taking them toward the main section of the house—and the exit.

The gunfire out front had slowed a little, but the shooting coming from the east side, where Clayne and Danica had gone, was as intense as before. There were occasional explosives going off, too. It sounded like Clayne and Danica were in trouble, but there was no way she or Jayson could go to their aid until they got all the girls out and over the wall.

They were hurrying through the living room, Layla starting to think their plan might actually work, when she picked up the scent of a lot of men coming their way—fast.

"Incoming!" she yelled, automatically slowing down and motioning behind her for Anya and the other girls to back up.

The girls slipped and slid on the marble floors but quickly moved backward into the cover provided by the arches that lined the eastern corridor.

Ten feet ahead, Jayson came to a stop in the middle of the living room and lifted his rifle just as four men came running down the central corridor from the west wing. She expected Jayson to start mowing the bad guys down the moment they came into view, but instead he hesitated.

Brian Powell's scent hit her like a ton of bricks and her mind fought to correlate what she was smelling with what she was seeing. Powell, his head still wrapped in a bloody bandage, wasn't a captive of the three armed militia soldiers. He was leading them.

She didn't understand how he'd done it, but the DCO agent had somehow escaped capture and put together a small team of men to rescue the girls. Maybe he wasn't so worthless after all.

Suddenly, the skin along the back of her neck burned as if it were on fire. Layla had never felt anything like it before, but she'd heard Ivy describe it often enough to know it was her feline intuition warning her that something was wrong.

"Watch out!" she shouted just as Powell lifted a small submachine gun and started shooting.

Jayson didn't know why Layla was warning him, but he trusted her instincts and dived for cover behind the big-ass sectional couch that dominated the middle of the room. He hadn't even hit the floor before bullets smashed into the sofa, sending shards of stone, chunks of wood, and cushion fluff everywhere. He gave a silent prayer of thanks that the base of the couch was so rugged. If it hadn't been for that, he'd have been dead. He'd always known Powell was a complete piece of shit, but fighting alongside Zolnerov's men against his fellow DCO agent was sinking to a whole new level of crap.

Jayson looked over his shoulder to make sure Layla and the girls had taken cover only to find her and Anya crouching behind the arches in the corridor trying to take out Powell and the men with him. Shit, they were only going to get themselves killed.

"Take the girls and go!" he shouted at Layla. "Get them outside and over the wall."

Layla shook her head, clearly hating the idea even as she had to jerk back when the stone edging near her face shattered into pieces from a bullet.

"Go!" he shouted again. "You two can't hold that position and you're just going to get yourselves and everyone else killed. I'll be right behind you, I promise."

Layla shouted at Anya to go, then gave him a hard look. "Don't you dare do anything stupid!"

Getting to her feet, she spun to follow the girls, herding them down the curving hallway.

Boots echoed hard and fast on the marble floor in front of the couch. Jayson jerked into a crouch and peeked over the top. One of the militia soldiers charged straight at him. The asshole must have thought Jayson would be so focused on Layla and the girls that he wouldn't notice anyone coming his way. But he had noticed, and he didn't hesitate to lay his AK across the back of the sofa and fire off a quick three-round burst. The man crumpled to the floor, his momentum taking him across the marble and slamming him into the base of the couch.

Jayson had barely ducked again when the sofa around him exploded in fluff and pieces of stone. Shards of marble peppered his left shoulder, making it feel like he'd been hit with a shotgun blast.

Shit. The man charging at him had been nothing more than bait to get him to poke his head out like a frigging turtle sticking its head out of its shell. No doubt Powell had ordered the charge. Jayson wondered if the militia soldier had known Powell was casually throwing his life away.

"Hey, Jayson." Powell's amused voice carried across the room as soon as the shooting stopped. "Pop your head up again. I promise I'll make it fast."

Jayson dropped the half-empty magazine out of his AK and loaded a fresh one. Then he yanked a handful of loose rounds from his pocket, dropped them on the floor, and shoved them in the magazine he'd just extracted. He wasn't stupid. Powell wasn't talking to him because he missed him. He was babbling to cover up the movement of the other two soldiers who were almost certainly moving around the room right then to get a bead on Jayson. He needed to be ready when they made their move.

"Is that how it's going to be then?" Powell asked with a chuckle that made Jayson want to kick him in the balls. "What, are you mad at me just because I tried to shoot you on that rooftop? It was nothing personal. I was just following orders. I'd expect a former soldier like yourself to understand that."

Jayson heard careful footsteps off to his right. One of the soldiers was moving toward the fireplace, trying to outflank him.

"You are so full of shit, Powell," he called. "You didn't try to kill me because of any DCO directive. You

did it because you're a piece of shit who gets off on killing. You figured you were about to die and you wanted
to make sure I went first."

Powell laughed again, the sound closer and slightly
off to the left. The jackass was getting ready to make his
move. Good. Jayson wanted to finish him and get out of
there. He didn't like the idea of Layla being out there
by herself. Anya had shown herself capable of firing a
weapon, but that wasn't the same thing as having actual
backup. That was Jayson's job.

"You might be right," Powell agreed. "I have to
admit, I never did like working with you shifter freaks. I
doubt you ever heard of him, but Jeff Peters was a good
friend of mine, and that psycho bitch Ivy Halliwell got
him fired from the DCO, then killed him. I've been
looking for a chance to off a shifter ever since. Even
if you're not much of one, you were the only shifter I
had available at the time, so I figured you were better
than nothing."

Jayson heard the guy by the fireplace edging a little
closer while Powell moved into position on the left. The
third militia soldier was still holding firm in the western
corridor, probably with his weapon sighted on the couch
in case Jayson popped his head up suddenly. Within seconds, Powell was going to have everyone in position and
this little show was going to get started.

"I figured it was something like that," Jayson said. He
didn't really care about the conversation, but he wanted
to keep Powell talking. "I'm just shocked you made it
off that roof in one piece. I thought the militia would
have killed you for sure."

Jayson wiggled across the floor to the right. When

everybody started shooting, he didn't want to be in the same place he'd been the last time they'd seen him.

"I almost didn't," Powell answered. "The militia could have killed me, but one of them recognized me as American and figured their colonel would want to see me. Zolnerov was about to execute me when I mentioned there was another American here with a diplomat's son from the U.S. embassy in Kiev. That got his attention damn quick. Then I told him about shifters and that really floated his boat. The idea of getting a feline shifter of his very own had him salivating. Telling him I could deliver the two of you on a silver platter made me his favorite person in the world."

Jayson's head was spinning. Powell had told Zolnerov about shifters—about Layla. And unless Powell was full of shit, this entire rescue mission was a setup for Zolnerov to grab a shifter of his very own—a very special female shifter.

Anger welled up in his chest. It was bad enough that Powell had tried to kill him, but now he'd betrayed Layla, too, setting her up so a sadistic piece of shit like Zolnerov could grab her. Jayson decided that shooting Powell was too good for the man. He would snap his frigging neck with his bare hands.

Jayson slipped his finger in the trigger guard of his AK, twisting around to head for Powell to kill him first. Then he heard the crunch of boots on marble fragments from behind him. *Shit.* Powell had been fucking with him all along, using his feelings for Layla to get him to do something stupid. And it had worked. Jayson had turned his back on the closest threat and was about to pay the ultimate price for it.

Layla herded the girls down the central corridor in the same direction they had just come from. "Find the first exit out of the building. It should be up on the right somewhere."

Leaving Jayson behind to face Powell on his own had been the hardest thing she'd ever had to do, but he'd been right. If she and Anya had stayed where they were, it would have only been a matter of time before one or both of them had been hit, and she had to get Anya and the other girls out of here. Once they were over the wall and safe, she would text Mikhail and let him know what was going on. Then she'd be able to get back in there and help Jayson.

She just prayed he'd be able to hold on that long against what seemed like overwhelming odds.

Up ahead, Anya quickly found an exit along the east wing corridor and urged all the girls outside. Layla caught up with them and hurried the group toward the pool area. They'd just gotten there when the concrete in front of them was chewed up with the impact of bullets. The girls screamed and scattered toward the only cover available—the raised flower beds positioned around the near side of the pool.

Layla cursed as she crouched beside Anya. Zolnerov and a handful of his soldiers were heading their way at a fast pace. The men had gotten between them and the south wall like they'd known Layla would be bringing the girls that way.

Zolnerov wasn't trying to kill them, though. He and his men repeatedly put round after round into the concrete in front of them, driving her and the girls closer to the pool. Layla's heart sank as she realized that he intended to recapture them. Of course he did. He needed the girls to pay off Kojot. With only two weapons, a limited supply of ammo, and nowhere to escape to, Layla had no doubt the colonel could do it. Even as she watched, some of the girls were forced into the pool as Zolnerov's men circled around her side of the pool and closed in. It wouldn't be long before the stone flower bed didn't provide any cover at all. When that happened, Layla would be forced to surrender.

That didn't mean she and Anya were going to give up. Maybe the men out there were hesitant to shoot at the girls for fear of injuring their valuable merchandise, but the reverse certainly didn't apply. Layla took aim with her 9mm and emptied her clip into the handful of soldiers coming at them. Beside her, Anya did the same with her assault rifle. The girl might not be able to shoot very well, but she could sure as hell make the soldiers duck and back up.

Even though Layla hit at least two of Zolnerov's men, there were too many left to simply run from. Layla loaded her last clip into her pistol and turned to Anya. The Ukrainian girl shook her head. She was almost out of ammo, too.

Layla glanced back at the girls. She couldn't let Zolnerov get his hands on them again. She had to give them time to get away.

"Anya!" she shouted. "I'm going to distract them. Get the other girls to the wall."

The Russian girl looked at her like she was insane. Maybe she was. But she couldn't think of anything else to do except charge at the colonel and his men, focusing their attention on her and praying her speed would make her difficult to hit. It was probably a suicidal plan, but it was the best she could come up with.

Layla was just about to dash forward when a hail of gunfire came from behind her. She was sure it was Jayson, Danica, and Clayne coming to their rescue, but when she turned, she saw Dylan, Olek, and Mikhail running toward them while laying down a steady barrage of bullets from the three Makarovs they'd just learned to shoot.

Layla couldn't believe what she was seeing, but she wasn't going to waste their amazing display of courage. She stepped out into the open and popped shots off at Zolnerov and his soldiers. Anya did the same, and suddenly, the tide began to turn. She had no idea if any of Zolnerov's men were actually hit by all the bullets flying through the air, but it sure as hell freaked them out. Within seconds, the majority of them turned and ran.

Without being told, the girls abandoned the protection of the pool and the flower beds and ran back toward the main house.

"Go after them!" Layla shouted at Dylan and the other boys, gesturing to the girls. "Get them moving toward the east side. Find Clayne and Danica if you can. Just get them out of here."

Dylan nodded, motioning Anya and the other girls toward him before turning to lead them to safety. Dylan wasn't the only one taking charge. Olek and Mikhail were helping girls out of the pool and urging them in the right direction.

The move must have pissed off Zolnerov because he began shooting straight at the girls, and this time, he was aiming to kill.

One dark-haired girl, who'd been late getting out of the pool because she'd been helping the others, got caught up in a hail of bullets and froze where she was. Layla turned to race toward her, but Mikhail was already sprinting across the open area. Suddenly, the Russian teen's leg twisted as bullets tore through his right thigh. Mikhail ignored the injury and lunged at the frightened girl. They both went down as another torrent of rounds annihilated the ground where she'd been standing.

A moment later, Mikhail was sitting up and aiming his Makarov at the nearest soldier, calmly putting a bullet through the man.

By the time Layla got to the two teens, the girl was trying to get Mikhail up on his feet so they could head for cover.

Layla grabbed the big Russian kid by one shoulder and dragged him to his feet, helping him over to the nearest flower bed. She didn't want to get trapped there again, but it wasn't like she had a lot of choices. There was no way she was going to get Mikhail out of there, not while they were getting shot at.

The dark-haired girl slipped herself under Mikhail's other shoulder and helped Ivy hurriedly move him toward the cover of the stonework, talking to Mikhail in Russian the whole time. Through clenched teeth, Mikhail said something back to the girl in their language, but she ignored him. Knowing Mikhail, it was likely something about wanting the girl to save herself and leave him. What a typical male.

Between the two of them, they got Mikhail to safety. Turning, Layla started shooting at Zolnerov and the two men with him again. Despite being injured and in obvious pain, Mikhail fired in their general direction, too. Another militia soldier went down just as the upper slide of her weapon locked back to the rear. Crap. She was out of ammo. She opened her mouth to tell Mikhail to conserve his, but it was too late for that. He was out, too.

Stomach clenching, Layla turned to regard Zolnerov and the last remaining soldier who now stood with him. The Russian colonel was standing fifteen feet away, a large pistol held casually in his hand as he stared back at Layla. In person, he was even more menacing. He and the soldier had moved around the pool area until they had a clear shot at her, Mikhail, and the dark-haired girl who was currently trying to keep the Russian teen from getting up. As crazy as it sounded, the fact that Zolnerov wasn't shooting them worried her. What was he up to? Whatever it was, she didn't think she was going to like it.

"You are not the beast I expected when your American friend told me about you," Zolnerov said.

Layla flinched. He knew she was a shifter.

"I will very much enjoy putting you in a cage and showing you off," he added, a sinister smile crossing his face. "Your friend said I would likely need to torture you to get the monster inside you to come out, but after what you have done tonight, you have made me very angry, so I think torturing you will be extremely easy."

She bit back a growl, furious that Powell had betrayed her and Jayson so completely. There was nothing she could do about it now, though. She and Mikhail might be out of ammo, but she still had to figure out how to get them out of this situation. Not only because of what Zolnerov had in store for her, but also because of what he would almost certainly do to Mikhail and the dark-haired girl.

"You two are about to see some things that you won't understand," she said to Mikhail and the girl in a soft whisper. "When I distract them, run. It will be your only chance."

Mikhail and the girl both shook their heads frantically, but she ignored them as she moved to the side, putting as much distance between her and the teens as she could. Every little bit would give them more time to get away.

Layla set down her empty pistol. If she was going to get out of this, she'd need to use her God-given weapons now. She'd done some hand-to-hand combat training with Landon and Ivy, but it had been mostly defensive stuff, like how to break out of a choke hold or separate from an attacker. Using her claws and fangs in a fight wasn't something Ivy had taught her yet, probably thinking that the idea of tearing into another person wasn't something Layla was ready for.

Ivy was right. Layla had never imagined having to do something like that to another person, but at the moment, she was out of options. She had to protect herself, give Mikhail and the girl a chance to escape, and most importantly, get back to Jayson.

Zolnerov and the soldier immediately moved toward her. Layla's body shifted instinctively, her claws and fangs extending. The night exploded with dozens of sensations as her inner feline came out.

Layla heard Mikhail and the girl gasp. The soldier with Zolnerov, on the other hand, looked terrified. She couldn't blame him. She must have made one hell of a sight standing there with her eyes aglow like a cat.

The soldier mumbled something in Russian, then turned and ran in the other direction.

Zolnerov lifted his weapon and shot the man in the back as casually as another person might turn off a light. The soldier fell to the ground, then lay there moaning for a few seconds before finally going still.

The colonel smiled at Layla. While he didn't have fangs, there was still plenty of menace there. "It's better this way, don't you think? Just the two of us?"

He lifted his weapon again, this time aiming it directly at her.

"Your American friend said your kind can survive a lot of damage and heal quickly. I hope he did not lie to me. I would hate to permanently mar such a pretty trophy."

Chapter 15

IF JAYSON DIDN'T MOVE ASAP, HE WAS DEAD—EITHER at the hands of the guy over by the fireplace or Powell. Unfortunately, he didn't have many options. Taking a deep breath, he jumped up and vaulted over the couch, doubting either man would expect that. He was right. The hail of bullets that were meant to kill him missed completely.

He hit the marble floor on the other side of the couch in a roll, the twinge of pain in his back a welcome reminder that he wasn't dead yet. He came up in a crouch, then drilled a long burst of 5.54mm ball rounds through the soldier standing in the western corridor. A clatter of gunfire from his right, along with an explosion of marble fragments, told him that the guy who'd been sneaking up from that side was still there and quickly correcting his aim.

Jayson rolled over the other way and emptied the entire contents of his magazine at the man, sending him backward into the glass enclosure of the fireplace. He didn't have time to verify if the man was completely out of the fight, though. No doubt Powell was lining up for the kill shot at that very moment.

Jayson dropped his empty assault rifle and rolled to the left, toward Powell, flinching as bullets sliced through the air mere inches above him. By moving closer to Powell, he'd temporarily screwed up the man's aim and kept the son of a bitch from getting a clean shot. But that trick wouldn't save him for long. Powell was probably already moving to put himself in a better position to put an ass load of bullets in him.

Jayson reached behind his back and pulled his 9mm, putting three rounds over the top of the couch in the general area he'd last seen Powell. If nothing else, he had a good chance of making the asshole duck at the very least. Then, before he had time to wonder whether it was a good idea or not, he climbed to his feet and leaped back over the same sectional. He could have tried to play hide-and-seek behind the couch, but with ten feet between them, at some point, even a shitty shot like Powell would get off a lucky pop. Jayson would rather take chance out of the equation and get in close to the other man to see if he had the stomach to stand and fight toe-to-toe. Jayson was willing to bet he didn't.

Powell was just coming up out of his defensive crouch when Jayson slammed into him, taking them both to the floor. In this kind of fight, the pistol Jayson had was better than the submachine gun Powell carried, and he was forced to drop his weapon and focus all his attention on keeping the barrel of Jayson's gun away from his body.

They struggled there in the middle of the floor, trading punches, head butts, and elbow strikes, both of them grunting and swearing as they tried to kill each other. Even with a weapon in his hand, Jayson couldn't gain the advantage, but fortunately, neither could Powell.

"Must be nice having your girlfriend out on a mission with you," Powell sneered. "Getting to bang her whenever you want. So, is Layla a hot lay or what?"

Jayson knew the other man was just talking shit to distract him. That didn't keep it from working. Cursing, Jayson tried to go for a punch to the throat. The next thing he knew, Powell caught his right arm in an arm bar and got a grip on the pistol at the same time.

"I guess that means she's not, since you're getting all sensitive and shit," Powell mocked. "You ever think that maybe it's because you're a cripple? I bet she'd warm up a little more with a real man. What do you think about me banging your kitty?"

Jayson drove his knee into Powell's gut, but only because he couldn't reach his balls. It didn't do much good. Finally, he had to give up his hold on the pistol or let Powell break his wrist. The weapon fell between them and Powell immediately lunged for it.

That was the mistake Jayson had been waiting for. He ignored the weapon and jumped on top of Powell just as the man rolled over, straddling his stomach and getting one hand locked in the man's hair, jerking his head back. Powell struggled, flailing his fists in an effort to hit him, but Jayson was too close for him to land any real punches. Gaze locked with Powell's, Jayson slipped his free hand down and got it under the man's chin.

Powell's eyes widened in fear. He brought one of his knees up sharply, trying to ram it into Jayson's back. The position was all wrong, and Powell couldn't get a clean shot at him. But even getting a knee slammed into his hip was enough to send immediate and intense pain flooding through him. A wave of darkness threatened to envelope him. But Jayson had become so familiar with pain and the shadow of unconsciousness that followed it like an old friend that he was able to fight it down, push it back, and hold it at bay like he had for most of the past year.

He leaned forward until his mouth was only an inch from Powell's ear. "Fuck you," he whispered, then yanked with one hand and shoved with the other, snapping the other man's neck.

The wave of darkness he'd been holding off started to crest over his head then, and he realized he probably wasn't going to be able to breathe through the pain this time. Powell had damaged something with those jabs to the back. The ache was continuing to grow, not ebb as it usually did.

A single shot sounded from just outside the french doors a few feet away from him. There had been plenty of shooting going on out there but this single shot was more resounding, more menacing than all the previous automatic weapons fire combined.

Layla.

Jayson grunted, shoving the pain and darkness away. Grabbing the pistol he'd dropped earlier, he ran out the doors toward the pool area just as a second shot echoed in the night, followed by a third. He was halfway there when he caught sight of a scene that froze his heart in his chest and knocked the air from his lungs.

Layla was locked in a hand-to-hand struggle with Zolnerov, much like he'd been with Powell, except the Russian colonel was the one holding a weapon, and Layla was the one fighting to keep the barrel from pointing her way.

She was fast, way faster than Jayson could ever hope to be. She drove a straight punch into the man's chest, knocking him back a step or two but at the same time giving him the space he needed to get his weapon up and pointed at her.

Shit. Zolnerov was going to take the shot.

Jayson lifted his weapon and aimed for the man trying to kill the love of his life, but even as he started to pull the trigger, he knew Layla was too close to the target. One wrong move on her part and his bullet would go through her instead of Zolnerov.

"Get down!" he shouted, praying Layla would hear him.

But Layla didn't take cover like he hoped. Instead, she launched herself through the air as the Russian fired multiple rounds at her. She was so close that there was absolutely no way Zolnerov could miss her, but then she twisted in the air like the big cat she shared her DNA with and, however impossible it seemed, she didn't get hit.

Jayson's heart was in his throat as she landed in front of Zolnerov and dropped into a crouch. She lashed out with her hand at the same time Jayson pulled the trigger of his 9mm, her claws slashing Zolnerov across the inner thigh even as the bullet pierced his chest. The Russian stared in shock, his weapon slipping from his nerveless fingers.

Jayson was sprinting toward Layla before Zolnerov hit the ground. Although his back hurt like a son of a bitch, he covered the distance between them faster than he ever thought he could.. Then Layla was in his arms, and he was kissing her even while trying to check her for injuries at the same time. He still couldn't believe Zolnerov hadn't hit her, but he was grateful as hell. She was just as interested in checking him out too, fussing over all the cuts and scrapes he'd gotten in the fight with Powell. As a result, the kiss ended up being something a little less than romantic, but Jayson wouldn't have traded it for the world.

"You really think it's the best time to be doing that?" a gruff voice said from behind them.

Jayson reluctantly broke the kiss to see Clayne standing there with an impatient look on his face. The wolf shifter's shirt was shredded to ribbons, and his chest, abs, arms, and shoulders were scratched up all to hell. It looked like he'd wrestled with a cheese grater.

"Damn, Clayne, I hope the other guy looks worse," he muttered.

Clayne chuckled. "Oh, hell yeah. When Kojot and I ran out of ammo, he thought he could take me down hand to hand. Last mistake that stupid fucker ever made."

Layla just shook her head, then hurried over to check on Mikhail. The dark-haired girl with him was already tearing strips off the bottom of Mikhail's T-shirt so she could bind his wounds. Both kids regarded Layla with eyes as round as saucers. Jayson couldn't blame them. He'd been like that the first time he'd seen Layla shift in front of him, too. And Layla hadn't just shifted—she'd gone completely ThunderCat in front of them. Jayson only hoped they could trust Mikhail and the girl to keep what they'd seen to themselves.

He turned back to Clayne to find him standing there grinning. If he didn't know better, he'd think the wolf shifter had arranged events so the fight with Kojot would come down to hand-to-hand combat. He couldn't imagine Danica had been too thrilled with that.

Jayson frowned. Where *was* Danica? He liked to

think Clayne wouldn't be standing there with a satisfied smile on his face if his fiancée was in danger, but maybe he should check anyway.

"Is Danica okay?" he asked Clayne.

The wolf shifter nodded. "She's fine. We intercepted Dylan and the rest of the kids as we were finishing up with Kojot. She got them off the estate while I came to help you and Layla. Not that you needed it." Clayne frowned as he looked at Mikhail. "Except for him. How the hell did he end up shot?"

Jayson was about to say he didn't have a clue, but the wolf shifter cut him off.

"You can fill me in later." He glanced at his watch. "We need to get the hell out of here."

"What's the rush?" Jayson asked. The shooting had all stopped, so that meant everything was over. "If any of Zolnerov's men survived, they're long gone."

"I'm not worried about Zolnerov's men." Clayne walked over to Mikhail and bent to pick him up. The Russian teen tried to act like he didn't need the help, but the wolf shifter ignored him and headed toward the french doors, giving Jayson, Layla, and the young Russian girl no choice but to follow. "It's the explosives I'm more concerned with. I rigged Zolnerov's entire munitions storage area to blow."

"What about the chemical weapons that Kojot brought?" Layla asked. "Won't explosives spread the chemical agent all over the place?"

"That's not going to be a problem," Clayne said. "Zolnerov looked like he was preparing for a really long war. Those buildings out there on the east side of the estate are all stuffed to the gills with high-explosive artillery shells, long-range rockets, hand grenades, and bulk explosives. The crates of chemical rockets Kojot was trying to sell him are sitting right in the middle of all that stuff. When those buildings go up, there won't be anything left but a big, smoking crater. The chemicals will be incinerated in the fireball, along with most of this estate."

"How much time do we have?" Jayson asked.

Clayne shifted Mikhail a little in his arms and looked at his watch again. "Five minutes. That's plenty of time."

Five minutes didn't seem like a lot of time to Jayson. Layla and the Russian girl must have agreed because they picked up their pace as they moved through Zolnerov's former mansion.

Clayne stopped when he saw Powell lying on the floor. "I thought you said Powell was dead already. What's he doing here?"

Jayson really didn't feel like talking about it now, but it was obvious Clayne wasn't going anywhere until he heard the story, even with the clock ticking on a building full of explosives. "He survived and sold us out to Zolnerov for a chance to get another shot at killing me."

"Huh," Clayne said.

They found Danica and the kids waiting for them outside the demolished main gate, along with a handful of pickup trucks and Range Rovers parked out on the street with armed men standing all around. That explained where all the gunfire he'd heard earlier had come from. Some of the vehicles had been shot up pretty good and so had some of their occupants, but none of the guys looked like they were seriously wounded. Standing at the head of their group was Victor Garin.

At the sight of them, the old cop ran forward and pulled the dark-haired girl beside Layla into his arms. It wasn't until Victor said her name that Jayson finally recognized her. She was Victor's granddaughter, Larissa. When he pulled away, there were tears in his eyes.

"Thank you," he said to Jayson.

Jayson gave him a nod. "We need to get out of here. Zolnerov's ammo stores have been rigged to blow and we don't have a lot of time to get outside the frag distance."

Victor nodded and started shouting orders in Russian. The men he'd brought with him immediately began getting everyone loaded into the vehicles. Victor started to lead his granddaughter to the truck he was obviously leaving in, but Larissa refused to leave Mikhail's side. Instead, she helped get the injured teen into the back of the pickup truck first, then climbed in with him.

When Victor gave him and Layla a questioning look, all Jayson could do was shrug. Larissa had obviously developed a strong bond with Mikhail. Having someone risk his life for you could do that.

He and Layla climbed in the back of the truck with the two teens. Moments later, they squealed away along with everyone else. They hadn't gone more than half a mile when the entire estate went up in a huge fireball that sent a shock wave through the ground that shook the vehicle. Clayne hadn't been lying when he'd said the explosion would incinerate anything and everything in the blast zone, chemical or otherwise.

Jayson leaned against the cab of the truck, easing the pressure on his aching back and pulling Layla close. She buried her face against his chest and hugged the hell out of him. He knew exactly how she felt. Rescuing those girls had almost killed both of them, but they'd done it. They still had to get Dylan, Olek, and Anya back across the border into Ukrainian-held territory, not to mention get Mikhail medical attention, but after everything else they'd been through, dealing with that didn't seem all that difficult. It was only after they got back to the States that things would get complicated.

He wasn't going to think about that. Right then, he was simply going to hold on to Layla and enjoy being with the woman he loved while doing the job he loved.

—∿∿—

"You ready to do this?" Landon asked Ivy as he pulled the SUV up in front of Thorn's mansion.

It was late at night—or early in the morning, depending on your definition of that kind of thing—but she had no doubt Thorn would still be awake since they'd called him about an hour ago and said they'd be dropping by with his stolen property.

Frasier opened the door before they could ring the bell. Thorn was waiting in the foyer, a frown on his face. He barely glanced at the diamond when she handed it over. Mostly because he was too busy glaring at them.

"Why the hell didn't you call when you figured out who stole it?" he demanded. "I thought I was quite clear that I wanted Frasier to handle the actual recovery?"

"You were," Landon said. "But to be truthful, we didn't know for sure the guy we were going to see tonight was the thief."

"We knew we were never going to find out who stole your diamond working with Hayes, and since the bodies of known thieves kept turning up, we did our own digging," Ivy added, elaborating on the story that she, Landon, and John had come up with. "We looked for other people who had the requisite skills but who'd been excluded from the detective's suspect pool for some reason."

"We came up with a couple people and went to talk to one of them—Daniel Abbott—down at his warehousing business near the Navy Yard tonight," Landon said. "Twenty years ago, Abbott was picked up and questioned in connection with nearly a dozen jewelry heists, but nothing ever stuck to him, even though the detective on the case back then was sure he was the guy."

"Wait a minute," Thorn said, holding up his hand. "Are you trying to tell me that it was some washed-up thief who broke into my home and stole my property? What, did he just decide to come out of retirement because his mutual funds had taken a beating in the market?"

When he put it that way, it did sound a little crazy. Ivy prayed that Kendra and Evan had done a flawless job on Abbott's fake background because she had no doubt Thorn was going to dig into the poor guy's former life with a microscope. In reality, Daniel Abbott was a marine salvage dealer who'd been unfortunate enough to pass away the previous night from a heart attack in his shop down near Washington Navy Yard. Other than the fact that the man had absolutely no family and very few friends, there was nothing remarkable about him. Which is why Kendra had selected him as their thief.

Ivy hated the idea of messing with a dead man's life by giving him a police record, making it look like he'd been involved with a string of unsolved burglaries in DC nearly twenty years ago, and creating a fake history that was going to live on forever. But it was either destroy one man's past or accept that Dreya Clark probably wouldn't have a future. It simply had to be done.

"We knew it was a long shot, which is why we didn't bother to call you or Frasier," Ivy admitted. "It wasn't until we got to the warehouse that we figured out Abbott was the guy. We caught him right in the middle of getting ready to leave the country with your diamond."

"Where the hell is he?" Frasier growled. "You better not have turned him over to the cops before Mr. Thorn gets to speak to him."

"It never got that far," Landon said. "We found out the hard way that Abbott had been planning to blow up the warehouse so it would look like he was dead. After we cornered the man, he tried to use the bomb he'd rigged to get away from us and ended up collapsing half the building on his own head."

Thorn's eyes widened. "Are you talking about the building that burned to the ground down by the Anacostia River earlier?"

Ivy nodded.

"How'd you get the diamond back?" Thorn asked.

"That was all Ivy," Landon said. "She ran into the building while it was still falling down and got Abbott's backpack before the fire took it. If it weren't for her, you never would have gotten your diamond back."

Thorn regarded her thoughtfully, as if wondering whether this was all too good to be true.

"We barely got out before the cops and firefighters showed up," Ivy added, trying to make it seem as if running into a burning building to retrieve a diamond had been no big deal.

"Did you find anything else in the backpack?" Thorn asked.

Ivy just knew Thorn was going to ask that. She made a show of looking at Landon with the proper amount of confusion. "You mean besides the diamond?"

"Yes. Besides the diamond."

Standing next to Thorn, Frasier eyed them suspiciously.

"The pack was mostly full of clothes," Landon said. "There was a black lockbox of some kind too, but it was badly damaged in the explosion. We pried it open some and found what looked like silver rocks in it. Ivy and I figured they were uncut stones of some kind from another job the guy had done. We thought we'd take them back to the DCO so they could figure out what kind of gems they are and who they belong to."

"The box belongs to me," Thorn said sharply. "Where is it?"

Landon frowned. "You never mentioned any other stones. If you had, it might have helped us find Abbott earlier."

Thorn's mouth tightened. "I was mostly concerned with the diamond and wanted you focused on that. Now, if you have the rest of my property, I'd like to have it back."

Landon exchanged looks with Ivy. "It's outside in the SUV. I'll go get it."

Thorn nodded to Frasier, indicating he should go, too.

While Landon went outside with Frasier, Ivy chatted with Thorn about Abbott and how they had tracked down the man. She kept all her answers vague, knowing that Thorn would verify every word she said later.

Landon came back a few moments later, Frasier in

tow. "I wish you'd mentioned the thief had taken something else besides the diamond. We might have been able to get this thing back undamaged if we had known about it."

Frasier walked over to Thorn and opened the outside pocket of the pack, showing the contents to his boss. Thorn glanced inside, then looked at her and Landon. Ivy held her breath. This was the moment of truth. If Lisa and Karl had done a poor job with their fake hard drive, Thorn would know it, despite how smashed up it was. Then who knew what the hell he'd do?

"I owe you two a very special thanks," Thorn said. "The fact that you recovered my property is of far more importance to me than the damage to it. I have a certain reputation to uphold, and by getting these articles back, that reputation is still well intact, even if the man who took them is dead."

She and Landon stayed for a few more minutes before Frasier showed them out. Landon didn't say anything until they'd climbed in the SUV and he'd started the engine. "I think that actually worked."

Ivy didn't answer. She was too busy looking in the side mirror at Thorn and Frasier standing on the front porch watching them drive away. Something about the look on Thorn's face suddenly had her feeling like a cat in a room full of rocking chairs.

"I guess we'll find out soon enough," she said.

Chapter 16

LAYLA FELT LIKE A ZOMBIE AS SHE AND JAYSON WALKED into the main DCO building. They'd been going non-stop for nearly thirty-six hours, since leaving Zolnerov's estate, and she was exhausted. She only prayed they wouldn't have to go through a full mission debriefing because she'd probably fall asleep in the middle of it. All she wanted to do was check in with Kendra, deal with the minimal amount of paperwork necessary, then fall into bed and sleep for twelve hours straight with Jayson at her side.

If they didn't run into John, of course. Their boss likely knew exactly what she'd done by now and he was going to be pissed. She should probably go see him and do some damage control before he came looking for her, but trying to talk to him when she was this tired was plain stupid. She'd end up doing more harm than good.

She glanced over at Jayson. He looked even more exhausted than she did. That wasn't surprising. He'd been busting his butt for the last few days, and after getting into a close-quarters struggle with Powell, then taking care of all the loose ends over in Ukraine, it was all finally catching up to him.

After getting away from Zolnerov's place, she and Jayson had slipped back into Donetsk to bring all the girls back to their respective families as well as to get Mikhail some much needed medical attention. No one wanted to take him to a hospital since that would have led to too many questions, but the two bullet wounds weren't anything that could be handled with a few bandages and some hydrogen peroxide. The reality was, the kid had needed surgery.

Amazingly, Victor had managed to find someone willing to operate on Mikhail right in the middle of his quaint, little living room. Larissa had planted herself firmly at Mikhail's side during the surgery and refused to move. Neither of her grandparents had been pleased with that, but it had quickly become obvious that no one told the young woman what to do. And when the doctor stated that Mikhail would need to stay flat on his back for at least two weeks, Larissa had announced the recovering teen would be staying on Victor's living room couch the entire time, and that she would be the one watching over him. Victor hadn't even tried to change her mind. Layla was glad. Mikhail was a good kid.

By the time she and Jayson had finally gotten out of the Russian-held territory with Dylan, Anya, and Olek, it had been midnight the next day. Getting the diplomat's son and his Ukrainian friends back to their families after that had been simple.

She and Jayson just reached Kendra's office when the woman came running out and almost mowed them over.

"Whoa!" Jayson said, catching Kendra before she lost her balance. "Where are you off to so fast?"

"The lab," Kendra said, quickly getting her feet back under her and hurrying down the hallway, leaving them both staring after her.

Layla exchanged looks with Jayson before they followed.

"What's wrong?" Layla asked when they caught up to her.

Kendra didn't answer as she pushed open the double doors and started down the sidewalk.

"Did someone get hurt?" Jayson asked.

Kendra shook her head. "No one got hurt, not yet anyway. Zarina just called to tell me that Dick found another test subject for his hybrid serum. The same doctors who injected Jayson are there right now."

Oh no.

"Who is it?" Jayson demanded. "Did Zarina give them the same antidote she gave me?"

Kendra did a double take, clearly surprised Jayson knew about the antidote. "It's Moore. And no, Zarina didn't give him the antidote. She hasn't even been able to make any more yet. It took months to make the batch she gave you. Plus, Dick's doctors tossed her out of the lab the moment they showed up. She didn't even have a chance to warn Moore about what he was getting into."

Layla frowned. Why the hell would Moore want to take the hybrid serum? He hated shifters and hybrids alike.

When they got to the medical building, Zarina was standing outside in the hallway, one of the DCO security guards keeping her out of the out of the lab. Layla didn't recognize the guy, but whoever he was, he definitely didn't look happy about what was going on inside.

"We have to get in there," Jayson told the man. "Moore is going to die if we don't."

A muscle worked in the guy's jaw, but he shook his head. "I can't let you in. The deputy director said that no one goes in there."

Jayson's eyes narrowed, and Layla knew he was half

a second away from physically moving the guy from
his post when a gut-wrenching cry of agony came from
inside the lab. It climbed higher in pitch before becoming a savage, pain-filled growl.

Cursing, Jayson grabbed the security guard by the
front of his uniform and tossed him aside, then rushed
into the lab. The guard followed them in, no doubt so he
could throw them out, but the sight that met their eyes
stopped all of them in their tracks.

Three doctors were restraining a struggling Moore
while Dick slowly backed away from the table. His eyes
widened as Moore bucked and thrashed like he was
being electrocuted. Moore's eyes were glowing dark red
and blood was running out of his mouth from the gashes
he'd inflicted on himself with his fangs. Stunted and mis-
shapen claws reached out to tear savagely at the doctors.
They weren't going to be able to control him for long.

Layla was right. A moment later, Moore punched one
of the men in the chest, knocking him halfway across the
room. Jayson and the security guard raced over to help
the remaining two doctors restrain Moore while Zarina
hurried over to do what she could to save Moore's life.

Even though Layla was no doctor, she knew it was
too late. Before the end, the poor man was shaking so
hard that it was all Jayson and the guard could do just to
keep Moore from falling off the exam table. He yowled,
in such horrible pain that Layla simply couldn't watch
anymore. It reminded her too much of what could have
happened to Jayson.

Knowing there was nothing she could do to help and
refusing to just stand there and watch the man die, Layla
spun around and hurried out of the room.

She was leaning against the wall outside the lab when Dick came out a few minutes later. His face was pale and his hands were shaking.

"I hadn't realized that Jayson was back," the deputy director said. "Or that you'd been with him. I can't say I'm surprised. I knew there was nothing that could keep you two apart for very long."

While Layla seriously wasn't ready for this conversation, she couldn't imagine having a better opening to talk to Dick about whether he was going to get in the way of her and Jayson being partners.

"No, there isn't anything that can keep us apart—not as a couple anyway," she said. "But you can certainly get in the way of our partnership. I suppose the question is, are you going to?"

Dick considered that. "I mentioned the possibility of you and Jayson being partners when I talked to him, but I didn't really give it much thought after that."

"Perhaps it's time you do."

He regarded her thoughtfully. "There are several factors that could make your partnership difficult, not the least of which is the fact that Jayson and Powell are technically a team right now."

"That isn't an issue," she said.

The deputy director opened his mouth, no doubt to ask what she meant by that, but Layla cut him off, saying "We don't have long to discuss this, so I'm going to get to the point. Jayson needs to stay in the field, and I need to be his partner. If you make that happen, I'm prepared to consider it a favor that I'd be obligated to return."

Dick's eyes turned almost predatory at the mention of her owing him something. Layla's stomach began to flutter like she just swallowed a bucket of butterflies. He probably would have said something to make her regret her decision, but Jayson came out of the lab, interrupting them. He glared at Dick like he wanted to kill the man.

Jayson might not have had any noticeable shifter or hybrid skills, but he moved damn fast regardless. One second, he was ten feet away; the next, he was slamming the deputy director against the wall and lifting him off his feet by the lapels of his suit jacket.

"You killed Moore," Jayson ground out. "You might as well have filled that syringe with cyanide and killed him on purpose."

Dick turned pale. "That was never my intent, I swear to you. After the success of the serum we gave you, the doctors were sure we were on the right path. All they did was increase the potency of the serum a small amount to improve overall performance."

Layla placed a hand on Jayson's shoulder before he did something he regretted. Jaw tense, he slowly let the man slide down the wall until his feet were on the floor. He didn't let him go, though.

"The success of the serum you gave me?" He snorted. "The serum wasn't a success. In fact, it was a complete and total failure."

Layla tensed. If Jayson admitted that Zarina had given him an antidote to counteract the serum, the Russian doctor would be fired within hours, no matter what John did to try to keep her.

"My body rejected the serum," Jayson said scathingly. "But you couldn't even wait to find that out. You just ran out and tested the next man willing to be your guinea pig, didn't you?"

Dick started to open his mouth, but Jayson closed it with his glare. "I'm nothing more now than the man I was before, and anything I accomplished on the mission in Donetsk was due to Layla's help and my own abilities."

Dick's eyes darted to her before going back to Jayson. "Layla was just mentioning that you two make a good team and that the DCO should keep you together."

Jayson glanced at her, clearly hating the idea of her talking to Dick about the subject of their partnership without him. He'd hate it even more if he knew she'd essentially sold her soul for him—again.

"Yes, we are a good team," Jayson agreed. "But we're both ready to walk away from the DCO if you think for a second about splitting us up."

Dick gazed at him for a second but then nodded. "Of course you'll remain a team. That's the promise I made you when all this started."

Jayson eyed the deputy director suspiciously. "You're not going to try to get in the way of that?"

Dick shook his head. "Of course not. Beyond the promise I gave you, there's also the simple matter of the respect I have for you and all that you've overcome. The fact that you were able to successfully complete the mission I sent you and Powell on without any hybrid abilities only convinces me more than ever that you're one of the most amazing men I've ever had the privilege to meet. I'm thrilled for you and Layla, and would never want to get in the way of all that you're sure to accomplish for the DCO and your country."

Layla thought she was going to be sick. This guy was good, she'd give him that. He practically had her believing his crap.

Jayson let the deputy director go and would have turned away, but Dick stopped him with a hand on his shoulder.

"I know you probably won't believe this, but I was hoping only for the best for Moore," Dick said. "For all the outward show of disdain he had for shifters and hybrids, I think the man was simply jealous of the abilities he could never have. When he came to me and asked to take the serum, I couldn't say no. No more than I could when I thought it was what you most needed. I was trying to help him the same way I was trying to help you."

Dick gave Jayson's shoulder a squeeze and headed back to the lab. At the door, he stopped and turned to look at them. "By the way, where's Powell?"

Jayson's eyes were cold. "Powell no longer works for the DCO."

Dick considered that for a moment, his gaze going back and forth between her and Jayson. Finally he nodded and walked into the lab, leaving her and Jayson alone.

"You ready to get out of here?" he asked.

Layla nodded, praying to God she hadn't done something incredibly stupid by making a deal with Dick. But she'd done what she had to do.

"I'm more than ready," she said. "But only after Zarina checks you out and makes sure you're okay."

It took a while for Zarina to come out of the lab and into the hallway, and by that time, John had shown up along with Ivy and Landon. While everyone was glad that she and Jayson had returned safe and sound, what had happened to Moore put a damper on the reunion.

As Layla suspected, John was pissed at her for dis-obeying orders. While he was happy she and Jayson made a good team, he let both of them know that he had no use for two agents who couldn't be trusted to follow his orders. Properly chastised, she and Jayson promised to be the model of trustworthiness from now on.

"Do you want something to eat?" she asked Jayson when they walked into her apartment an hour later.

"As long as it's something simple and fast," Jayson said, coming up behind her to wrap his arms around her and pull her close. "I'm too tired to cook something or even get takeout."

She agreed entirely. All she wanted was to climb into bed with him and sleep for a week—with a few breaks for lovemaking in between of course.

Layla couldn't help but notice the bandage around his forearm as he hugged her. She didn't mention the vials of blood Zarina had taken because she knew he didn't want to talk about the tests the Russian doctor had run. The results of the blood workup that would tell him how much shifter DNA he had in his body after taking the serum were sealed inside a yellow envelope in her purse, but Jayson didn't want to look at those either.

"I already know what I am and what I'm not," he'd said before they left the DCO complex. "I don't need to see a blood test to tell me anything. I'm your partner now. That's all that matters to me."

She grabbed a box of Ritz crackers and a brick of cheddar cheese while Jayson poured two glasses of milk. As they sat at the kitchen island, she realized she was going to have to get a lot more guy food. On the way over, they'd already decided that Jayson would move in here with her. Not only would that mean going to bed with him every night and waking up beside him every morning, but also the money they would save on not paying for two apartments could go toward their first vacation to Hawaii.

Layla was still daydreaming of lying out on beautiful white sand beaches when Jayson wrapped up the block of cheddar.

"You're not hungry anymore?" she asked as he put it back in the fridge.

She couldn't believe he'd be satisfied with a handful of crackers and a couple bites of cheese.

"Oh, I'm hungry." Grinning, he took her hand and urged her to her feet. "But not for food."

Layla smiled as he led the way to her bedroom. She liked the sound of that.

Jayson skipped the overhead light, going for the lamp on her bedside table instead. Good choice. The soft glow provided the perfect mood lighting.

Without a word, he took her into his arms and kissed her gently, his tongue delving into her mouth to caress hers. She moaned against his lips, the desire she felt for him completely washing away her previous exhaustion.

As one, they slowly took off each other's clothes, undoing buttons and belt buckles. Somehow she ended up naked before she'd even gotten Jayson's jeans down. Figuring he needed to catch up, she dropped to her knees in front of him and tugged them down, then did the same with his underwear.

That put her eye level with his erection. Since she was already down there, she might as well help him with that too.

He let out a good imitation of a growl as she closed her mouth over the head of his cock and took him deep. Who said he didn't have any animal DNA in him? He definitely seemed like an animal in the bedroom.

She wrapped her hand around base of his shaft and made a few animalistic sounds of her own as she reveled in the taste of him on her tongue. He was so delicious that she naturally sped up, taking him deeper with each bob of her head. Jayson threaded his fingers in her hair, guiding her movements and making sure she took it nice and slow. That was obviously his way of saying he wanted to make this last. Maybe she should remind him that John had given them the next two days off. No need to rush.

Jayson's hand tightened in her hair then, gently pulling her away so he could tug her to her feet.

"Hey," she protested. "I was busy down there."

Jayson grinned and nudged her backward onto the mattress. "Trust me, I noticed." He scooted her back a little, then climbed between her legs. "That's why I stopped you. This is our first time together in our place. I want it to be memorable."

Layla laughed, appreciating the thought. Of course, if she'd been able to finish what she'd been doing, it would have been memorable as well. That said, she was eager to see what he had in mind.

She found out a moment later when Jayson slid down until his face was even with her pussy. Lowering his head, he closed his mouth over her clit and began to lick with firm, steady swipes of his tongue.

Sighing, Layla buried her fingers in his hair to control his movements just as he'd done, but it didn't matter.

He seemed to know exactly where to focus his efforts to make her go crazy without guidance. She clutched the sheet with her free hand, rolling her hips in time with his tongue as the sensations in her clit got stronger and more intense. Jayson cupped her ass in both hands, got a good grip, and held on tight, refusing to let her go anywhere.

Layla threw her head back and went with it, loving the way he took control. As her orgasm approached, her claws and fangs slipped out of their own accord. It was so beautiful being with a man she could let herself go with. It made everything he was doing feel even better.

She was so caught up in the moment that when her climax hit, she let out a feline yowl. It was a relief not to have hold it in like she had in the library in Donetsk. This time she could be as loud as she wanted and she didn't have to care if anyone heard.

Layla wasn't sure how long her orgasm lasted, but when she opened her eyes, she found Jayson lying with his cheek resting comfortably on the inside of her right thigh, his mouth turned up in a smile, his blue eyes twinkling.

"I'm going to enjoy watching you come like that for the rest of our lives," he said softly.

She smiled. "I'm completely good with that."

He pressed a tender kiss to her thigh. "Any chance you have condoms, or are we thinking of going the unprotected route again?"

The idea of feeling him come inside her again and the possibility of the pregnancy that might come with it wasn't an issue for her, but the reality was that they had things they wanted to do as a couple before starting a family, so that called for birth control.

"Top drawer of the nightstand," she said. "I've been saving them for this moment."

Jayson rummaged around until he found what he was looking for. Layla spread her legs wide, purring when he slid in deep a few moments later.

"You feel so good," she whispered as she brought her arms and legs up and locked them around him.

Jayson placed his arms on either side of her, gazing into her eyes as he slowly began to move in and out. She reached up and pulled his head down, capturing his mouth with hers at the same time she squeezed tighter with her legs, urging him to go harder and faster. He refused, driving into her with those perfect, careful thrusts that seemed designed to drive her insane.

His mouth trailed from her lips, down to her neck, then over to her left shoulder, nibbling and nipping as he went. She let him play, entertaining herself by tracing her claws slowly up and down his triceps, which were bulging and flexing nicely as he kept himself poised above her. She liked the way his body trembled when she did that. It made her hot knowing her touch turned him on like this.

She had to be the luckiest woman in the world. It took her breath away when she thought how close she had come to giving up on Jayson and how close he had come to giving up on himself. That welling of emotion was what drove her to finally yank him down harder into her with her heels. He didn't try to resist this time, but instead thrust deeper and more forcefully at her urging.

After the slow buildup, it didn't take long for either of them to peak. She came hard in a long, drawn-out climax that brought tears to her eyes, and she wrapped her legs tightly around him, never wanting to let him go.

"I love you, Jayson Harmon," she whispered in his ear as she pulled him close and shuddered against him.

"Almost as much as I love you, Layla Halliwell," he said softly.

Burying his face in her neck, he plunged as deep as he could go and held himself there as he groaned his own release.

She and Jayson didn't have to say anything else after that because everything had already been said. They simply held each other and enjoyed the feeling of being with that one perfect person each was meant to be with. Layla smiled as she fell asleep in his arms, content, happy, and in love.

She woke up some time later to realize that Jayson had turned off the bedside lamp and gotten them both under the covers. She turned in his arms to look at his face. He was so incredibly gorgeous that it was all she could do not to lean over and kiss him. But he was exhausted and she didn't want to wake him, so instead she lay there and watched him sleep.

She probably would have stayed like that the rest of the night, but unfortunately, nature called. Even though it meant getting out of the warm bed and Jayson's arms, she slipped from under the covers and tiptoed into the adjoining bathroom. He was so wiped out that he didn't even move. Then again, she was a cat shifter. She knew how to move quietly.

When she came back out, she took a quick detour into the kitchen to turn off the light and caught sight of the yellow envelope sticking out of her purse. Before she realized what she was doing, she pulled it out and ripped it open.

Zarina had been nice enough to put everything in simple English, even the technical stuff. The final bottom line results of all the blood work were right there, circled in red ink.

Layla stared at it for a while, then turned and went into the guest bedroom that doubled as her home office. Closing the door, she walked across the room, flipped on her, thankfully, quiet shredder, and slowly fed the report into the machine. Once it was gone, she walked out and turned off all the lights, then tiptoed back into the bedroom to join her partner-slash-lover in bed. She climbed in, almost moaning at how warm it still was under the blankets. She was so going to love sleeping beside this man for the rest of their lives.

Jayson's arm instinctively wrapped around her, pulling her close. Layla wiggled around until she was pressed up against his hard body, nice and tight; then she closed her eyes, happier than she had ever believed possible. She and Jayson were going to be incredible together…in every possible way.

Epilogue

FRASIER WALKED INTO THORN'S OFFICE TO FIND HIS BOSS sitting at his desk, his fingers steepled before him, his gaze fixed on the crushed black box there. Of the two things the thief had stolen from the former senator, the hard drive had been by far the most valuable.

Frasier had taken to calling the digital storage drive Thorn's "little black box" because it reminded him of those little black books that people used to carry around back in the day, the ones in which they wrote down the names of all their lovers and former lovers. Thorn's box did much the same thing, only on a much larger scale. That hard drive had contained secrets on many of the richest and most powerful people in the world, including Thorn. Frasier liked to think there was even a whole section in there somewhere dedicated just to his own misdeeds. He knew he certainly had more than a few.

Beyond the trove of personal data, the drive had also held an uncensored log of every single action the DCO had ever taken part in or instigated, official or otherwise.

Frasier had never understood why Thorn would keep something like that around. Frasier didn't doubt there had been enough in it to put the former senator and hundreds of other people in prison for a million years. But collecting and keeping secrets was Thorn's thing. He'd been doing it for a very long time. Now that the box had been destroyed, all those secrets were gone.

Maybe.

"Did the techs from the company confirm it was your little black box?" Frasier asked.

Thorn didn't answer right away, and Frasier didn't push. He had learned long ago that his boss always thought before speaking.

"They can't be one hundred percent sure because the damage from the blast and the fire destroyed all of the internal markings," Thorn finally said. "But they feel relatively certain it's my storage drive. It's the only one in existence, and they doubt that anyone could make a copy in anything less than week."

The doubt that crept into the former senator's words immediately put Frasier on guard. Thorn had an uncanny instinct when it came to situations like this. If his gut was saying something was wrong, Frasier needed to look into it.

"Do you think Donovan and Halliwell took the real one and somehow slipped you a fake?" he asked.

Letting the DCO agents get so close to Thorn and his contracting company was something else Frasier had never understood. He personally didn't trust the shifter and her partner.

"Perhaps." Thorn met his gaze. "But if so, they didn't do it on their own."

Frasier snorted. "John Loughlin."

"Possibly." Thorn picked up the black box, tilting it so that a silvery chunk of crushed silicon fell onto the desk. Frasier supposed he could see how someone might consider the material to be uncut jewel stones of some kind.

"What would you like me to do about it?" Frasier asked.

He knew what he thought should be done, but it would be up to Thorn.

Thorn continued to study the box. "Right now? Put a few more people on Loughlin, see if you can get someone close to him. It might be nice to finally get somebody in that damn penthouse apartment of his. As for you, find out if he actually has the box and whether there's any chance he can get into it."

"And if I find out that he does?"

Thorn didn't look up from the box. "Then the current director of the DCO will have to be eliminated."

Frasier was glad Thorn was focused on the box instead of him so the other man didn't see the smile on his face. When the time came to kill Loughlin, he was going to enjoy every moment of it.

*Keep reading for an excerpt for the
next book in the SWAT series*

WOLF
UNLEASHED

Dallas, Texas, Present Day

"IF WE DON'T GET ANYTHING IN THE NEXT FIFTEEN MINUTES, I'm calling it a night," Sergeant Rodriguez said, his voice rough as sandpaper in Alex's earpiece. "We knew it was a long shot that our dealers would come back to this same location anyway."

Thank God, Alex thought. He and his spotter, fellow werewolf and SWAT officer Remy Boudreaux, had been lying motionless on this rooftop for most of the night, and he for one was more than ready to be done with this op. It was a bust—again. If they wrapped this up quickly, he might be able to grab a few hours of sleep on one of the cots at the SWAT compound before taking Tuffie to her appointment at the vet in the morning.

Of course, not catching the bad guys tonight meant they'd be back on some other roof tomorrow night providing oversight for this snipe hunt.

"I don't know how narcotics puts up with this crap," Remy said from his position a couple of feet farther along the roofline. He sounded just as frustrated as Alex felt. "Another night, another frigging waste of time."

Alex silently agreed. He and Remy, along with Max Lowry and Jayden Brooks, had been working with Sergeant José Rodriguez of the Dallas Police narcotics division on this task force gig every night for nearly three weeks now. The duty schedule wasn't Rodriguez's fault. If you wanted to catch people selling designer drugs, you had to do it on their schedule—which seemed to be directly associated with those hours when the rest of the world was tucked in bed all happy and oblivious.

"How the hell can it be so hard to find the dirtbags selling this new drug?" Remy asked in his distinctive Cajun drawl. "This stuff is killing people who use it. You'd think there'd be a line a mile long willing to give up these dealers."

"No kidding," Alex said. "But something tells me the people who use this crap are more afraid of losing access to their supply than they are of dying from an overdose."

That was why they were out here trying to catch the guys selling the drug that had killed eight people in the last month and put more than twenty others in the hospital. Because no one would talk.

Alex leaned over the edge of the roof to scan the group of people gathered down on the corner. There was a good chance that some of them were simply hanging out, but at this time of the night—in an area well known as one of the city's go-to locations for drug deals—there was an equally good chance that a few of them were looking to buy some of those drugs. That was why the narcotics division had one of their undercover officers buried in the middle of the group, risking his life to get any information he could on the people responsible for putting fireball on the street.

Users supposedly called the stuff fireball because it burned through you like fire, making you feel an incredible rush of heat and energy, only to leave you drained and wrung out when you came down from the high. No one in the Dallas PD had even known there was a new drug on the streets until the bodies started showing up at the hospital—and the morgue. At first, everyone thought it was simply a strong batch of heroin or some of that nasty krokodil crap coming out of Eastern Europe. But they'd quickly figured out it wasn't either of those things when a derivative of fentanyl, a type of synthetic opiate, showed up in the toxicology reports. Fentanyl was one hundred times more powerful than heroin and would have been bad enough by itself, but whoever was making fireball was cutting in other drugs like codeine, caffeine, and ecstasy, along with a whole bunch of crud that had chemical names Alex couldn't even pronounce. In addition to creating an intense and long-lasting high, fireball was so addictive that people were out looking for more mere hours after almost dying from an overdose.

Alex couldn't understand why someone would put crap like that into their bodies, but within weeks, fireball had spread to the club scene and college campuses. If the cops didn't get it off the street ASAP, it would only be a matter of time before the stuff started showing up in the local high schools.

Luckily, SWAT had a good working relationship

with the DPD narcotics division. Mostly because Mike Taylor, one of their squad leaders, had spent a good portion of his career working undercover for them. So when Rodriguez had come looking for help, Gage Dixon, the SWAT commander and alpha of their pack of werewolves, had quickly agreed. Mike's relationship with the narcotics division wasn't the only reason Gage had been so willing to loan out Alex and teammates. The way Gage saw it, SWAT was partially responsible for this latest drug epidemic.

Over the past year, the Dallas SWAT team had taken out some major crime figures. Gage had killed Walter Hardy, destroying a syndicate that controlled most of the crime in the southwestern United States; Alex's squad leader, Xander Riggs, had taken down a major bank robbery ring; Eric Becker had single-handedly wiped out the Albanian mobsters who'd moved in to take over; and Landry Cooper had ended up putting a family full of arms dealers in prison.

All of that was great, but by taking out all those big fish, the local ocean had become swarmed with dozens of little fish all trying to get their piece of the pie. With so many small fish running around doing business on their own, it was damn near impossible to keep an eye on them all. That was why the task force hadn't been able to find the people distributing this new drug yet. There were just too many new players in town.

"Five minutes and we're finally out of here," Remy muttered, glancing at his watch.

Alex lifted a brow. "What? You have a date or something?"

Remy flashed him a grin, his hazel eyes twinkling. "I wouldn't call it a date. More like a booty call."

"At three o'clock in the morning? Who the hell would be awake now and looking to hook up?"

"That would be Vivian." Remy's smile broadened. "She's *always* ready for a hookup."

Alex dug through his memory, trying to figure out if he'd ever met Vivian. After mentally scrolling through the Rolodex of Remy's girlfriends, he gave up. The man had a lot of women in his life. Alex didn't know if it was Remy's accent or what, but it seemed like every time he turned around, women were throwing their panties at the guy left and right.

It wasn't that Alex was a monk or anything—not by a long shot. He enjoyed the company of a beautiful woman as much as the next man, but he needed something beyond the physical to hold his attention.

"Is she the tall one with long, dark hair?" he finally asked.

"Nah. That's Leslie." Remy shook his head. "Vivian's the fiery redhead who drives the Ferrari."

Alex opened his mouth to ask why the hell a woman who could afford a Ferrari would hang out with a SWAT cop whose paycheck probably couldn't even cover the detailing on a ride like that when a dark blue Toyota came down the street. It slowed to a crawl as it passed the small group gathered at the corner, then pulled into a parking lot a few hundred feet away. Not much chance they were stopping for gas or munchies, since the old Gas-n-Go that used to be there had gone out of business a long time ago.

The people on the corner stood up a little straighter,

practically bouncing on their toes as three men climbed out of the Toyota and surveyed the area. Well, if that didn't scream they were up to something shady, Alex didn't know what did.

He leaned over his rifle, using the low-light scope to see details that even his werewolf enhanced vision couldn't pick up from this distance. Apparently, the men must have thought the coast was clear, because one of them ducked into the back of the car and came out with a handful of small plastic bags that he casually shoved into the pocket of his jacket.

"We're hot," Alex said into his mic. "The big guy with the mountain-man beard just tucked several baggies inside his right pocket."

The other cops listening in immediately started talking among themselves, their voices a jumble over the radio.

"Relax and maintain position," Rodriguez said softly, as if he were worried the dealers would hear his rough voice. "The guys are going to take a little time to feel out their customers first and make sure there's nothing fishy going on. We wait until my undercover guy confirms they're dealing fireball, then move in when he gives the signal. And remember, don't blow his cover. We arrest him along with the rest of them and make sure he spends a night or two in lockup like everyone else."

"Talk about a crappy job," Remy muttered. "I wonder if he gets overtime for that."

Alex turned off his mic. "I doubt it. Mike said that having narcotic cops spend time in jail is good for their street cred—or at least the street cred of their under-cover identity."

Remy made a face. "That's a pretty harsh price to pay for a little street cred. Remind me never to request a transfer into narcotics."

Alex didn't argue with that as he peered down his scope so he could keep an eye on the three dealers—and Rodriguez's UC officer. Everyone in the group down on the corner was talking like they were all old friends. Unfortunately, no one seemed to want to bring up the reason they were standing on a dark street corner at oh dark thirty in the morning—drugs.

COMING DECEMBER 2016

Acknowledgments

I hope you enjoyed *Her Rogue Alpha*! I knew Layla and Jayson were going to end up together the moment I introduced them, but I realized it would take a while to do it because they both had some stuff they had to work through. And for those of you keeping track, Dreya and Braden will meet up in the sixth book in the X-Ops series. Something tells me those two have a pretty good story to tell. Oh, and this isn't the last you'll see of Thomas Thorn and that mysterious black box, either.

This whole series would not be possible without some very incredible people. In addition to another big thank-you to my hubby for all his help with the action scenes and military and tactical jargon, thanks to my agent, Bob Mecoy, for believing in us and encouraging us and being there when we need to talk; my editor and go-to-person at Sourcebooks, Cat Clyne (who loves this series as much as I do and is always a phone call, text, or email away whenever I need something); and all the other amazing people at Sourcebooks, including my fantastic publicist Amelia, and their crazy-talented art department. The covers they make for me are seriously drool-worthy!

Because I could never leave out my readers, a huge thank-you to everyone who has read my books and Snoopy danced right along with me with every new release. That includes the fantastic people on my amazing Street Team, as well as my assistant, Janet. You rock!

I also want to give a big thank-you to the men, women, and working dogs serving in our military, as well as their families.

And a very special shout-out to our favorite restaurant, P.F. Chang's, where hubby and I bat story lines back and forth and come up with all of our best ideas, as well as a thank-you to our fantastic waiter, Andrew, who gets our order into the kitchen the moment we walk in the door!

Hope you enjoy the sixth book in the X-Ops series coming soon from Sourcebooks, and look forward to reading the rest of the stories as much as I look forward to sharing them with you.

If you love a man in uniform as much as I do, make sure you check out my other action-packed paranormal/romantic-suspense series from Sourcebooks called SWAT (Special Wolf Alpha Team)!

Happy Reading!

About the Author

Paige Tyler is a *New York Times* and *USA Today* best-selling author of sexy romantic suspense and paranormal romance. She and her very own military hero (also known as her husband) live on the beautiful Florida coast with their adorable fur baby (also known as their dog). Paige graduated with a degree in education, but decided to pursue her passion and write books about hunky alpha males and the kick-butt heroines who fall in love with them.

Visit Paige at her website at www.paigetylertheauthor .com.

She's also on Facebook, Twitter, Tumblr, Instagram, tsu, Wattpad, Google+, and Pinterest.

Don't miss the next book in Paige Tyler's
pulse-pounding X-Ops series

Her True Match

by Paige Tyler

New York Times and *USA Today* bestselling author

———

Working as a feline-shifter cat burglar, Dreya has always
disliked authority figures—especially cops. After stealing from
a congressman in a big heist, she lays low for a little while,
happy to get that pesky yet sexy cop off her back.

Braden and Dreya have a long history of cat-and-mouse.
When Dreya is forced to take a deal and work for the police,
Braden is torn between his need to put her behind bars and his
strange desire to protect her. With danger hot on their heels,
the two must keep their growing attraction at bay—how long
can they last?

———

Praise for Paige Tyler's X-Ops series:

"Does it get any better than this? Tyler…is an
absolute master of the genre!" —*Fresh Fiction*

"Nonstop action and thrilling romance."
—Cynthia Eden, *New York Times* bestselling author

"Sexy, smart, and suspenseful—Paige Tyler just keeps
getting better!" —HelenKay Dimon, bestselling
author of the Bad Boys Undercover series

For more Paige Tyler, visit:
www.sourcebooks.com

Billionaire in Wolf's Clothing

by Terry Spear

USA Today bestselling author

—⁓⁓—

He wants answers...

Real estate mogul werewolf Rafe Denali didn't get where he is in life by being a pushover. When sexy she-wolf Jade Ashton nearly drowns in the surf outside his beach house, he knows better than to bring her into his home and his heart. But there's something about her that brings out his strongest instincts.

Rafe has good reason to be suspicious. Jade Ashton and her baby son are pawns in an evil wolf's fatal plan. How can Jade betray the gorgeous man who rescued her? But if she doesn't, her baby will die, and her own life hangs in the balance.

To get to the truth, Rafe is going to have to gain Jade's trust. If he can do that, he just might be her last—and best—hope...

—⁓⁓—

Praise for Terry Spear:

"Terry Spear has a gift for bringing her *lupus garous* to life and winning the hearts of readers." —*Paranormal Haven*

"Spear has created a fascinating and interesting world that I enjoy visiting every chance I get." —*For the Love of Bookends*

For more Terry Spear, visit:

www.sourcebooks.com